DARK ZEAL

Other Books in The COIL Series

Dark Edge, Prequel
Dark Liaison, Book One
Dark Hearted, Book Two
Dark Rule, Book Three
Dark Vessel, Book Four

Books in The COIL Legacy Series

Distant Boundary, Prequel
Distant Contact, Book One
Distant Front, Book Two
Distant Harm, Book Three

✝

Other Books by D.I. Telbat

Arabian Variable
Called To Gobi
God's Colonel
Jaguar Dusk
Primary Objective
Soldier of Hope
The Legend of Okeanos

Coming Soon

Fury in the Storm
Tears in the Wind
Steadfast: America's Last Days

DARK ZEAL

A CHRISTIAN SUSPENSE NOVEL

Book Five in The COIL Series

D.I. Telbat

In Season Publications
USA

Publisher's Note: This is a work of fiction. Names, characters, places, and incidents are a product of the author's imagination. Locales and public names are sometimes used for atmospheric purposes. Any resemblance to actual people, living or dead, or to ministries, businesses, companies, events, institutions, or locales is completely coincidental.

Discounts are available to place D.I. Telbat paperback books in church or prison/jail libraries. Contact Dee at ditelbat.com/contact/.

Printed in the United States of America

Dark Zeal/D.I. Telbat. -- 1st ed.
The COIL Series, Book 5, Christian Fiction

ISBN 978-0-9864103-5-2

Book Layout ©2013 BookDesignTemplates.com
Cover Design by Streetlight Graphics

To God's people
Inside and outside Gaza

Israel – Gaza City

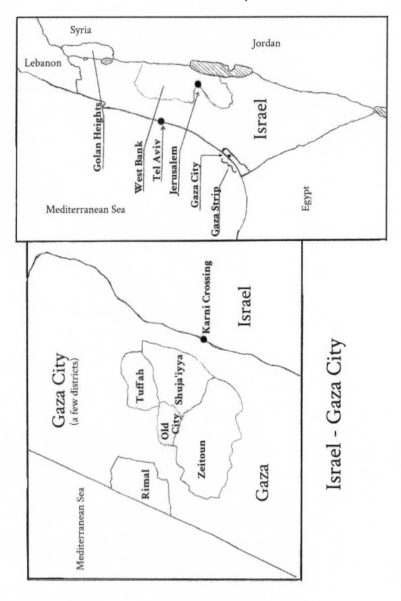

Hamas Tunnel

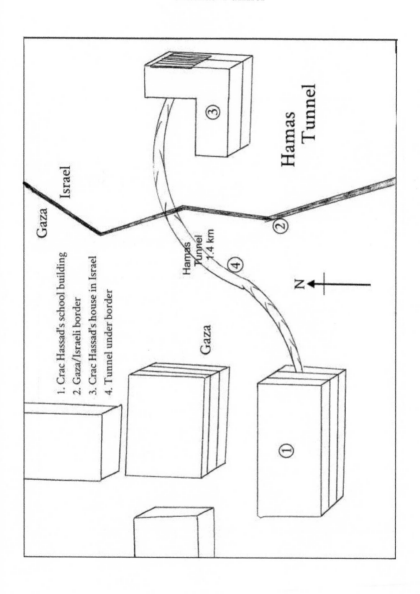

1. Crac Hassad's school building
2. Gaza/Israeli border
3. Crac Hassad's house in Israel
4. Tunnel under border

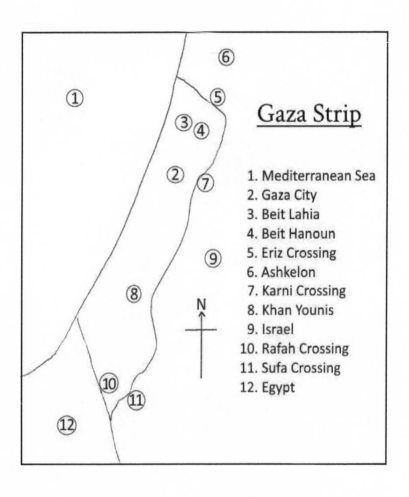

Gaza Strip

1. Mediterranean Sea
2. Gaza City
3. Beit Lahia
4. Beit Hanoun
5. Eriz Crossing
6. Ashkelon
7. Karni Crossing
8. Khan Younis
9. Israel
10. Rafah Crossing
11. Sufa Crossing
12. Egypt

†

Gaza City seemed peaceful that morning. The sun was shining and there was a breeze drifting off the Mediterranean Sea. Children walked with their parents down the street and a woman hung laundry on a clothesline.

The morning was interrupted by a man crossing the street with a weapon in hand. Then three more soldiers crossed, with ten others behind them, each carrying a rifle or RPG launcher.

Sohayb Hassad, nephew of the great Hamas tactician, Crac Hassad, was their leader. None of them wore traditional Palestinian clothes, and their rifles weren't the inaccurate AK-47s their allies usually smuggled to them. Rather, they wore stolen IDF uniforms and their weapons had also been taken from Israel Defense Force captives.

"This street!" Sohayb yelled at his men, some of them only in their teens. "Spread out and hide!"

He stood at the corner of a bombed building that had two crumbled walls left standing. His men dispersed along the street to do what they had been trained to do: ambush, maim, kill—and when necessary, die. The Palestinian civilians who were present knew the signs of impending conflict. Children ran with their parents for cover, and a woman who carried a

1

bucket dared walk no farther—nor leave her bucket behind. Sohayb watched her crouch behind an overflowing dumpster to wait for the violence to end.

With his men hidden, Sohayb dropped to the ground and wiggled under the rusty hood of a car. He steadied his breathing and prayed to Allah that the blood shed this morning would bring him honor. In moments, Sohayb would kill as he had killed before. The bodies of the dead would be found with Israeli bullets in them. The world would blame Israel as they had blamed Israel before.

Uncle Crac had told Sohayb to leave someone alive to point the finger at Israel, but everyone else could die. It didn't matter that the convoy they were about to ambush were UN observers, many of them sympathetic toward the Palestinian cause. An infidel was worthy only of death, and anyone who didn't fight the Jew and Christian was an enemy of Allah.

Sohayb waited for the convoy to rumble down the quiet street. Nothing on earth would take away his hatred for Israel and Westerners. They had killed his father, mother, and sisters. Nothing on earth could remove his lust for blood and vengeance. Nothing on earth.

†

CHAPTER ONE

EASTERN MEDITERRANEAN / GAZA

An explosion lit the night sky. Far away, Gaza City was illuminated by the flash. Shrapnel in the form of sparks showered the low clouds like a grotesque fireworks celebration. Corban James Dowler stopped paddling the sea kayak and counted the seconds until he heard the rumble of the precision missile's detonation. Five seconds. Continuing toward the bombarded city, he knew he was still over a mile from the beach.

Though nearly sixty years old, well under six feet, and soft around the middle, Corban's strokes with the paddle were still powerful, his aging muscles recalling rigorous conflict of recent years.

He stopped paddling again. An Israeli Sa'ar 4.5 class missile boat four hundred yards to the north fired a volley inland, punishing Hamas terrorists who were probably spotted by an Israeli Hermes drone far overhead. Corban hoped he couldn't be seen in his small carbon-fiber kayak. Though he wasn't an enemy of Israel, his mission would be more easily executed if the Israeli Defense Forces, also known as the IDF, didn't interfere.

The wind shifted and Corban gagged. Raw sewage from al-Shati and Jabalia refugee camps had been dumping into the Mediterranean Sea for months. Due to lack of electricity, fuel, and spare parts, Gaza's treatment plants and sewage management systems had been abandoned. Israel had been forced to tighten the blockade on the narrow Palestinian strip of land, and Hamas and other terrorist organizations seemed committed to taking every civilian in Gaza down with them.

Whatever the odor or risk of disease, Corban had to push through it. Like other missions, this one was more important than his personal safety.

Corban drifted in the dark current, feeling his cargo of two forty-pound waterproof packs fastened behind him. Lives depended on their immediate delivery—even if it meant walking into the barrels of Hamas rifles.

When he began paddling again, he was careful to breathe through his mouth. The stench was overwhelming, seeming to penetrate his dry suit and cling to his skin and hair.

Twenty minutes later, Corban rode a wave onto a sandy but littered beach. Careful not to tip his cargo into the pollution, he stepped out of the kayak and dragged it beyond the high tide mark. He set the narrow boat against a retaining wall that once supported a thriving restaurant. If he needed to exfiltrate by sea, he doubted the kayak would be bothered before noon the next day. Finally, he peeled off the kayak skirt and dry suit, and tucked them into the hollow bow.

One on top of another, Corban strapped the two forty-pound packs high up on his back for maximum mobility. Only then did he draw an NL-1 air pistol from his belt. Using the light from a series of inland flashing explosions, he checked the non-lethal weapon. Its pellets contained a knockout toxin that, if inhaled, would render a target unconscious for twenty minutes. The NL-1 held thirty pellets adjacent to a CO_2

cartridge inside the pistol grip. The weapon wasn't much against live rounds from a Hamas rifle, but Corban hoped he wouldn't come across the militants at all.

From the other side of his belt that held up his black cargo pants, he tugged his satellite phone and checked the screen. It was still dead. The Israelis were jamming every signal in and around Gaza. But that didn't matter. Corban clipped the sat-phone back onto his belt. As long as he was in and out in twelve hours as planned, nobody would miss him.

Corban didn't need a GPS for guidance as he left the beach on an eastern route. He knew Gaza City well, having set up a safe house in the neighborhood of Rimal two years earlier. The refuge had also been a center of operations for three other missions. No one lived at the house, but Lord willing, his Christian contact would be there to escort him to his primary destination.

The Old City of Gaza sat on a low-lying round hill forty-five feet above sea level, two miles east of the beach and port. Between central Gaza City and the beach lay the residential district of Rimal, originally built on the sand dunes that now caused cracks in the street pavement and blew in swirls through bomb craters. It was around one of these craters that Corban skirted as he moved down an empty street. Stepping onto a crooked sidewalk, he placed his back against a stucco building. Bullet holes peppered the wall at his back, but Corban's eyes were on the dark sky, more concerned about the Israelis mistaking him for a Hamas "freedom fighter."

He peeked around a corner and saw two Palestinian soldiers dart from a doorway toward him. The sky was dark, but the two men were visible from nearby fires and distant explosions. Each soldier carried an AK-47, the mass-produced and disastrously inaccurate rifle. Corban waited until they were ten feet away, then he emerged from his corner and fired at their chests. They brought their rifles up while still running, but the tranquilizing toxin acted before their trigger fingers could react. They crumbled at Corban's feet and he dragged them to the wall. One of the soldiers appeared to be a teenager. The other one had a thin beard and a Hamas identification card. The Hamas terrorist group—religiously rather than politically-driven—had been voted into Gaza office in 2006. Gaza had never been in worse hands. From the card, Corban confirmed the need to completely avoid the militant. More cautiously now, he jogged down the street, his packs jostling against his shoulder blades.

When he reached a darkened apartment building that was covered with shrapnel divots, he ducked through an archway and ran down the sidewalk. He ascended steep stairs to the third floor and knocked twice, then twice more. The door cracked open and a familiar face peered out.

"Open, Jachin," Corban said in Arabic. "I'm here."

"God be praised!" Jachin Numan threw open the door and kissed Corban on each cheek. "Come!"

Corban closed the door and locked it. He ensured the windows were adequately sealed with black plastic as Jachin lit a candle in the single bedroom apartment. They were alone in the COIL safe house. Kneeling, Corban unstrapped his packs. Jachin lifted each pack off and set them on a splintered table—the only furniture in the haven besides a mattress leaning against the south wall.

"You brought everything, Corban?" Jachin's hands worked

at a pack's zipper so shakily that Corban had to unzip it for him. "Huldah has only one day of insulin left. We have to get to her tonight!"

"There's enough here for six months." Corban ran his fingers over vials packed in foam. He understood the man's desperation since Corban had a daughter with medical needs as well. "Be still, my friend. Let me look at you."

Jachin tore his eyes from the life-saving medication and gazed into Corban's eyes. Both men flinched as a bomb exploded a few blocks away, shaking the walls and dusting the floor.

"My daughter owes you her life, Corban." Tears welled in his eyes. "My whole family owes you."

"No, my friend. You owe me nothing. I serve God by helping you, so I'm the one who is thankful." Corban zipped up the pack. "You're thin, Jachin. Have you been eating?"

"Chard and lentils . . . without the lentils." Jachin grinned, the thirty-four-year-old's malnourishment showing in his discolored gums. "Your presence has filled me."

"How's your wife? And your son, Levi?"

"Leah is eternally beautiful, and Levi, even at twelve, keeps the family fed. His courage frightens me when he runs for food and water, but he knows the streets better than me now."

"And Huldah? She's still embroidering with the needles I brought last time?"

"She is. Look." Jachin lifted his chin to show his name embroidered in Arabic on his collared shirt. "She's a wonder with the cloth. The neighbors pay us in rice for her patchwork. God has given us amazing children."

"I have more gifts for them." Corban patted the second pack. "And Bibles. How is the church, my friend?"

"It's a struggle to meet, but we pray together at three o'clock every day, whether we are all in one place or many. Tell me, Corban, what's that smell?"

"I arrived by sea." Corban sniffed his black turtleneck. "It was the safest route, but my friends must pay the price for my odor."

"Oh, it's nothing. Shall we leave? It'll be difficult to reach my house before dawn."

"Give me a moment."

Corban moved the mattress away from the wall and used the candlelight to find a lever at the foot of the partition. He yanked on the lever and the wall clicked. A hidden counterweight allowed Corban to swing the entire wall panel up to the ceiling where he braced it open. Behind him, Jachin moved closer and whispered words of amazement.

The removed wall panel, as large as a garage door, exposed a shallow space packed with NL weapons, water and food rations, and other emergency COIL gear. Corban selected a briefcase and opened it next to the candle. He used a clear adhesive to glue a full beard onto his face, then closed the case. From a stack of vacuum-sealed clothing, he chose a T-shirt with a Lebanese footwear emblem on the front.

"How do I look?"

"You look Palestinian, like a loyalist. The Israeli missiles will target you before me."

"The Israeli missiles will target me as it is." Corban chuckled. "I just don't want to look too Western where we're going."

"Perhaps you should bring a bigger gun." Jachin nodded at the cache of non-lethal weapons much grander than the air pistol now under Corban's long shirt. "Where we're going, we'll see only Hamas."

"I can move faster without one."

Corban closed the secret panel and the room returned to its humble appearance. Jachin blew out the candle and Corban helped him into the lighter of the two packs. After Corban shouldered the other one, he opened the apartment door. They stood in the doorway a moment listening to the gunfire amongst the explosions.

"They're close," Jachin whispered. "There are rumors Hezbollah will join Hamas in the offensive against Israel. Hamas from here and Hezbollah from Lebanon. Even ISIS is involved, they say, by smuggling weapons to Hamas."

"Syria and Iran can join if they want," Corban said. "My money is still on Israel. Look. A Saraph helicopter. It's hunting."

The men watched the Israeli gunship, sister to the American Apache, sweep a street with its mini-guns. It flew on, leaving nothing alive.

"If anything happens to me . . ." Jachin set a hand on Corban's shoulder. "Be sure to get my daughter the insulin. Huldah will not last another week."

Placing his hand on Jachin's, Corban prayed.

"Lord God, You know our mission in these wicked times. Watch over us, we ask, and bless Jachin and Your servants for their faithfulness in this violent land."

"Amen."

Corban led the way down the stairs and across the first

street. Though he couldn't see the military's eyes far above, he continued to glance skyward. He was now twice as visible with Jachin in tow, but Corban couldn't carry both packs all the way to the Palestinian Christian's house. The young man was weak, but he didn't complain under the heavy load.

After three blocks, Corban paused to study the next street before crossing. Even without consistent electricity in the city, countless fires acted like street lamps. They were traveling south toward the Zeitoun neighborhood where Jachin's family lived near the football field. Buildings towered around them. When Corban glimpsed a ground force moving south through the rubble a block to their left, he told Jachin.

"Israeli or Hamas?" Jachin asked at Corban's shoulder.

"I'm guessing Hamas. Israel wouldn't continue to shell the area if their own ground troops were here." Corban studied Jachin. "How are you not winded? I'm exhausted."

"My family. I'm compelled beyond exhaustion."

"You're a machine, Jachin." Corban saw a dozen more dark figures cross the street in the distance. "Whoever they are, a conflict is sure to meet them soon. We should distance ourselves from them. We'll have to go farther east. It'll set us behind, but we don't have a choice."

Together, they darted across the pavement. But before they could reach cover, Corban was thrown into the building in front of them. He landed on his side and rolled over to look into Jachin's frightened face.

"You okay?" Corban helped Jachin to his feet and noticed a crater the size of a car in the street where they had been an instant earlier. "I think that missile was meant for us."

"My ears are ringing!" Jachin yelled, checking his limbs.

"Maybe we should wait until daylight!"

"Too many people will be about during the day. Besides, Israeli spy planes see in the day or night. Come. Stay close to me."

Corban dusted off his jacket and crept against the building as he led the way east. He wondered if he would ever retire from this call on his life. Someday, he would have to leave the stealth missions to the younger generation of Christian operatives. But so many were in need around the world. Every available laborer had to be in the field. That meant him as well, Corban mused, even though he had to spend more time away from his wife and daughter.

"Janice," Corban said aloud, tightening his pack straps, "I hope you're praying for us . . ."

†

CHAPTER TWO

SOUTH GAZA CITY, ZEITOUN DISTRICT

"**D**o I really have to wear this thing?" Annette Sheffield adjusted the chin strap on her United Nations helmet. "There's obviously not a battle right now."

In the morning light, Belgian Luc Lannoy glanced at Annette. He licked his chapped lips at the sight of the tall American model seated next to him in the Humvee. Though he did prefer she had the helmet off so he could better admire her profile and auburn-colored hair, he had to pretend he cared for her well-being.

"Regulations, Miss Sheffield," Luc said in his Walloon French accent. At thirty-seven, he was fit, and he appreciated that most women found his trimmed jawline beard irresistible. But Annette hadn't paid him any mind. He shifted his hand closer to hers. "The Israeli butchers have fired on UN convoys before. The helmet is for your own protection."

Annette's eyes strayed from the war-torn Gazan countryside outside Gaza City to Luc's hand. She moved her knee away from him. Luc looked out his window, snarling at Annette's reluctance to open up to his advances.

"How long have you worked for the UNRWA, Mr. Lannoy?"

"Please, call me Luc." He smiled broadly and touched her leg for balance as the Humvee bounced over ten-year-old potholes. "I volunteered for the Relief Works Agency two years ago. The Palestinian people need a voice and they need help. They can't fight the Israeli cowards alone."

"Aren't UN observers and aid workers supposed to remain neutral, Mr. Lannoy?"

"So naive, Miss Sheffield. You're a weekend humanitarian. Your camera crew in the next vehicle will take pictures of you in the middle of al-Shati, then you'll go home. You'll not see the slaughter of these forgotten people by merciless machines in the sky. If you stayed another week, I'd show you the real face of terror."

"Are you angry because I can't stay longer, or are you upset that I want to see both sides of this conflict?"

"We're entering Gaza City, Miss Sheffield," the driver said. He was a British sergeant in full UN uniform.

Annette leaned forward to see out the windows. Luc had seen the devastation before, but he hadn't seen a beauty like Annette in a long time. When he'd picked her up at Ben Gurion Airport, her identification had barely been checked while she signed autographs. The actress/model was an international celebrity, far too consumed with herself and her "world peace" mission to truly care about the Palestinian crisis. Yet, Luc still couldn't help but lick his lips. She wasn't skin and bones like most models, and she was at least six feet tall. A goddess!

"Why are these people on the street if it's so dangerous?"

Luc leaned forward to brush against her shoulder.

"Now that it's morning, they search for food and water. When the fighting resumes, they'll hide anywhere they can. Most have only holes in the ground since there are no bomb shelters in Gaza. The Israelis have hundreds of bomb shelters, but these people are left in the open to be slaughtered."

"But the world has given the PLO and PNA millions of dollars. Why doesn't Hamas build shelters to protect the people instead of buying M-75 rocket components that don't even fly straight?"

Luc eyed her carefully, shocked that a mere beauty could reason through the situation, even if he didn't like her conclusion.

"What do you know? If you have no compassion for these victims you see in rags, then go back to America." Luc sat back, pouting. He really hated her now. Of all the sympathizing celebrities, he had to get stuck escorting a Zionist!

The four-car convoy slowed through the Zeitoun District. A bullet struck the side of the Humvee. Luc instinctively reached for his sidearm. He'd been ordered to use the weapon only if fired upon, but lately, he hadn't cared much for following orders. Maybe now would be his chance to kill some Jews!

"Ambush!" the driver screamed as gunfire erupted all around them.

The Humvee in front of them exploded. Annette screamed and cringed against Luc as burning debris and bullets battered their vehicle. He shoved Annette against her own door to give himself room, and peered out the window, searching for Israeli Defense Forces uniforms.

"Where are they?" Luc ground his teeth, hungry for just one kill. After twenty-four months of quiet escorts, now was his chance for action. In all the confusion, no one would know a UN escort had killed an Israeli. "All I see are Gazans!"

"They're trying to kill us!" Annette screamed and tried to hide on the floor. "Get us out of here!"

The driver swerved the Humvee forward. Thrusting his pistol out the window, Luc fired at who he guessed were Jews dressed as Palestinians. He withdrew his arm suddenly as an RPG zipped toward their vehicle. Luc saw the grenade detonate on the front of the Humvee. A flash of light and a force that took his breath away threw him backward. He felt weightless for an instant, then found himself lying on the ceiling, fiery smoke choking him. A chopper with a fifty-caliber gun kicked up dust nearby. The Israelis were trying to kill them all!

With bullets peppering the burning vehicle, Luc gripped Annette's wrist and dragged her unconscious body out of the overturned Humvee and pulled her on top of him. He was six-three and weighed twice what she did, but she still made an adequate human shield.

He was blinded by dust as the chopper hovered down the street. After firing blindly at the sound, Luc climbed to his feet, dragging Annette by the arm, and struggled to the side of the street into a bombed-out shop. Coughing, he checked Annette's pulse. She was bleeding from the brow but seemed otherwise uninjured. With little effort, he hefted her over his shoulder and kicked through a back door as he fled the Israeli gunship.

Three blocks later, he dropped Annette through the broken window of a closed textile factory. The street was clear at the moment. Luc climbed through the window and hid behind the wall while watching the street.

Suddenly, two men came from around the corner outside. They each carried a pack. The first man was bearded and wore a T-shirt. He carried a pistol. The second one looked sickly and appeared unarmed. Luc wasn't taking any chances after the scrape with death he'd just had.

Snarling as he fired, Luc emptied his gun at the two men. Both went down, but only the second one was a sure kill. Luc jumped out the window and sprinted to the men. By the time he reached them, his pistol was reloaded.

"Stay down!" Luc yelled in Arabic. He kicked the bearded man in the ribs and picked up his gun. Luc frowned at the light-weight air pistol. An air pistol? It was useless in this war zone. He threw it aside. "Come on! Come with me!"

Luc unclipped the man's heavy pack so he could support him easier, then walked him across the street. Enjoying the opportunity to flex his strength, Luc pushed the injured man inside the window and jumped in after him.

"You're making a mistake," the bearded man said in Arabic. He sat against the wall, holding his chest wound. "I'm not whoever you think I am."

"Shut up!"

"I saw the ambush on the UN peacekeepers. You're European, right? Let's speak English. My name is Christopher Cagon. I'm British Red Cross. Those packs out there have medicine for these people. You're UN. We have nothing to do with this conflict."

"Shut your mouth!" Luc said in English. He thrust his gun into the man's face. Now that he was face to face, he could see the injured man wasn't Middle Eastern at all. "Everything's gone wrong. I was supposed to meet someone."

The wounded man ignored his own condition once he noticed Annette, and moved to check her vitals.

"She might have internal injuries. We should get her to a doctor. The Israelis are just a few blocks away. If you—"

"The Israelis just tried to kill me!"

"No, you're mistaken. I was watching, friend. Hamas attacked you. They've done it before. Later, they'll blame it on Israel. The IDF gunship came to your rescue."

"You're wrong! The IDF are murderers." Luc rubbed his eyes and gazed out the factory window. "We can't move, anyway. Both sides are liable to shoot us out of panic!"

"Like you did to us? That's my friend, Jachin, out there. Let me go see if he's okay. Let me take the medicine to his daughter. She'll die without it."

"You English call that collateral damage. There are greater things happening today. I have a meeting to get to."

"Let me go. I'll take this woman. We'll only slow you down, friend, whatever it is you have to do now."

Luc licked his lips and studied the shorter man. He was surprisingly calm for a wounded Red Cross ambassador. The man's British accent sounded authentic, but he had also spoken flawless Arabic, which was suspicious.

"No."

"Why?"

"I might need you."

"I see." The bearded man nodded. "A UN official needs two hostages. Now we understand one another."

"What?" Luc turned slightly. "What do we understand?"

"That I'm not the only one who isn't who he seems to be."

"If you have enough energy to speak, you have enough

energy to move Miss Sheffield behind that wall. We need better cover."

"Sheffield? Annette Sheffield? I thought she looked familiar."

Christopher Cagon pulled Annette into his arms. The front of the man's shirt was bloody, but he was surprisingly mobile. Luc held a gun on his captives as they moved deeper into the factory. As soon as Chris was situated in the next room, Luc took Chris's water bottle from his belt. He found the sat-phone as well, but knowing the signal was jammed, he dashed it against the wall. With his finger on the trigger of his pistol, he stood against a doorpost to plan his next move. Maybe the convoy ambush could work to his advantage . . .

†

CHAPTER THREE

EGYPT / GAZA

"It ain't easy being a Gazan civilian, huh?" Titus Caspertein shielded his eyes from the morning sun as he peered northeast from Egypt into the Gaza Strip. "I'd hate to be the fools going into that war zone."

"We are the fools, remember?" Oleg Saratov said with a scowl. His accent was rich, unlike his appearance. Titus would've been embarrassed to be seen with the short, stocky Russian if he weren't so reliable. "Let's go tunneling."

Titus looked away from Gaza's Rafah Crossing blockade to his partner's broad back. At forty-five, Oleg was an ugly creature, carrying as many scars as Titus' thirty-nine-year-old frame. Oleg's most notable scar was on his left nostril, as if scissors had cut a slice of flesh from his face.

With his back to the blockade, Titus followed his partner through the crowd to an Egyptian merchant shop. Food and supplies for sale at expensive rates were piled on the Egyptian side of the border, waiting for the Israelis to open the border into Gaza. But the blockade wasn't stopping those who had a little ingenuity.

"He says we were expected sooner," Oleg said to Titus as they stood before the merchant. Titus spoke Arabic as well, but Oleg preferred to translate. "You sure about this?"

"Does this look like a joke?" Titus patted a canister

19

strapped over his shoulder. Though it was already seventy-degrees, Titus wore a jean jacket to cover his shoulder holster where he cradled a Glock 18, loaded with deadly parabellum rounds. He felt cockier than normal with the fully automatic handgun. Besides the case and the hidden gun, he carried only a water bottle on his belt, like everyone in the Middle East who knew the dangers of being caught without one. "Tell him to let us through."

Oleg translated in near perfect Arabic to the merchant, but the man still didn't permit the Westerners into the store.

"Tell him to let us through or we'll tell Crac Hassad he hindered our meeting with him."

"Crac Hassad?" the merchant asked without a translation. His eyes widened and he opened the door.

"We'll try that name first next time." Oleg led the way around piles of rice bags, some already priced to sell for ten times their worth to their Gazan neighbors. Fuel containers were stacked to the ceiling.

The merchant pointed to the floor against the back wall of the storeroom. Titus brushed his blond hair out of his eyes and tugged at a dusty ring on the floor. A well-oiled trapdoor swung open, exposing a light that shined on a ladder leading straight down. At the bottom of the tunnel shaft, a youth jumped to his feet and aimed an assault rifle up at the merchant.

"Selah!" the merchant yelled. "Wake up!"

"I'm awake, Papa."

"You go first." Oleg moved aside for Titus.

"I went first in Iran."

"But I went first in Libya."

"Okay, you win." Titus rubbed his hands together, eyeing the tunnel with uncertainty. "It ain't easy being an arms dealer. Look what we have to go through."

"You could always join one of the resistance groups you supply with arms."

"Do I look like someone who likes to get shot at?"

Hand over hand, Titus descended, with Oleg following. The second Oleg's giant head lowered into the hole, the merchant closed the trapdoor above.

"*Salam Alaykum.*" Titus greeted the boy at the bottom with a clap on his shoulder. "How far to the other side?"

"Two kilometers, *caphir.*" The boy wasn't shy about keeping his muzzle on Titus. "Go die in Gaza, *caphir.*"

"Mouthy little kid, isn't he?" Titus said in English, frowning at Oleg. "Do me a favor and take that gun from him."

"Not me." Oleg chuckled. "He probably knows how to use it better than either of us."

Titus ducked his head as they entered the narrow horizontal section of the tunnel. Light bulbs hung from a thin cord along the ceiling. The floor was packed hard from constant foot traffic over several years.

"On any other day, this tunnel would be crowded," Titus said, maintaining a brisk pace. "You'd think with Israel bombing tunnels, we'd consider another route into the country."

"If you think this is foolish, Titus, you're welcome to skip across the border above ground."

"And miss the experience of a cave-in initiated by a missile? Never!"

Less than half an hour later, they reached the end of the tunnel with a ladder leading up to another trapdoor.

"Any idea where that opens into?" Oleg scratched his unshaved jaw. "Just curious who's going to shoot you when you show your head like a gopher."

"We're almost twenty miles from Gaza City." Titus checked his watch. "I don't have time to be shot. We have a noon appointment and we still don't have a car."

Titus climbed the rungs quickly and threw open the trapdoor. Three young men with new beards scrambled from a domino game to their carbines that leaned against a footlocker. They each aimed at Titus, displaying their bravest faces.

"Crac Hassad," Titus said, ready to duck back into the hole if bullets started flying.

"Crac Hassad?" One of the men stepped closer. "You American?"

"I have a meeting with Crac Hassad."

"Crac Hassad is not here, American."

"I know Crac Hassad isn't here. He's in Gaza City. He's waiting for me. I'm his favorite American."

"What's your name, American?"

"You may call me the Serval."

"Serval? The cat?"

Titus climbed completely out of the hole and turned to offer his hand to Oleg, but the man slapped it away.

"You shouldn't tell people you're the Serval," Oleg said in Russian. "That's not for their young ears."

"It probably doesn't mean anything to them. They're too young to know or care who I am, really."

"I'll take you to Crac Hassad, Serval, but you tell Crac Hassad I helped you. I am Seif. I will fight for Crac Hassad one day, if he finds me worthy."

"There's a man with his priorities straight," Oleg said in English and slapped Titus on the back. "You could learn something from him."

"What? Fighting for Crac?"

"No, being worthy of something."

Titus shook his fist at Oleg as they followed Seif out of the shack. The two other men exited the shelter and climbed into the back seat of what Titus recognized as a Toyota Land Cruiser, silver-colored with rust peeking through the paint around bullet holes. He glanced at Oleg.

"Stolen IDF vehicle. We climb into that, Titus, and we're targets."

"We're in Gaza. Everyone's a target."

"I drive." Seif patted the hood and climbed into the SUV. He could barely see over the steering wheel.

"This isn't exactly low-profile, Titus," Oleg said, still not climbing into the vehicle.

"You're welcome to walk, *caphir*." Titus winked and held the front door open for Oleg to take the middle seat. He looked south toward the border they'd walked under. Slum shacks crowded the Rafah Crossing blockade where Israelis had barricaded themselves safely inside steel-plated buildings.

"What are you thinking?" Oleg asked as Titus climbed in and closed the door. "Something wrong?"

"I've never been inside Gaza before, but I imagined it'd be more difficult to get in."

"Israeli Satan-dogs bomb one tunnel," Seif explained as he

floored the Toyota, "so we dig another. It is a game we will win."

From Rafah, Seif drove west to the coast. The Palestinian man was the average age for all males in the Strip. Seif was intelligent and desperate, and Hamas offered a cause, which made Seif also willing and dangerous. Dangerous or not, he knew how to drive, throwing Titus and Oleg against one another at every swerve around corners, bomb craters, and burnt vehicles. They reached the coast in twenty minutes, then flew north on the empty Rasheed Coastal Road.

"No gas," Seif said as he pushed the needle to ninety. "No gas, no cars."

"Did you imagine the Eastern Mediterranean would smell like that?" Oleg asked Titus. "Like a summer breeze in an Austrian meadow?"

Titus took a sniff and choked.

"No plumbers," Seif said. "No toilets."

Thirty minutes later, Seif drove onto Gaza City's Rimal Salah ad-Din Street and slammed on the brakes.

"Saraph!" Seif cursed and gazed at the object cruising over the city a mile away. "We stop here."

"We can't go by foot to Crac Hassad." Titus elbowed Oleg. "Where's his sense of adventure?"

"No, we stop here. Too dangerous. You want Crac Hassad? You walk to Crac Hassad."

"I don't feel like walking." Titus slipped his Glock out of the holster. "You feel like walking, Oleg?"

"Not really. When I was climbing that ladder, I think I pulled my—"

Titus turned on the two men in the back seat faster than

either of them could raise their carbines. On cue, Oleg placed his own Beretta pistol against Seif's temple.

"We drive, you walk," Oleg said.

"Leave your guns and walk away, boys." Titus gestured with his pistol. "You're too young for me to kill, but I've killed younger, so don't tempt me."

Seif and his companions sulked as they slid out of their seats. Oleg scooted into the driver's seat as Titus collected the carbines.

"You drive, you die!" Seif spit at the SUV. "The Saraph never misses."

"You stand, you watch." Oleg laughed. "You've never seen me drive."

He hit the gas as Titus buckled in and checked the carbines.

"Doesn't hurt to have more firepower, huh?" Titus threw one rifle out the window. "That one was destined to jam."

"Whenever you have firepower, you always want to use it."

"So?" Titus slammed a fist on the action of another rifle. The Palestinians were sold the worst military gear at the most expensive rates. Maybe, he considered, he could smuggle them more reliable and accurate rifles for cheaper rates. It wouldn't be the first time the Serval had undersold greedy Egyptian and Syrian arms smugglers.

"We don't want to get caught in the crossfire out here, Titus. We meet your guy who leads us to Crac Hassad. That was the deal. Then we sell that thing strapped to your shoulder, and we walk away rich. This chaos is not our fight. If we shoot anyone, then we have to take a side. I hate taking sides. We can't leverage one side against the other if we take sides."

"I think we took sides when we agreed to sell this baby to Crac Hassad and his Hamas puppets." Titus patted his canister, then looked out the window. The few people on the streets or in their doorways were watching the chopper over the skyline. "I know what you mean, though. Don't worry. It's still about the money for me."

"But you know what Crac Hassad will do with that thing."

"I can't think about that. This isn't my first sale, Oleg. Quit acting like you have a conscience. You want to get paid as bad as me. We're early enough. The sooner we can find our guy, the sooner we can sell this thing and leave."

Oleg was cruising at close to sixty near the Old City when he crested a tiny bump in the Salah ad-Din Street. As if purposefully planted to discourage speeding vehicles, the Toyota's front axle plummeted into a shallow bomb crater. The front wheels hit the far side of the crater and buckled. Oleg was thrown against the steering wheel as Titus tested the seat belt with all his weight. The SUV flipped forward at an airborne sideways angle and landed on all four wheels, facing the opposite direction.

Coughing from smoke that boiled from the open hood, the two men crawled from the cab. Oleg held his chest as he rounded the vehicle to collapse next to Titus. Titus wasn't injured, but his water bottle was split open.

"The axle is broken." Oleg took a deep breath, wincing. "I think my lung is, too."

"You can't break a lung, Oleg." Titus checked his canister for damage. His cargo was safe. He found his feet and helped

Oleg to stand. They stared mournfully at the billowing white smoke from the Toyota. "Nothing like a little smoke signal to let everyone know we're here."

The Saraph gunship circled closer to investigate the smoke.

"As Seif would say," Oleg said with a groan, "you stay, you die."

Titus and Oleg abandoned the carbines in the vehicle and dashed for cover as an air-to-ground rocket blew the Toyota into scrap metal, nearly clearing the street of the obstacle. Mini-guns simultaneously spit bullets that slapped the pavement where Titus and Oleg had last stood without cover, but they were quickly a half-block away behind an empty car garage. They stopped with their backs to the wall.

"We might get paid," Oleg said, still holding his chest, "but we'll be stuck in Gaza without a vehicle. Please tell me you know where we are and how we can get out!"

"I only know Gaza by map, but I think we're just outside the Old City." Titus studied the sky to the south. "Our guy should have signaled us by now."

Gravel crunched under a boot nearby. Titus turned and fired without identifying the target. There could be only enemies around, anyway. He hadn't come this far to get shot by some militant with a third generation grudge.

A man in green fatigues crumpled at the corner of the garage. Oleg moved wide, his Beretta drawn, as Titus approached the man directly.

"Please, mercy," the man begged in Arabic. He appeared to be in his mid-twenties with curly dark hair. A wound high on his chest was leaking blood. He didn't reach for his IMI Negev light machine gun as Titus placed his gun muzzle against his skull.

"What do you know, Oleg? It ain't easy being an IDF soldier all alone in Gaza City. Honestly, I thought he was Hamas."

"You're . . . English?" The soldier gasped in accented English. "Please. I was separated from my unit overnight. Every time I try to signal a Saraph, Hamas closes on me." He moaned and pulled his hand away from his wound and stared wildly at the blood. "I need a hospital!"

Titus met Oleg's eyes. They switched to Russian.

"You pull that trigger, Titus, and we officially take sides."

"We can't walk him to al-Quds Hospital. And even if we could, they wouldn't take an Israeli soldier."

"His chances are better in a Palestinian hospital than bleeding to death here."

"Then we'll do the humane thing." Titus' finger tightened on the trigger, then he stepped away. "I can't do it. You do it."

"I'm not shooting him!" Oleg shoved Titus away from him, as if he were offended Titus even asked. "Why'd you shoot him in the first place?"

"I told you, I thought he was a Hamas soldier! It was a reflex."

"If Israel finds out you shot him, we're finished. And I'm not digging your bullet out of him."

Titus rubbed his brow.

"This isn't part of the plan. We can't get wrapped up inside Gaza!"

†

CHAPTER FOUR

<u>*SOUTH GAZA CITY, ZEITOUN DISTRICT*</u>

Annette Sheffield gained consciousness long before Luc Lannoy or the bearded man knew she was awake. Her head hurt and she felt blood caked on her hairline. The bearded one, who called himself Christopher Cagon, had lain her against a crumbled cement wall. He sat against the opposite wall in view of the window from where she could hear Luc mumbling in French to himself.

"Remain still, Annette," Chris said in his British accent. "Your UN friend is holding us as leverage for something. If he sees you're awake, he may hurt you. I've seen the way he looks at you."

"Then I'll play dead," Annette said. "Just give me a signal when he's coming."

"This will be the signal." Chris touched the corner of his eye. "I removed your cracked helmet. How's your head?"

"It's throbbing a little. Your chest looks worse, though."

"I irritated it to make it bleed more. Luc believes it's bad, but I can move if I need to. Can you?"

"Yeah, I can run. I ran track in college."

"Good girl. It may come to that. What distance?"

"Fifteen hundred."

"Endurance, huh?"

"Well, that was twenty pounds and thirteen years ago."

She smiled, wondering if he was keeping her talking to settle her nerves. "Luc called you Chris. Who are you?"

"British Red Cross."

"You look Palestinian."

"Just blending in."

"What's he going to do with us?"

Chris touched his eye. Annette tensed, closed her eyes, then relaxed. She heard Luc move to their side of the wall.

"You were talking. Is she awake?"

"I'm a praying man. Does she look awake? That head wound doesn't look good, friend. There could be brain swelling. Her life is in your hands. Let me take her to a hospital."

"No, and stop asking."

"Who are you waiting for?"

"None of your business." Luc returned to the window.

Annette opened her eyes but didn't move.

"What does he need us for?"

"Nothing good, I'm sure."

"You said you're a praying man." She smiled at old memories. It felt strange to smile in their situation. Chris seemed to have a calming effect on her. "I went to a Bible camp when I was a kid. In Montana. I remember a rope course and a counselor named Arianna. She was so cool. She called me her little sister. I learned to pray from her. Well, she prayed every night. I just listened. That was the best week of my life."

"Not many know that peace. Sometimes tragedy happens to remind us of those more important memories. I gave my life to Christ a few years ago. I was lost and hell-bound, but

He forgave me and set me on a new path."

"Really? I used to think I'd have regrets if I ever took that, you know, leap of faith."

"It can be scary, sure. The world is against us, so it's only natural to struggle, emotionally, physically, and spiritually. But the end is already written plain enough for us to read. You understand?"

"The Bible."

"You got it."

Annette flinched as Luc fired his pistol out the window. A man screamed and fell silent. Luc laughed, then cursed.

She tried to remember everything she could about Gaza and Hamas soldiers. They were known to think little of a woman's life, especially a non-Muslim woman. The Palestinians were a desperate people, she had come to see for herself. Hopefully, the worst rumors about Hamas weren't true—that they kidnapped foreigners, beheaded enemies, and sent children strapped with bombs into crowds.

"Tonight, when it's dark, we'll escape." Chris pointed briefly to his left. "I don't know where that corridor leads, but I'm sure there's an exit somewhere."

"You know where to go?" Annette trembled with fear.

"Yes, I know where to go." Chris touched his eye.

"Hey, you, Chris." Luc approached Chris and yanked him to his feet. Chris groaned and swayed on his feet. Annette watched, squinting covertly. Luc gave Chris a green signal flare. "Take this fifty yards down the street and let it burn. Don't light it near this building or it'll draw the wrong company. Can you do that?"

"I don't think I can. My chest—"

"You look fine to me. Light it and drop it against that far wall. If you do anything wrong, I'll shoot you. You want to get shot again? Walk back here when you're done."

Chris glanced at Annette.

"Don't touch her."

"I don't have time to touch her, yet. Just do what you're told."

"You're going to get us all killed." Chris shook his head at the flare in his fist. "Everyone in the city is going to see this."

"That's the point!" Luc clubbed Chris on the side of the head and stood over him as he fell. "Get up!"

Bleeding from the new cut over his ear, Chris stood and leaned against the wall.

"I'm sorry, friend. Just don't hit me again. I'll go."

Luc cursed in French and kicked at Chris as he walked to the front room. Annette listened, too afraid to peer around the wall to see what happened next. She expected a gunshot, but moments later, she heard Chris climb back through the window.

"I knew I was keeping you around for something. Good boy." Luc shoved Chris into the back room. "Stay there and tell me if she wakes up."

As soon as Annette heard Luc walk away, she sat up.

"Your head is bleeding, Chris. We can run now and see where that hallway goes."

"It's too dangerous in the daylight, but we may not have a choice if Luc attracts too much attention with that flare. In this city, that's about the dumbest thing to do."

"I'm pretty sure whatever he's doing has nothing to do with his UN position."

"Yeah, I agree. He said he wants to meet with someone. He's hiding behind the window, watching to see who comes to the flare. It's burned out by now, but thousands would've noticed the smoke—Israelis, Hamas, Islamic Jihad, probably even ISIS and Hezbollah." Chris gazed to his right at the corridor. "That hallway is tempting, but we'd be caught before we could ever get to safety. Right now, we just have to worry about one crazed man with a gun. In a few minutes, a whole unit could be on us, and if they're friends of Luc's . . ."

"Hey!" Luc suddenly yelled then whistled out the window. "Hurry! Here! It's me, Luc Lannoy."

Annette trembled as she listened to more bodies climb through the window.

"We need to get out of sight," a stranger said with a Southern accent. "That signal will draw everyone in Gaza!"

As if on cue, two Israeli gunships could be heard circling over the factory. Annette prayed they would move on, rather than pound the building with missiles, since no one was visible. In moments, the thumping rotors moved to the west.

Annette was too shaken and nervous to play sleep now. A tall blond man with a canister on his shoulder stepped into the back room. With him was a short muscled man, maybe in his forties, carrying a wounded Israeli soldier.

"Who is this?" Luc pointed at the soldier as the muscled man set him down next to Annette. "This isn't a hospital, Caspertein!"

"Could've fooled me." The blond man winked at Annette. "Hey, darlin'. Have we met? Titus Caspertein."

"That's Annette Sheffield. She was in my convoy when we were ambushed by Israelis. She's mine."

"The Israelis didn't ambush you, Luc," Chris argued, drawing the attention of the newcomers. "Hamas fired on you. The Israeli gunship moved in to help you, but it was too late."

"The name's Oleg," the muscled man said, and extended his hand to Chris.

"That one's my prisoner, too!" Luc slapped Oleg's hand away from Chris.

Oleg turned to face Luc more directly, but Titus stepped between them. Annette watched the tall blond man carefully. He looked more like an athlete or model than someone who would be acquainted with the likes of Luc Lannoy.

"We have lots to do tonight. Let's stay focused, huh, Oleg?"

"All I was going to say was that sounds like Hamas. They're probably already blaming Israel for shooting up the convoy on *Al Jazeera* television."

Annette knelt in front of Chris to study his chest and skull wounds. Titus knelt beside her, his shoulder against hers. A moment ago, he had winked at her, and now he was closer than he needed to be.

"Titus, I said don't pay any attention to him," Luc said. "He's just some Red Cross worker I'm keeping until I don't need him anymore."

"Red Cross, huh?" Titus frowned. "What're you going by, old man?"

"Christopher Cagon out of Great Britain."

"Nice. Did this idiot here stumble onto you, or are you here for me?"

"What?" Luc's voice cracked. "You know him?"

"So, old man, what do you say?" Titus chuckled and lightly

nudged Annette with his elbow. She didn't see the humor. "Never thought I'd meet this guy, especially way out here."

"I haven't played that cat and mouse game for a few years," Chris said. "I went private. But you know what they say."

"Yeah, I do." Titus nodded. "You never actually leave the Agency."

"*The CIA?*" Luc gasped.

"Meet Corban Dowler, everyone." Titus tugged at Corban's beard and the right side detached. Annette's mouth gaped. *Was no one who they seemed to be?* "He's an ex-spy hunter and tracer for the CIA. I've worn enough of those beards to recognize a fake one." Titus rose to his full height and faced Luc. Luc seemed to shrink in the man's shadow, though they were nearly the same height. "Lannoy, imagine a man who can summon the most powerful resources in the world from all available countries at a moment's notice. Imagine that man minding his own business in a war-torn region. Then imagine some idiot drawing this very unique man into a deal that is vitally important to a number of bank accounts, particularly mine."

"I—"

"Yes, Luc Lannoy, you're the idiot in that story, and Corban Dowler is the agent of our impending destruction." Titus turned from Luc and paced the floor. Oleg moved closer to Luc, causing Luc's eyes to dart nervously about.

Now less afraid of Luc, Annette crawled to the IDF soldier with a chest wound. She doubted Luc would do anything to her with Titus there, who seemed to have the situation well in hand. Wherever Titus went, Annette wanted to stay close to him, even if he was some sort of greedy businessman.

"Luc, you've turned a potentially dangerous situation into an impossible situation. The only thing I can think of that would make Oleg and me feel better about this impossible situation is if he and I split half your cut." Titus stopped pacing in front of Luc, pinning the UN officer between himself and Oleg.

"I'm only getting what?" Luc glanced from Oleg to Titus. "Now I only get five-percent?"

"And you live," Oleg added. "Seems reasonable."

"What about us?" Annette asked Titus. "You'll let us go now, right?"

"Too dangerous, Miss Sheffield. Tell her, Corban."

"She knows." Corban tugged off the rest of his beard. "She just wants to know that we're not prisoners."

"And you know the answer to that, too, don't you?" Titus chuckled. Annette couldn't understand why the blond man seemed to be enjoying himself so much. What was there to laugh about? "Tell us, Corban. What are the stakes?"

"We know too much. You can't let us go until your deal is done." With surprising agility, Corban rose to his feet. He tugged the loose, bloody shirt off and examined the bullet hole in his chest through the black turtleneck. Without flinching, he reached into the hole and plucked out a flattened bullet. Annette held back the vomit rising in her throat. Corban tossed the bloody thing to Luc. "You didn't actually hit me, Luc Lannoy. That was from a ricochet off the wall."

"You . . . pretended a near fatal injury?" Luc fingered the bullet. "Why?"

"Luc, I told you." Titus stood in front of Corban. "This man is a legend. He could have taken you at any time. The only reason he didn't is because there was no point. He wouldn't want to move around Gaza City in the daylight, and he wouldn't leave a female American citizen behind. So tell me, Corban, how much trouble are you going to be for me?"

"I'm only here to deliver insulin to a diabetic girl, and Bibles to an underground church."

"Bibles? You found religion?"

"Christ found me, because I was lost." Annette followed Corban's eyes to the canister strapped over Titus' shoulder. "Regardless of my original mission, I'm obligated to ask what you have there? Cyanide to put in an Israeli water supply? Ricin? Potassium chloride?"

"So you know your poisons, old man. It doesn't matter. You're not stopping me."

"Just kill him." Luc raised his pistol, but Oleg pushed his arm down. "What? He's a witness. A bullet will solve this problem! Let me kill him."

"The problem is worse than another bullet," Oleg said.

"How much time do I have before people notice you're missing?" Titus asked Corban.

Annette listened and watched the men intently. Though Titus was clearly in charge, the respect he showed the older man, Corban Dowler, was startling. Titus seemed more and more like a villain, but the casual nature with which he approached every moment suggested to her that she could actually depend on him to keep her safe.

"I'm expected to call in by noon."

"It's nearly noon now."

"Then calls will be made on my behalf."

"But you said you worked in the private sector." Titus

placed his hands on his hips. "How much trouble can you Christians be? Maybe the people who scare me the most won't know you're missing until much later."

"Okay. Except . . . I founded COIL."

"COIL?" Titus glanced at Oleg. Annette wondered what the new revelation meant. "Did you know he founded COIL?"

"I know international agencies envy COIL's network behind closed borders."

"What's this COIL?" Luc asked.

"The Commission of International Laborers," Titus said. "A team of case workers out of Manhattan manage a network of field operatives who make the Iranian Pasdaran writhe in fury. They're like spies with Bibles who carry non-lethal weapons. And this entire time, you've been running it?"

"Since I left the Agency a few years ago." Corban stepped forward. "I wish I could introduce you in such a flattering manner, Titus, but I have an insulin delivery. A life hangs in the balance. Tomorrow may be too late."

"Who's the dead man across the street?"

"Jachin Numan, the diabetic girl's father."

"Nice shooting, Lannoy." Titus shook his head at the Belgian. "Of all the bad people in Gaza, you manage to shoot only the good ones."

"The insulin, Titus," Corban said. "That girl doesn't have long."

"I have a meeting. Let me make this deal and everyone can go their separate ways. Besides, it's too dangerous to move right now."

"People are looking for me, too," Annette said, her hand on the wound of the IDF soldier. "It's only been a couple hours, but the American embassy will stop at nothing. My family is very important in the United States. Titus, please?"

"I'd be more concerned about Aaron Adar." Oleg pointed at the IDF soldier. "Israel is the muscle here. They'll tear up the whole city looking for their missing man."

"Which is why we give them no indication as to where we are." Titus glared at Luc. "Except you, Lannoy. Ten-percent is back on the table for you if you go tell Crac Hassad the meet is here." Titus placed his hand on the canister. "And I'll keep this safe until you return."

"Me?" Luc licked his lips, then doused his face with water from Corban's bottle. "I don't have the weaponry to reach the district of Tuffah. And I never set up a signal with Hassad. I'm supposed to take you to him."

"The only reason you're part of the deal is for you to set up the meet. If you can't do that, what do we need you for? I can go to Hassad myself when the heat cools down outside."

"No, I'll do it. Ten-percent?" Luc moved around the wall and looked out the window. "I can probably find a rifle somewhere. It's only about a kilometer or two."

"Thata boy. Tell Hassad to meet us here at three o'clock tonight. That's 0300. And tell him to bring some food and water. We're pinned down here with nothing."

Luc checked his handgun and ammo, then eased up to the window. Annette watched him climb out, hoping she never saw him again.

"It ain't easy being Luc Lannoy." Titus laughed with Oleg. "Okay, everyone out of sight. Oleg, check that back corridor. I don't want anyone sneaking up on us through some back door."

Annette met Corban's eyes, and he nodded. He wouldn't abandon her. If he really was a Christian, Annette guessed he had some sort of luck. She was even tempted to pray right then herself.

†

CHAPTER FIVE

<u>*MANHATTAN, NEW YORK CITY*</u>

Forty-five-year-old Chloe Azmaveth cracked her knuckles as she watched the clock turn to five a.m. in her Manhattan office. That made it noon in Israel and Gaza. Corban still hadn't checked in from his Gaza City mission. She reached for the phone and dialed a number she dreaded calling. It wasn't that Chloe dreaded bothering people. As COIL's public relations manager, she did that for a living. What she did dread was news of Corban's death or capture. He insisted on the most dangerous missions for himself. One of these times—and this could be it—he wasn't coming home.

"*Shalom,*" a man answered. "This is Colonel Yasof."

"Kalil, it's me, Chloe."

The line was silent for several seconds.

"This is unexpected, Chloe. You're not due to report for another week, and certainly not on this line."

"I wish I was calling to visit, Kalil, but I've been watching the news. Gaza City looks bad, even worse than normal."

"Hamas has made it bad, Chloe. Hezbollah is gathering its forces in Lebanon, and there is rumor of a biological weapon in the hands of Muslim sympathizers backing Crac Hassad. Yes, Gaza City is bad. We wish there was peace, but the attacks keep coming."

"I hear you're in charge of the incursion to hunt Hamas

41

extremists. The media says they're hiding amongst civilians to fire their rockets."

"Yes, I'm in charge of Forward Command in Ashkelon, living in a bunker for the past week. Regardless of our air strikes, Hamas is still launching rockets at our cities and digging tunnels into Israel. Their rockets are hitting Tel Aviv almost regularly now."

"Have you noticed any reports of a foreigner spotted in Gaza City?"

Silence again. Chloe popped her knuckles against her leg. She didn't want to tell him anything about their COIL operation, but she knew she'd have to.

"Which foreigner? We had a UN convoy disaster earlier this morning. Hamas used our own captured armaments to destroy four vehicles full of peacekeepers and humanitarians. An investigation will show that IDF weapons shed the blood. There were several foreigners in the party. A couple aren't accounted for, but we're still securing the site."

"I'm actually looking for a foreigner who wasn't in the convoy. He was an unofficial aid worker, Kalil."

"Unofficial? Chloe, the last time you called me unofficially, you wanted help with your new organization. You're not still acting as Mossad's eyes and ears just to use us whenever you want."

"I know, and I don't mean to jeopardize your position, but no one in the IDF knows about Corban Dowler going into Gaza."

"Oh, Chloe. In Gaza? Did he go under the name Corban Dowler?"

"No, he's under the name Christopher Cagon, a Red Cross

ambassador out of London. He missed his scheduled call."

"Of course. We're jamming everything in Gaza. No one can call in or out."

"He was supposed to be well out of Gaza by now. If he could have, he would've at least sent a message, because he knows I'll send in the troops for him. He would do it for me. He's done it for others."

"And what exactly do you want from me?"

"I can mobilize three COIL units within twenty-four hours. Can you authorize me?"

"No! Even if it were up to me, no. Israel wouldn't allow covert foreign troops into Gaza, not intentionally. Give me an hour, Chloe. I'll look for a report of this Christopher Cagon. We have IDF in Gaza, some on foot. Someone may have crossed him."

"I'm sending you my sat-phone number. I scheduled a flight while we've been talking. I'll be in Tel Aviv by the time your sun sets."

"Don't come, Chloe. If your agent is here, give us time to find him."

"I can help, Kalil. Don't forget, I worked in the field for twelve years. Those were our glory days, huh?"

"That's what I'm afraid of. I don't want to have to monitor your activities while I need to command our troops. The world is watching."

"Then don't ignore me. I'll definitely cause a scene."

Yawning, Chloe hung up the phone. The COIL office that filled two suites over Times Square was as crowded at that hour as it was during the day. It was always daytime somewhere around the world. At any given time, COIL had no less than thirty field operatives smuggling medical supplies or Bibles into a country, or whisking a missionary family out of harm's way. Sometimes those operatives were soldiers armed with the NL weapon series, and other times COIL sent in one man or woman to make a difference, like Corban.

Chloe dialed her phone again. Her husband, a micron gold miner and salesman, didn't pick up. She left him a voicemail: *"Hey, Zvi. I'm needed overseas. Corban missed a check-in. I'll call when I can. Praying your Australian convention went well. Hope to be back by this weekend. Love you."*

She didn't have time to go home, so she shouldered her overnight bag and headed for the elevator. Though she was worried, she wasn't panicked. Corban had gone missing before, and she had responded by searching for him. Hopefully, his wife, Janice, wasn't panicked, either. Chloe would have to call her before she left, even if she couldn't tell her where Corban was.

...†...

Luigi Putelli couldn't sleep, but that was nothing new. He sat at his computer monitor and popped three pieces of bubble gum into his mouth. He still craved cigarettes, but the gum was helping.

On his desk, he adjusted a photo of Heather Oakes. She'd once tried to arrest him in New Jersey, but Luigi had since gone legit. Well, mostly. He was doing his best to avoid the wicked contacts from his past and live up to his commitment to Heather and his old spy friend, Corban Dowler. Heather now worked for COIL, so Luigi's whole social circle was easy to track in one location, but that didn't bring him any closer to marrying Heather.

Marry Heather? Luigi looked at the wall where he had a tranquilizer dart hidden behind a picture frame. He figured he should tranq himself right then and there for even thinking about marriage, but his heart was winning this battle.

The distance between him and Heather wasn't geographical or even emotional. He knew she had feelings for him, even if they were borne from sympathy. They had shared a meal the first day they'd met, and since then, he hadn't imagined growing old with anyone else. No, their distance was spiritual, and she was the one who insisted they couldn't be a couple because he wasn't committed to God.

Luigi wasn't against God. One of his other favorite people in the world, Corban Dowler, was a man of God. But Luigi couldn't thrust all his evils onto a holy and good God. No one would deal with his sin but himself, Luigi decided. And yet, that kept him from drawing closer to Heather.

He clicked a desktop icon on his computer screen that resembled an ear. A number of new calls had been placed to and from people he'd been monitoring. Just because Corban and Heather had saved him from a livelihood as an assassin didn't mean he had given up all forms of espionage.

The first message was from his sister to a friend upstate. It was in Italian. Luigi found himself smiling as he listened to the women gossip and laugh. For several years, Anna had been a chain-smoking recluse, but now she had built friendships in America, thanks to her connection with Janice Dowler. Anna and Luigi even talked once a week, but he never gave any indication that he'd been eavesdropping and watching over her.

After listening to the phone calls, which were mostly by

Corban's neighbors and potential COIL enemies, Luigi pushed away from the computer. He rubbed his short hair and wondered if he should grow his hair out like the old days. No, he'd just have to update all his new identities and passports. He would keep it short for now.

His computer chirped and he hit a button. It was an incoming call to Zvi Azmaveth. This early in the morning? Luigi counted the rings, anticipating who the caller could be. He guessed it was Zvi's wife, Chloe, though Zvi had many international contacts. Corban and Janice were friends with Zvi and Chloe, but Luigi doubted Corban would be calling Zvi at that time. Corban had disappeared three days earlier on some mission overseas. The COIL offices were impossible to bug, since Corban had them swept twice a week, so Luigi usually had to find out Corban's whereabouts through secondary surveillance.

A message was left for Zvi, and Luigi noted the details that interested him. Chloe was going overseas in search of Corban, who had missed a scheduled call.

Luigi pulled up Chloe Azmaveth's file. He'd met her first in Malaysia, then again when they had worked in tandem to rescue Corban in the Caribbean.

After Chloe's call to her husband, Luigi's computer chirped again, and he eavesdropped on a call from Chloe to Janice Dowler.

"I don't want you to worry, but Corban missed his last check-in. It's probably just something simple, but I'm heading out the door for the airport to be sure."

"Oh, Chloe, please tell me where he is."

"I'm sorry, Janice. You know I want to tell you. But I'll call as soon as I have news, okay? You just pray and . . . well, God knows."

"Corban doesn't make it easy on me. After twenty-five years, you'd think I'd be used to this."

"I debated even calling you . . ."

"No, I'm glad you did. Stay safe, Chloe. Bring him home. I'll be praying."

Luigi had already traced the call's origin: Manhattan. But he got no further than that, which meant Chloe was calling from the COIL offices. With his heart racing, Luigi fingered two more pieces of gum into his mouth. Even after so many years, it still excited him to help his old friend, Corban, though he knew the risks were great. But where was Corban? Chloe would know.

He played the phone messages over twice more, but Luigi still found no clues that would help him locate Corban. His better sense told him to let COIL handle the dilemma, but he was tired of sitting on the sidelines for almost a year, listening to wire taps, and occasionally meeting with government men to assure them he wasn't an active agent. Since his debriefing with the CIA, they had checked on him, and he had remained obedient, mostly for Corban's reputation, who had vouched for him. But he missed the action! No one was targeting the Dowler family at the moment, so he felt he deserved to be at Corban's side, wherever he was.

Collecting his laptop and phone, Luigi packed light, careful to include his weaponized belt. The buckle face held jagged edges coated with a tranquilizing agent not unlike a gentle scopolamine. Because of Corban, Luigi didn't own a firearm anymore. Corban wouldn't want his help if he did. Though Luigi wasn't a Christian, he'd grown comfortable with COIL's non-lethal policy: "God's people can't show God's love if they are intent on killing their enemies."

Luigi rode a taxi to JFK International and took a seat in the lobby entrance with a magazine in his lap until he spotted Chloe enter with a carry-on backpack. He let her pass, his head down, then he followed her into the terminal. He'd gained weight and a little hair since they had last seen one another, but he knew the pretty woman with curly black hair and bold eyes was no civilian. She'd been a field agent for the Mossad and spoke more languages than he did. Her file showed she was Krav Maga trained, and most importantly, she was still Corban's right hand. Corban wouldn't let her remain at his side at the top unless she was still on her game. Thus, Luigi figured Chloe had already spotted him.

Chloe stopped at the counter offering flights to Berlin with a connection to Tel Aviv. Standing in a bookstore across the terminal, Luigi computed his next move. If she were going to Berlin, he'd need only his passport under the name Francis Malvao. But if she was going on to Tel Aviv, he'd need a visa as well. Luigi had been monitoring the news and hadn't seen anything happening in Germany, or its neighboring countries. However, Chloe had dual citizenship with Israel.

Stepping into the men's room, Luigi locked himself in the spacious handicapped stall. He connected to the airport's wifi and informed the new Canadian embassy in Tel Aviv that the Canadian citizen, Francis Malvao, would be on real estate business in Israel for an indeterminate spell. Next, Luigi purchased an expensive last-minute ticket on the flight that left in an hour. Finally, Luigi used a razor to shred and flush the other identities he'd brought along—since he'd determined where Chloe was headed. A pocketful of passports would set off all kinds of alarms in Israel, which had the most secure customs border in the world.

He made it through security with no problem, then found his gate and sat a few seats down and across from Chloe to await boarding. They were seated in a quiet area. Her face betrayed her anxiety and weariness; she had dark circles under her eyes. Instead of busying herself with a book or the phone in her lap, she kept popping her knuckles every few minutes.

"They say that causes arthritis," Luigi voiced with a smile. He wasn't used to speaking to people face to face, but Chloe was no stranger.

"Luigi Putelli." She smiled with what Luigi guessed was tolerance. Not everyone was happy to see him, but he didn't mind. "Why do I only see you when there's turmoil somewhere in the world?"

"That's just an old wives' tale, though," he said. "The popping sound of the knuckles is just air squeezing over cartilage or something."

"Oh." Chloe frowned at her hands. "I don't think about it. I hate these long flights, you know? Database crash in Germany's COIL office. When the boss says go, I have to go."

"Germany. Huh. You're sticking with that cover story?" He picked up a novel left behind in the next seat. "Well, while you're going to Germany, I'm heading for this plane's next stop: Tel Aviv. A friend in need. Did they seat you well?"

"First class was open. Gotta love those early morning, mid-week flights. Practically empty."

"Me, too. First class. The spoiled life." Luigi pretended to read his book, enjoying their reunion on behalf of Corban.

"Do you go to Israel often?" She barely masked a smile.

"It's been a while. I'm from Ontario, Canada, and I don't travel as much as I'd like. And you should probably call me Francis Malvao."

"Francis Malvao again? Ontario. That explains the French accent."

"Oh, my accent . . ." Luigi laughed and feigned embarrassment, touching his mouth with his fingers. "I've lived in New York so long, I thought I'd lost it."

"It's nothing to be ashamed about."

"How about you? Ever get to Israel?"

"I've wanted to, but never got the chance."

Luigi nodded, wondering what her plan was. She had to be going to Israel. Israel's Palestinian thorn was the only thing in world news. It was too explosive for Corban to avoid. He would find someone to help in the midst of the missile strikes. Why was she being evasive when she could use his help?

"It's beautiful—Israel." Luigi sighed. "But, I'm not there to sightsee. I just don't want to get lost in the middle of Gaza, right?" Luigi made the sound of an explosion.

"Oh? You'll be near Gaza?"

"Might be." Luigi fought the urge to smile. He loved the game! "Depends on where exactly my friend is. He went off the radar three days ago and missed his last check-in." Luigi shrugged. "It's tough to say for sure. My Arabic isn't that good, but if the Arabs got him, I'll have to do something, right?"

Chloe stared at him with her coldest look.

"You're gonna make a mess of this, aren't you?" she said

quietly, then surveyed the terminal. "Tell me what's going on. Did Corban contact you? I thought you retired from this business. I thought they made you retire."

"I don't retire from my friends, Chloe. Aren't we friends?"

"Just tell me what you know about Gaza."

"It's just deductive reasoning. I'm tailing you."

"You haven't changed. Look, I have people in Israel. I can't have someone tailing me for this. The Mossad never really got over me leaving."

"Janice and Jenna are safe. Let me tag along. It sounded serious on the phone. Corban might need some muscle. I want to help."

"You were listening in?" Chloe scoffed. "You're better than I thought if you have a bug on a COIL phone."

"No." Luigi shook his head. "It was on Corban's home phone. You called Janice. I couldn't hide a bug at the COIL offices, and I'm the best there is."

"Well, this is nothing, Luigi. The phones are down in Gaza. That's all that's happened. Corban's fine."

"I'm restless. And I think you need company, Chloe. You may call me your assistant."

"Yeah, right. You have spook still written all over you. The IDF will know you're not Francis Malvao. The people I deal with won't have the patience for your games."

"Well, I am a spook. I have no need to hide it from you. I owe Corban my life. Tell me how I can help, and I won't get in your way."

"No killing."

"I know that much."

"You do as I say and keep your spook mouth shut."

"I have nothing important to say to anyone but you."

"Then I'll allow you to tag along."

"Excellent. To Germany we go?"

"Funny. You knew I was going to Tel Aviv all along."

"Yes. Yes, I did."

✝

CHAPTER SIX

<u>*SOUTH GAZA CITY, ZEITOUN DISTRICT*</u>

"He needs surgery," Corban said as he withdrew bloody fingers from Aaron Adar's chest wound. His Gaza op—just a quick insulin run—had been derailed, but he was doing his best to roll with what God was guiding him to do. It seemed he was there for Titus. "I've done all I can with what we have here."

"Nobody leaves, Corban." Titus stood over them with his Glock in his fist. "Not until the deal's finished. You know the drill."

"I don't want to die." Aaron struggled to breathe. His hand shot out and gripped Corban's collar. "Elizabeth . . ."

Annette pulled Aaron's fist from Corban's shirt. Corban was growing impatient with Titus. The infamous weapons cowboy was risking lives.

"He's helping you, Aaron. You understand?" Annette cast a hateful glare at Titus. Corban had noticed she seemed attracted to the handsome smuggler, but now even she was growing intolerant of Titus' stalling. "He's just a boy! What were you thinking?"

"Survival," he mumbled and left the room. Corban watched Titus check the window. Both Palestinians and Israeli patrols had passed the factory building in the last hour, but both had been under fire and had moved on quickly.

"We should've never left." Aaron fumbled with his words, tears in his eyes. "I told them it would only get worse."

"Is he delirious?" Annette mopped Aaron's brow with the tail of her T-shirt.

"No, he's not delirious." Corban checked his watch. It was three in the afternoon. Three hours past his scheduled deadline. Chloe would be on the move by now, he figured. "He's talking about Israel's unilateral pullout of the Gaza Strip a few years ago. The Palestinians talked the world into the solution, and the world pressured Israel into the move. Most in Israel knew the Palestinian terrorists would take control of Gaza and assault Israel even more. And now, statehood? It's a mess. Good people on both sides have died."

"So that's what all this is about? All those rockets from Gaza firing into Israel?"

"Right. All those rockets."

"I was one of those settlers." Aaron squinted at the ceiling. "I met Elizabeth that year. We were just kids then, but I asked her to marry me last month."

"You hold onto that, Aaron. We're going to get you back to Elizabeth." Annette looked at Corban. "Right? Titus knows you. You can talk him into getting Aaron help. Just look at that Titus! He came in here so smug and confident. He's probably used to winning everyone over when he walks into a room. Well, he's not winning me over! You have to use what he knows about you to turn him. You have to!"

"He knows me, and I know him." Corban eyed the pieces of electronics against the wall. "Luc broke my phone. I have another one nearby, but the IDF is still jamming communications."

"Why's he doing this?" Annette growled, her voice low to keep Titus from hearing. "He doesn't seem that dangerous. I mean, he's nothing like Luc Lannoy, right?"

"Don't be fooled by his wit. Titus Caspertein is a world-renowned thug. The CIA used him for a while, but he went rogue again. If it's valuable and can be sold, you can bet the Serval is planning a heist."

"The Serval?"

"It's an African cat, like a lynx, but smaller. It survives by stealth and resilience. Titus is known as the Serval by those who've hunted him. I knew men in the CIA he outsmarted, but I never crossed him myself. Different assignments. He has powerful friends, mostly underground. Those friends made it difficult to actually prosecute Titus in the US, which is why he was exiled permanently years ago. His own family in Arkansas disowned him. After heists and arms deals, he's wealthy beyond imagination, but instead of retiring, he continues to pull jobs. He's an adrenalin junkie—addicted to the next risky sale. You're seeing him do what he loves."

"Seems like he has so much potential, a guy like him, and this is the life he chooses?" Annette sighed and shook her head. "That case on his arm—he's selling it to the terrorists? He hates the Jewish people that much?"

"Help me stand up!" Aaron begged. "Together, we can stop him!"

"Rest, Aaron." Corban placed a firm hand on the young soldier. He looked from Aaron to Annette. "We must be patient. Things are not as they seem."

"What?" Annette leaned closer. "What do you mean?"

"Quit whispering." Titus entered the room. "Corban, your

two packs are still across the street with that dead Arab."

"His name was Jachin. He was a better man than you or me."

"Maybe, but he's not anymore. Anything in those packs we can eat or drink?"

Corban rose to his feet. If he was going to save Annette and Aaron, he would have to force the situation from Titus' hands.

"Let's not talk about food and water, Titus. This boy's dying here from your bullet. You really want his blood on your hands?"

"It's a war zone, Corban. You already know I didn't mean to shoot him. And I could've left him out there."

"Well, it's time to make things right." Corban prayed that God would reach into Titus' heart and plant a seed of compassion. "It's time to do the right thing, Titus."

Titus' eyes drifted to Aaron, whose face grimaced in pain.

"I've got a deal in a few hours." Titus used his gun to scratch his cheek. "You have a plan that doesn't jeopardize me or my retirement?"

"That's all you think about!" Annette leaped to her feet to stand in front of Titus. Her fists were flinched. Corban hoped she didn't attack him; Titus was twice her size and strength. "He's dying, and all you can talk about is your bank account!"

Titus smiled, which only made Annette angrier.

"It ain't easy being a famous model, is it, Miss Sheffield? All that money you have while people are dying all over the world. You and I live with the same conscience."

Annette swung with a lightning-fast hand, but Titus caught her wrist before it connected. He squeezed her wrist until she whimpered. Corban considered stepping in, but he had to bide his time. Besides, Titus' tone was more flirtatious than dangerous, as he goaded her.

"I'm nothing like you!"

"You're right. I sell stolen commodities. You sell your body."

"You—!" She tried to strike him with her other hand, but Titus shoved her backward to land on her backside next to Aaron.

"What's going on?" Oleg asked as he strode into the room from the dark corridor. "Are you trying to bring attention to us?"

"Just setting a hypocrite straight," Titus said. "How's the back door?"

"I hear gunfire now and then. Seems nobody's clearing the buildings, yet."

"This man needs medical attention soon," Corban interrupted. "At sundown, we'll have a chance to move. You'll have to shoot me to stop me from getting him help, and I already told you about the girl who needs insulin. Time's not on your side, boys."

"What did you have in mind?" Oleg asked.

Corban watched the Russian's face carefully. There was a wariness in his eyes that confirmed Corban's hunch about the man.

"I have a plan," Corban said. "Let me go."

"Assuming Luc confirms our meeting," Oleg said, "we have an appointment later tonight, Titus. Let's keep our priorities straight."

"That has nothing to do with me," Corban stated. The only

clout he had was his past reputation. He hoped it continued to threaten Titus' plans.

"Well, you're not leaving here alone." Titus shook his head. "You may have retired, Corban, but I know you. You'll still try to disrupt the meet. If you're going somewhere, I'm coming with you."

"Titus—" Oleg lifted a hand.

"No, Oleg. These self-righteous Christians irritate me. I'll show them they're not better than us. You can stay here with the girl and Aaron. I'll leave the case. We'll be back in time. So, Corban? What'd you have in mind? It's you and me."

"I have a safe house west of here in Rimal."

"That means we have to go through about a mile of battle zone I don't want to be a part of."

"There's food and water and some medical equipment, maybe enough to save Aaron."

"And what about the insulin?"

"First, we'll go to the safe house, then return here. Once Aaron is stable, we'll deliver the insulin. We need to avoid the Salah ad-Din Street which runs east and west. You know it? We can stick to alleys. Figure one hour for each run, if we hustle." Corban guessed it would take much longer, but Titus didn't seem to know Gaza City that well.

Titus looked at Oleg.

"What do you think?"

Corban watched the Russian's face. There was clearly something afoot, much more than even Titus knew about. For years, Corban had stayed alive by reading people in the shadows, discovering their secrets before they knew they'd revealed them. Oleg had a secret.

"You don't have to do this," Oleg said. He glared at Corban, as if trying to send him a message. Corban thought he finally understood. "Titus, Corban won't be a problem if you let me put a bullet in his leg. Forget the diabetic girl. We have other priorities!"

"Oleg, you said it this morning." Titus slipped the canister strap off his shoulder and handed it to his partner. "We're fools for being here, anyway. Maybe for me, it's boredom. I can't sit here doing nothing while they judge us."

Corban winked covertly at Annette. Their moral authority had definitely bothered Titus' conscience.

"Just be back by three." Oleg shouldered the canister. "I don't want to deal with Crac Hassad alone. I can't. You hear? He'll have an army with him, and Luc Lannoy isn't someone I trust."

"We'll be back." Titus turned and patted Corban on the cheek. "Rest up, old man. We leave at sundown."

Oleg returned to his post, down the dark corridor out of sight, and Titus kept watch by the window. Corban took Titus' suggestion and relaxed next to Aaron. Annette sat on the other side of the wounded Israeli.

"I can't believe you're leaving me alone with Oleg!" she whispered just loud enough for Corban and Aaron. "I can tell he's a pig. Look at the way he carries himself. A total slob. What am I supposed to do if he tries something? He wanted to shoot you again!"

"Oleg won't bother you. He has other things on his mind." Corban crossed his arms and tried to hold his chest muscles still. His bullet wound was superficial, but he didn't want it opening up again. "He's a professional, regardless of his sloppy appearance. Titus might be crooked in every other way, but he's always fancied himself as a ladies' man. He wouldn't tolerate a partner who wasn't halfway decent."

"*A ladies' man?* Hah! There's nothing attractive about him for a lady, believe me. I thought you didn't know him that well."

"I know his file."

"Well, you do have a plan, right? I mean, you're not going to let them sell that case to the terrorists, are you? It could be a nuke, or a biological weapon."

"Getting him alone is a first step." Corban remained prayerful in the silence, yielding constantly to the Spirit's guidance. If he operated as just a man in such a situation, he was headed for a wreck. But if he operated as a Christian, he was relying on his invincible God. "Maybe no one ever took the time or had the chance to share Christ with him."

"Yeah, like he deserves forgiveness for the things he's done!" Annette scoffed and grumbled under her breath.

"God doesn't discriminate against those who respond in faith to the proclamation of forgiveness, so we can't either, can we?" Corban checked Aaron's pulse as he rested. If he could keep Aaron alive, it would ease Israel's anger against him for being in Gaza, which was certain to become an issue now. "I've crossed some evil people over the years. I was one of the worst. But God is in the fixing business. He could turn Titus around if Titus yields. He has to first recognize his sin is an affront to our holy God. It's easy for us to judge people, but to God, hating a man is the same as killing him. That makes Titus, and the terrorists he's selling to, condemned men under God's wrath, like you and I would be without Christ. God changed me, made me a new man. He can change them."

"And you're okay with that?"

"Why wouldn't we be pleased to hear that someone who was evil is now a repentant believer?"

"Sounds nice, but Titus seems far from a repentant believer!"

Shadows gradually closed on Gaza City. Corban did his best to doze against the wall, but the necessity to pray felt greater than the need to sleep. Souls were in the balance.

As the sun arced into the Great Sea in the west, the fighting outside intensified. To the north and east, in the Old City, the battle was at its peak. Occasionally, a mortar round or rocket slammed into the factory's vicinity and shook dust from the ceiling onto the hiding party.

"You ready, Corban?" Titus called from the front window. "It's time, old man."

Corban checked Aaron's condition one last time and whispered a prayer over the young soldier.

"I'll be back," Corban said to Annette. "Stay close to Oleg if anyone else shows up."

She nodded, her face a shadow in the fading light.

With Oleg watching Annette and Aaron, Corban joined Titus at the window. There were just too many to save in one night, Corban thought. God would have to watch over those he couldn't.

"Let's do this, Titus."

"You sure you can stay up?" Titus raised his eyebrows. "I'm not going slower for you, old man."

"Why not? Do you know where we're going?" Corban smiled and nodded at the arms dealer. "So, just who's leading who here? You'll go as slow as this old man needs to go."

Corban climbed through the window with practiced agility and crossed the street. Titus, who seemed much more nervous, checked the street before crossing to join Corban, who knelt and touched his dead friend's body. *Another needless casualty of the Gaza conflict.*

"He's gone, Corban. Let's move!" Titus aimed his Glock down the street as shots were fired two blocks away. "Do you know how many killers are flooding the streets right now, preparing for a night of fighting?"

"Hamas militants, Palestinian Police, Islamic *Jihad*, ISIS, and probably some Hezbollah antagonists sponsored by Iran."

"Okay, so you know the score. Can we go?"

Corban glanced east, and Titus followed his gaze toward a building close to total collapse. As soon as Titus looked away, Corban darted west, the other direction. He couldn't help but smile as he heard Titus curse and rush to keep pace with the older operative.

Settling into a silent, moderate pace, Corban crouched as he jogged through alleys and across streets. Still dressed in black, he felt in his element, his eyes adjusting quickly to the dark city avenues. When Israeli planes bombed or gunships fired rockets in the northwest, Corban looked away from the flash or closed his eyes, maintaining his night vision. When he paused at each building corner to survey ahead for roving bands of soldiers, he often glanced behind to see Titus struggling to keep up. Corban was being a little reckless, he knew, but lives depended on his speed.

Reaching the edge of Rimal, the stench of the sea reached his senses. Corban ducked into a doorway as three men nearby were illuminated by a rocket detonation a quarter-mile away. Since the three hadn't fired, they probably hadn't seen him, but Titus was in the middle of the street, twenty yards from the prowlers. Titus had nowhere to go.

The men shouldered assault rifles and yelled in Arabic at Titus to halt. Titus cursed and dropped his pistol on the cracked pavement. The gunmen advanced on Titus rapidly, passing Corban in the doorway. Corban knew if he wanted to get rid of Titus, this was his chance, but as a Christian, grace was in order—favor that Titus definitely didn't deserve. Without making a noise, Corban slipped into the street behind the Palestinians.

"My daughter," Titus claimed in Arabic, "she needs immediate medical attention. Please, let me pass . . ."

Corban didn't wait to see if the men bought Titus' ruse. He kicked the first gunman on the side of the knee and punched the middle one in the kidney. As the third one turned, Corban shoved the man's muzzle into the sky as the gun fired a volley of automatic rounds. Kneeing the man in his hip, Corban temporarily paralyzed the nerve on his left leg. Titus recovered his pistol and covered Corban as he collected the three frightened militants' rifles.

"Run!" Corban ordered the Palestinians. They hobbled quickly away. "And don't look back!"

"We should've killed them," Titus said. "They would've killed us, and now they'll fetch their friends."

"They don't know who we are or where we're going." Corban hurled all three rifles onto the nearest roof. "Besides, they were just kids. You don't kill kids, do you, Titus?"

"Why'd you throw those guns up there?" Titus leaped for

the awning of the roof, but it was too high. "I needed those!"

"Oh, so you can get us caught in a gun battle?"

A Saraph gunship thumped overhead, urging Corban down the street. Titus ducked as large caliber bullets split the stucco wall over his head.

Ten minutes later, Corban climbed over a rock wall and dropped into the courtyard next to a familiar archway. Titus tumbled over the wall, landing next to Corban.

"You don't look like you're in this good of shape, old man." Titus panted for air.

"Maybe I'm just scared. Come on. Third floor."

Corban climbed the stairs two at a time and rushed to the safe house door. Using the key from the door frame, he unlocked the door and closed it behind them as Titus dove inside.

"We made it!" Titus laughed hysterically, checking his body for wounds. "Did you see that military unit to the west? They're coming this way."

"We'll let them pass in the darkness. Besides, you could use the rest before we leave."

Titus didn't answer, and Corban knew the younger man was seeing things a little differently already. Danger had a way of clarifying one's purpose. Letting Titus rest on the floor, Corban closed his eyes and prayed for safety. Every minute alive in that neighborhood was a gift from God. With so many needs crying for his attention, he couldn't die tonight.

†

CHAPTER SEVEN

Colonel Kalil Yasof adjusted his black beret and brushed bunker dust off his decorated uniform. His subordinates glanced skeptically at the ceiling, which had just taken a direct hit from a Hamas Grad rocket.

After serving with honors in the Mossad, and through two conflicts in the IDF, Yasof was once again in charge of the Gaza incursion. Militants needed to be arrested, and missile launch sites and tunnels needed to be bombed. He wasn't sure if he should be happy about the assignment, or if he should start penning his resignation. The situation wasn't improving in Gaza City, and things were only getting more complicated if Chloe Azmaveth was really on her way.

"Was that a lucky shot or are Hamas rockets getting more accurate, Captain?"

"I'm sure it was luck, Colonel. We'll keep the pressure on them."

Yasof nodded, dismissing one of his logistics officers, and stepped up to a large console. He fit a headset over an ear to listen to the communication channel of Aleph Team in Northern Gaza. That one encrypted channel wasn't jammed; contact with the ground forces needed to be carefully maintained. The fighting had been particularly harsh the last few nights, and Yasof knew why. Everyone was on edge and concerned about the rumors. Hamas had a biological weapon, and they had a way to launch an unprecedented attack against Israel. It was supposed to be a game-changer, but none of their informants or prisoners knew the details. The Shin Bet Security Agents had been applying every tactic to discover what the militants were planning, but the current Hamas military leader, Crac Hassad, was keeping his intentions quiet.

Because Yasof believed the threat was real, he had convinced Central Command of his need for more troops in Gaza. Twenty more Merkava battle tanks and ten more Saraph gunships had been placed under his command.

Beit Lahai, the Northern Gaza town where the majority of the rockets had been originating lately, was under bombardment by the Israeli Air Force, so Yasof had been able to focus his attention five miles south to Gaza City. As if his troops didn't have enough to deal with by trying to locate Crac Hassad and the biological weapon, he now had to find Chloe's missing American operative. Anyone who had been connected to intelligence circles the past twenty years knew of Corban Dowler. Yasof would have enjoyed helping the veteran agent any other week, but this week, with other urgent priorities, the pressure was almost too much to manage. He simply couldn't deal with another dilemma right now.

Yasof scratched at the nubby knuckle of his missing left pinky finger. He narrowed his eyes at the console which bore images from their high-flying drone. A large force of men was moving south through the City of Gaza.

"Captain, who is that force west of Omar Mukhtar Street? If those are Palestinian Police Forces, I want our troops to stay clear of them. Most of them are loyal to Hamas factions, but we've agreed to give them space to police their districts if they're active."

"No, Colonel. They have no police units anywhere west of Omar Mukhtar Street all the way to al-Nasser. The fighting was too bad last night, sir. They pulled out and asked for armored support."

"I want confirmation that it's a Hamas army, Captain. Then I want a two-by-two Saraph sweep from east and west. If that's a Crac Hassad force, I want to cripple and pin him down. He could be transporting more rockets to fire on us. Just tell the pilots to watch out for RPGs. We can't afford any downed planes, not in that beehive."

"Yes, sir."

"Sir?" A sergeant appeared at Yasof's elbow. "I've arrived from the airport with Chloe Azmaveth and her associate."

"Associate?" Yasof stood tall and turned to see Chloe at the door of the Forward Command bunker. At fifty, he was five years older and had always enjoyed the confident beauty from his younger days. She had avoided his advances since she was married, but he still held out hope.

He marched toward Chloe, scoping the lanky man with black eyes behind her. The man gave Yasof a chill, and he was reminded that Chloe continued in the covert arena even though she'd left the Mossad. Yasof knew she still had military contacts, old friends higher than he was, even if he was her IDF contact since her departure. Zvi, her husband, was no slouch, either, when it came to influence in Tel Aviv.

"*Shalom*, Chloe." He shook her hand. "Welcome back to Israel. I expected you to come alone."

"I'm Francis Malvao, Colonel," the gaunt man said, though he offered no hand. He chewed a giant wad of gum, visible as he chewed with his mouth open. "You'll hardly notice me."

"Of course. Welcome." Yasof made a mental note to have the man's file reviewed immediately. He turned his attention to Chloe, gazing into her daring brown eyes. "I was just speaking with my father last week about the Lebanese operation so long ago, how my unit's invasion distracted Hezbollah and the media for you to extract the hostages."

"I'm certain I was never in Lebanon, Kalil." Chloe glared at him. "And even if I was, it never happened, remember?"

"You should stay up on your Knesset briefings, Chloe." He winked and smiled. "That operation was declassified last year. You're a hero. Maybe if you visited more, we could—"

"We are not visiting, Colonel." Francis Malvao spoke firmly, raising his eyebrows for emphasis. "This is an urgent matter."

Yasof grit his teeth. This was his command post. He did the pushing. No one pushed him, and no one ever, ever interrupted him. But, he felt crippled by the unknown, the mystery of Chloe's presence and her dark-eyed friend.

"Did you find Corban Dowler?" Chloe asked. "Please tell me you've found him and we can get out of your hair."

"Our men on foot in Gaza are hunting Hamas terrorists, not checking identifications, Chloe, unless they come across a corpse, of which there are plenty. My units are spread thin across twenty-five miles. When they see someone armed in the street, they know it's an enemy. It's all I can do to keep them from killing civilians, especially since Hamas regularly uses the residences of loyalist families to launch attacks.

Hamas loves a high body count. Besides, Corban isn't exactly in Gaza legally, so this is difficult."

"He avoided protocol to get into Gaza to deliver medical supplies," Chloe said. "If you're checking identifications of the dead and you haven't come across Christopher Cagon, then Corban is still alive."

"But still, as you said, he avoided protocol. Chloe, he was smuggled somehow through our blockade. He entered illegally to distribute unauthorized equipment. To whom?"

"I don't like what you're insinuating, Kalil! COIL only helps civilians, especially the Christians, the non-aggressors in this war. He had a safe house somewhere in Rimal, but he was moving east on foot after he went to the safe house."

"East of Rimal?" Yasof walked to the console. "The whole city is east of Rimal. How do you expect us to find him if he doesn't want to be found?"

"At this point, he wants to be found. It's procedure to make contact any way possible on schedule. He's missed three check-ins now. If he hasn't been found dead, he's been captured."

"We did have our share of kidnappings early yesterday. We're still missing those two UN personnel from an ambushed convoy. Luc Lannoy and Annette Sheffield. That was here, in Zeitoun." Yasof pointed at the screen. "West of there, about here, we lost an infantry soldier named Aaron Adar, sometime last night. We have to assume they've all been kidnapped. Crac Hassad is the leading extremist across the city. Nothing happens in Gaza without his knowledge. Having said that, no demands or prisoner exchange offer has reached my office."

"Isn't that rare?" Francis asked. "No one has claimed responsibility for two missing UN people and an IDF soldier?"

"It's a bit rare. But the fighting has been extreme and communications have been down."

"Someone usually takes credit for an abduction by now, right?" Chloe held a palm open, as if begging for something she could use. "You're missing three people in the same vicinity as Corban, with no trace of their whereabouts. That doesn't seem odd?"

"Maybe. It may mean the obvious as well. Hamas may have them all. Or one of our BLU-109 bunker-busting super bombs disintegrated them. I'm not being insensitive, only honest."

"If you had to guess," Francis said, "where would Hamas be holding these captives if they did have them?"

"Perhaps south of the Old City. A large force we think is Hamas has mobilized with that heading. Something is definitely happening. We just don't know what."

"So the question is," Chloe asked, "why would a bunch of Hamas militants be moving south of the Old City on the most dangerous night of fighting?"

"We're trying to figure that out. Listen: the district of Zeitoun is swarming with Hamas. This large force is zigzagging, but definitely headed in an intentional direction. Maybe they've been summoned. It must be some of Crac Hassad's men. He's not even Gazan. He's Iranian, which is probably why he's caused more Gazan deaths and Israeli turmoil than anyone since Arafat. Hassad is more vicious than usual. He's kidnapped or imprisoned dozens of women and children, holding them somewhere. We're being blamed for countless civilian deaths or missing people, but it's probably this sadistic commander using the civilians as human shields or slave laborers."

"You said this force may have been summoned." Francis leaned forward, studying the console. Yasof didn't like him prying. "Summoned for what?"

"Crac Hassad would probably want to distance himself from any hostages his men may have, but there's word they have a biological weapon. Crac Hassad would want to have that in his own hands. He worked with munitions in Iran. His profile reads like he's a human detonator."

"So, they're in the district of Zeitoun." Francis stepped away. Yasof was glad the strange man who chewed too much gum was out of his way. Now he could focus more on Chloe.

"Could you lift your transmission jammer over Gaza City?" Chloe asked. "Corban has a sat-phone. Just give him ten minutes. He may be in hiding, waiting for a way to contact us."

"Ten minutes?" Yasof shook his head. "That's ten minutes we'd give Crac Hassad to communicate as well. We can't risk such a move. Corban isn't more valuable than the threat of a coordinated biological attack on Israel."

"What if it meant finding your biological weapon?"

"What are you talking about?" Yasof browsed the command room. Where was Francis? He pulled Chloe aside to talk quieter. "Do you know something about the weapon?"

"You know Corban's an experienced field agent. If he got wind of a biological weapon, he wouldn't ignore that threat against Israel. He's in Gaza City, Kalil. He may know where the weapon is. Lift the transmission blockade for just ten minutes. Do you have a better way to find the weapon?"

Yasof scratched the knuckle of his missing pinky again. He didn't like the espionage factor in this incursion. He preferred guerrilla or urban warfare instead of Chloe's undercover tactics any day.

"Interpol lost contact two weeks ago with someone who is close to the weapon." Yasof rolled his eyes, uncomfortable about trusting her with such sensitive intelligence even over some of his own people. "If I didn't know you already, Chloe, you'd never hear me say this, but your Corban Dowler is out there. And Interpol is out there somewhere, too."

"What? An undercover Interpol agent in Gaza? That's how you know the weapon is here?"

"That's how we know it was scheduled to be here by now, transported by the Interpol agent and an arms dealer called the Serval."

"Never heard of him."

"Is Corban resourceful enough to stop a biological threat if he and the Interpol agent worked together?"

"Corban is the best. If the weapon is local and he's identified it, he'll give his life if he must to stop an attack. The Interpol agent and he can work together, but he'll never know who the agent is if we don't lift the transmission blockade. We have to contact him!"

"Okay. I may be able to talk my superiors into this." Yasof's eyes searched the room again for Francis. "Where is your friend, Francis Malvao?"

Luigi Putelli spit his gum onto the ground outside the Forward Command bunker and shoved three new pieces into his mouth. He watched an IDF tank commander speak Hebrew to a number of ground troops, fully armed. Luigi didn't know Hebrew, but he could tell fresh foot soldiers were soon to be deployed into the Gaza Strip to reinforce the raging battle at its apex that night.

Trailing behind a few yards, Luigi watched a lone IDF soldier carry his pack and M-16 assault rifle into a mobile bathroom trailer. The soldier seemed to be about Luigi's height, maybe a little thicker in the chest. Luigi wandered over to the trailer, then glanced back to find the tank commander and his audience paying him no mind.

Inside the trailer, Luigi counted three toilet stalls. Only the last one was occupied. Luigi washed his hands at a single sink until the soldier emerged from the stall. Luigi cupped his hands and threw water into the man's face. The soldier recoiled at the assault and was about to scream out when Luigi jabbed a fist at the man's unprotected diaphragm. While the soldier gasped for air, Luigi raked the man's hand across the toxic belt buckle. Within seconds, the soldier fell unconscious and Luigi dragged him into the stall and stripped him of his uniform, pack, and rifle.

Five minutes later, Luigi walked past the tank commander, saluted, and hopped onto the back of a moving Namer heavy armored personnel transport headed toward Gaza. Luigi pulled his helmet down over his eyes and crossed his arms to cover his loose uniform. Twenty other soldiers chatted excitedly as they anticipated their duty in the coming ground assault.

Luigi blew a bubble with his gum and smiled as the transport jostled over a pothole. How would Corban react at the sight of him? He figured Corban's God was taking care of his old friend, but Luigi hoped he could help Corban in a way that meant something to Corban. After all, Corban had saved Luigi's life more than once. The least Luigi could do was risk his own for Corban.

†

CHAPTER EIGHT

WEST GAZA CITY, RIMAL DISTRICT

"You saved my neck back there," Titus whispered in the darkness. He lay next to Corban on the floor of the safe house, listening to occasional gunfire in the street. For a moment, he couldn't speak. His heart was beating like a locomotive. Death had never been so near. "Don't think I'm not grateful. Those three boys would've messed up my good looks with a few bullets to my forehead."

"Don't thank me." Corban paused as a fighter bomber rumbled overhead, its ordnance shaking the neighborhood like an earthquake. "Thank your Creator, Titus. If I were still the man I was before He changed me, you'd be dead."

"Tough words from a man without a gun in his hand." Titus tapped a finger on his own handgun. "Remember, I'm doing you a favor on this medical run."

"You're doing your conscience a favor." Corban chuckled. Titus didn't like being laughed at. "And quit threatening me with your gun or I'll take it from you and give you a fatherly whipping with it."

"Think you could, old man?" Titus felt his pride stepped on, and he was tempted to teach Corban a lesson. "You've got some mouth on you for a Christian."

"God told me to love my enemies, and I do. He didn't tell me to cower before them, and I never have. I know the weight of a loaded Glock 18, Titus, so just put it away. You've had an empty clip all day, probably since you shot Aaron."

Titus tested the weight of his handgun in his palm. How could someone know that without touching his gun? He shoved it into his waistband.

"You're good, Corban. I ran out of bullets last night. You knew it and you didn't jump me. I can't figure you out."

"I prayed about you. You seem like a reasonable man. God's used greedy crooks before, and I couldn't make this run alone."

"So, you think you have me all figured out, huh?" Titus' anger started to rise again, feeling like he was talking to his brother, Rudy, who never stopped preaching to him, claiming to know Titus' sinful condition so well. "You don't know me at all."

"Titus, you're an outcast. You sacrifice everything for the thrill of money and action. At the end of the day, after every job, you're still dead inside, wishing you had just one person in the world who could understand your loneliness, someone you could trust with everything. Twenty years ago, Titus, I was you. That's how I know you. That's how I know you're nothing special, just like I was nothing special. We're just broken vessels without Jesus Christ. You want to feel right inside? You won't find that satisfaction from things in this world. That void has to be filled by Christ."

A gunship circled the apartment building, hunting. A ground RPG zipped through the air, sending the gunship east.

"If you knew I was out of bullets all day . . . why didn't you do something about the canister I had on my shoulder?" Titus' throat felt dry. He guessed it was guilt, but he brushed it off, resisting what he figured were Corban's mind tricks. "You had to know what was in the canister."

"Do you really believe the Israelis would permit a biological weapon into their protectorate?" In the darkness of the safe house, Titus flinched when Corban placed his hand on his arm, but he didn't pull away. "I know many of your clients have been Arabs, and most of them want to wipe the Jewish people from the face of the earth, but I believe you've gambled one too many times. I've realized God has sent me here to reach you. You're spent, Titus, and this is your wake-up call."

"Do you know something about the canister I don't?" When Titus' voice cracked, he guessed he was being as vulnerable as he'd ever been with anyone. He'd done his best to control the scene for himself in front of Annette, but Gaza was clearly Corban's area of expertise. "You think there's some cosmic reason you and I have met? I don't think so. Like you said, I'm not that special."

"Maybe you're blinded by greed, Titus. It's been right in front of you."

"You're bluffing. You're trying to make me paranoid by messing with my mind. You just don't want me to make the sale. Let me guess: you're a Zionist."

"Do you mean, do I stand with the Jewish people? Yes. While I'm a Christian first, I do realize God's plan for His Chosen ones. But I'm here tonight for more of God's people— the Palestinian Christians."

"If the IDF knows I'm in Gaza, that changes conditions for my deal." Titus squeezed his eyes shut. He wasn't ready to retire or go to prison. Money was all he had. His whole family was successful. They probably didn't think of him anymore, but deep down, he'd wanted to prove himself to them. "It doesn't matter. It's worth the risk. Besides, Syrian investors already put a down payment on the merchandise."

"Why don't we pray about all these things that are out of our control?"

"What?" Titus shrank away, but Corban kept his hand on his shoulder. "*Pray?* What is this, Sunday School?"

"Lord God, we are simple, prideful men with many flaws. Even now, we hide like serpents, afraid for our lives. Titus doesn't serve You, Lord, but I ask that You open his eyes as he risks his life to help Christians among the Palestinians. We have far to journey over dangerous ground to deliver the insulin and Bibles, Lord, and we need Your protection. Please watch over Aaron, Oleg, and Annette as well. May they see Your hand, even in this violent place. I ask also that You spare everyone from harm caused by Titus' selfish intentions, including himself. I don't envy the decisions before him, Lord, so direct his heart, I ask. In Jesus' Name, amen."

A mortar round exploded, shaking the building. An infant wailed in an apartment nearby.

"So now we're invincible?" Titus scoffed. "Quit trying to sway me from the deal, Corban. Your mind tricks won't work on me. I heard enough of that stuff growing up in Arkansas."

"Listen. The battle is moving north again." Corban rose to his feet and pulled Titus up with him. "I know your mind is too strong to be touched by mind tricks, Titus, so it must be your conscience getting to you."

Titus moved aside as Corban lit a candle on the table. Their shadows flickered on the walls.

"An empty room? All this for nothing? Look at this place! You've been robbed, old man!"

Corban moved a mattress, then bent low and clicked something against the wall. There was a sound of pulleys straining against a counterweight, and the wall rose to expose a massive cache of weapons and gear.

"Don't touch anything," Corban ordered as Titus stood speechless before the hardware.

Though Titus had safe houses all over the world, he'd never seen anything like this. It was completely unexpected in Gaza City! He watched Corban index the equipment, calling out what they would need. Old man or not, Titus was glad he was with Corban Dowler

Corban selected two machine pistols off the safe house wall and handed them to Titus. To Titus, they felt like toys—and he couldn't wait to play with them.

"These are the NL weapon series. Non-lethal. This is the NL-2. Fully automatic or single shot selector. Two hundred and fifty round clips with a maximum effective range of fifty yards."

Titus raised his eyebrows as Corban handed him a dozen clips.

"What kind of rounds are we talking about here?"

"Water-soluble tranquilizer pellets that vaporize on impact. The target needs to inhale the vapor. Knockout time won't be longer than twenty minutes for a grown man." Corban picked out two assault rifles, the size of M-14s. "This is the NL-3. You can select between fully auto, five-round bursts, or single shot firing. Five-hundred-round magazine. Same load as the NL-2. This'll get us through the troublemakers down on the street within one hundred yards."

"Nice, but what's that?" Titus' arms were full with four NL weapons and clips, but he still managed to point at an even more impressive rifle on the wall. "It looks like a fifty-caliber!"

"That's the NL-X1 sniper rifle. Twelve-round magazine, five tranq darts within each round with a spread of five feet at one thousand yards. Figure a one hour knockout time for these biodegradable tranqs."

"One thousand yards? A non-lethal sniper rifle. Huh. Who would've thought?"

"Can't figure on accuracy after one thousand yards." Corban adjusted the cylinder on top of the sniper rifle. "A 4x20 scope with night vision adapter. I'll bring it along, but most of what we have to do is close street fighting."

"I . . . don't know what to say." Titus set all the weapons on the floor to familiarize himself with them in the candlelight. "I've heard of these, but didn't believe they were real."

"They'll do in a pinch, and the target only wakes up with a little hangover." Corban selected two packs off the wall and packed them with medical gear, emergency rations, and water containers. Finally, he took a spare sat-phone off the wall and turned it on. Titus heard the dial tone. "Listen! Israel stopped jamming!"

Titus clutched an NL-2 machine pistol and aimed it at Corban's face. But when Titus looked down at Corban's other hand, he saw the old man was already aiming an NL-3 at Titus.

"Put it down, Corban! I swear, I'll shoot you!"

"Back off, Titus." Corban dialed with his thumb. "We don't know how long communications will be up. This might be our only chance to save Aaron and get Annette to safety."

"Put the phone down!"

"It's already ringing. When your deal goes south, I'm the only thing standing between you and an Israeli Tavor assault rifle. And we need each other for what's ahead."

Titus pressed his lips together in frustration. Nothing was right about this. Corban was supposed to be his prisoner. Finally, he lowered his weapon. Conceding to anyone was so foreign to him. He was the Serval!

"Just because these are non-lethal weapons doesn't mean I won't hurt you if you say anything about the deal. Don't say anything!"

"Be quiet." Corban turned his back on Titus, but Titus still put his head next to Corban's to hear everything. "Chloe? Are you there?"

"Corban! Thank God! We have three more minutes of jammer-free time. I'm at Forward Command in Ashkelon with Francis Malvao."

"I'm at the safe house in Rimal. Jachin is dead. I'm going to his place to make the insulin drop. Keep your eye on Francis Malvao."

"Actually, Francis has already disappeared. Sorry. I should've never let him tag along. IDF Colonel Kalil Yasof wants me to ask you if you came across a guy named Crac Hassad or rumors of a biological weapon."

"Um . . . Paul has connected with an Athenian with the idol." Corban paused, and Titus clenched his teeth. It was some code between them. "It's all covered."

"You're sure? The threat is real?"

"I doubt it. Paul was in the idol's presence and witnessed

an advocate of King David nearby, so I'm assuming the idol is a fake to catch the governor."

"Governor?" the woman named Chloe asked. "Okay, I understand. Praise God. We're nearly out of time."

"Tell your colonel I have Aaron Adar and Annette Sheffield south of the Old City. Aaron is wounded but stable. He needs—Hello? Hello, Chloe?" Corban clicked the phone off. Titus moved away, uncertain of how much Corban had jeopardized his deal. "Lost the connection. Didn't even get a chance to call in an extraction for Aaron and Annette."

"Fine by me." Titus shrugged. "You would've only led them to Oleg. What was that about Paul and some idol?"

"Just Bible talk. You ever read the Bible, Titus? You mentioned Arkansas."

Corban held up one backpack. Titus thrust his arms through the shoulder straps, then tightened the torso belt.

"Sure, when I was a kid. I did the Sunday School thing with my brother and little sister."

"I bet now you wish you would've paid attention, huh?" Corban smiled and shouldered his pack without help. "Then you would've known what I said on the phone to my contact."

"All I know is that you didn't say my name or tell them where Oleg is. How about that Francis Malvao guy you told your contact to keep an eye on? What's his story?"

Corban lowered the secret wall, leaned the mattress in place, and blew out the candle.

"Francis Malvao is a false identity for an ex-assassin from Italy. He's been off the grid for a while, but he's watched my back for years, ever since I didn't kill him when I could have. We've traveled some together. You could say we have a sort of distant brother relationship. You'll want to watch out for him, more than the Saraph gunships if he catches up with us, especially if you still have it in your mind that I'm your prisoner."

"That's all I need. More enemies."

Corban chuckled and opened the door, then stood with Titus to study the dark street below. Far away, choppers traversed the skyline, seen only in strobes of exploding rockets. Strapped over Corban's pack was the NL-X1 sniper rifle. Titus was aching to fire it. An NL-2 machine pistol hung from each of their shoulders, and NL-3 rifles were in their hands—their primary weapons.

Titus hadn't been this well-armed in his life, but around Corban, he was learning that nothing would be easy.

"I'll take point," Corban said to Titus. He was feeling the pressure of completing his mission in Gaza: to deliver the insulin. "Cover formation. Aim for the chest, neck, or chin, or they won't inhale the tranq."

"I get it. But how do we take out the gunships? And those drones will spot us as soon as we step outside."

"Another reason you should be thanking the good Lord, Titus. My contact is in Ashkelon. Now that she knows approximately where we are and where we're going, she'll track us across the city. She'll keep the Saraphs off our backs as long as she doesn't lose us. I can't say the same for any ground resistance, IDF or otherwise. They'll shoot to kill."

Instead of waiting for Titus to respond, Corban darted from the doorway and headed for the stairs. When he was on ground level, he looked up to see Titus hadn't moved, covering him like a pro. Now, Corban covered Titus as he descended. Both men moved like the elite operatives they were, rifles leveled and sweeping only where their bodies faced. Regardless of the danger, Corban couldn't deny the exhilaration of working with a skilled agent, even if Titus wasn't a COIL man.

One block later, Corban held up a fist and eased up to a bombed media store. Titus stepped into the doorway of a shop behind and across the street from Corban, covering him over open sights.

Corban peered around the corner once, then quickly withdrew his head, allowing his mind to process the scene after the fact. Eight to twelve men stood around the corner under an awning where the satellites or drones couldn't see them. That made them non-Israeli, and probably not Palestinian police. He guessed they were Hamas.

With a signal, Corban brought Titus up to a parallel position across the street. As soon as Corban saw Titus moving, he turned his attention back to the men they had to somehow pass. Corban quickly ensured his rifle selector was on five-round bursts, then stepped around the corner. He fired on the nearest men before they saw him. The clicking of the NL-3 chamber and CO_2 burst of air was no louder than a silenced pistol. Because there was no obvious gunfire or muzzle flash, there were three men slumped unconscious on the ground before the first man noticed danger was near, and shouldered his AK-47. At that moment, they noticed Corban, but then Titus was firing, his pellets whipping down the street at a cycle rate of six hundred rounds per minute.

Two men managed to fire at Corban, but they were

frantically aiming and the bullets spit dirt to Corban's right.

As soon as the men were down, Corban ran forward—
with Titus covering—and collected their rifles. There were
eleven men down, mostly in their twenties. Since his arms
were already full, Corban couldn't carry the rifles away to
dispose of them, so he threw them onto the nearest roof and
ran back to the east-to-west street. Titus gave Corban a
thumbs-up, then Corban took point again. He checked his
watch. It was already after ten o'clock. Five hours until Titus'
deal with Crac Hassad at the factory. He prayed for God's
hand to be upon Annette and Aaron.

SOUTH GAZA CITY, ZEITOUN DISTRICT

Aaron Adar was dreaming. He was six years old, and next
to him on the train seat was his father, a hardened Russian
Jew. The train ride south was too long for the man. His wife
hadn't packed enough food. His shoes were too old to set foot
in their new country of Israel. The man seemed to never stop
complaining, but not without reason. He held up one foot and
wiggled his exposed big toe. Aaron giggled and his father cast
him a stern look, shutting his mouth.

"Sorry, Papa."

"You may laugh now, Aaron. I will laugh later when these
are your shoes." His father smiled, breaking the tension. He
ruffled Aaron's hair. "And somehow, even wearing these
holey shoes as a man, we will find you a fine Israeli wife, like
Eliezer found for Isaac."

"Elizabeth . . ." Aaron mumbled in his fevered sleep.
"Elizabeth . . ."

Aaron opened his eyes to an angel, but not his angel. His dream melted away and he focused on Annette, with explosions and gunfire and terror nearby.

"Are you okay?" She mopped his forehead. "You were calling for Elizabeth. Oleg said I should wake you before you draw attention to us. Anyone could be coming up the street outside."

Looking past Annette, Aaron saw the shadow of the stout, ugly man they knew as Oleg. The only light in the deserted factory was from the window, and that light came in strobes from artillery and sweeping Saraph spotlights.

"I was dreaming." Aaron shook his head. "I will never see my Elizabeth again."

"Don't say that. Corban and Titus will be back any minute. They'll get us out of here."

"Titus shot me. He doesn't care if I die."

Aaron turned his face from Annette and squeezed his eyes shut to the battle outside. His breathing made wheezing sounds. He knew he was dying.

"Keep him talking," Oleg ordered Annette. The man's accent reminded Aaron of his father's voice, though he'd never learned English. "I can hear his breathing. He'll die if he sleeps again."

Annette shook Aaron's leg.

"Hey, Aaron. Why don't you tell me about Elizabeth? I bet she's pretty, huh?"

"Pretty?" Aaron rolled his head back to look at Annette. If he were about to die, he didn't mind sharing his happiest thoughts with the strange woman and a Russian arms dealer. "She's the sparkle of morning sunlight on the Jordan."

"How did you two meet?"

"At my work." Aaron tried to inhale deeply, but it hurt too much. "I was a resident doctor of physical therapy. She came to me as her leg was healing after a climbing accident up in Galilee. We had met as children, but now we were meeting as adults. She could've picked another therapist, but she picked me. It was the year we pulled out of Gaza. This was our home. Life was . . . perfect."

"That's a beautiful story. I'm sure your parents are so happy for you."

"Yes. Except they were killed by a Qassam rocket last year. Crac Hassad is committed to killing all Jews. He started with my parents. I told them they lived too close to Gaza. The Palestinians took our land and now want our blood."

"Not all Palestinians. You know that. Corban said there are Palestinian Christians who love their Israeli neighbors. Where do you plan to take Elizabeth on your honeymoon?"

"Quiet!" Oleg whispered. "Someone is coming!"

Oleg knelt next to the wall and aimed his pistol at the window. The canister was nestled on his back with the strap across his chest. Aaron hardly breathed. If it was Crac Hassad, then he was dead. Everyone knew Hassad had killed other captured Israeli soldiers. Their mutilated bodies had been put on display through the media.

A chickadee whistled from outside. It was a beautiful sound of nature that softened Aaron's face. He hoped this was the sound of the afterlife.

Oleg cupped his hand around his mouth and whistled back. He stood, and Titus and Corban dove through the window, both breathless from running. Aaron sat up with

Annette's help, surprised the strange older man and Titus had actually returned with packs full of gear.

"We got everything we need, except a doctor." Corban knelt next to Aaron. He pulled out a bag of fluids and tapped Aaron's arm for a vein. Behind him, Titus gave Oleg and Annette food ration packs. Aaron winced as the needle eased under the skin. "Just relax, Aaron. We'll have that bullet out in a little while."

"Corban, we don't have time," Titus said. "If you want to deliver that insulin, we need to leave now to be back in time for the deal."

"Wait. No." Annette wiped her mouth with the back of her hand. "Corban, you have everything here. Why would you leave Aaron to die after risking your lives to bring all this? I don't know how to help him!"

"It won't take more than a half-hour." Corban continued to work on Aaron. "I can get that bullet with what we have."

"Oleg can do it." Titus gestured at his partner. "He's a genius with a knife."

"No!" Aaron grit his teeth through the pain. "He's not touching me!"

"I could do it." Oleg took a swig of water to wash down his food. "But I'd first like to know where you got those guns and why Corban is armed."

"Don't sweat it, Oleg," Titus said. "They're tranq guns. Can you get this kid back on this side of the grave? I don't want his condition interrupting the deal in a few hours."

"Do I have to wash my hands?" Oleg wiped his hands on his jeans. Titus laughed as Aaron stuttered a protest. "Take off. Annette, you're my nurse."

"Please, Corban, don't leave!" Annette said. "Titus, look at Oleg. Are you serious?"

Titus glanced at his partner.

"Just because he doesn't like to bathe doesn't mean he doesn't know how to gut a fish." Oleg and Titus laughed. "Relax, kid. Oleg's no beginner. Corban, we need to roll."

"It's okay." Corban nodded at Annette. "Their joking around relaxes their nerves, even when it's tasteless. The bullet's between his ribs. You guys can do it. Just hold the light low so no one sees it outside. I can finish up when I get back."

"If you get back!" Annette reached over Aaron to grab Corban's arm, but Corban stood and moved toward Titus.

"Get back before Luc Lannoy returns with Crac Hassad," Oleg said over his shoulder as he rolled up his sleeves. He still hadn't taken off the canister. "Annette, hand me the disinfectant. There should be an antibiotic drip in that bag. Put it in his IV. Hold it up higher."

Fighting panic, Aaron looked to Corban for help, but Corban had already left with Titus, abandoning Aaron to the likes of Oleg Saratov. Annette touched Aaron's shoulder as he began to tremble in shock, and Oleg sat his bulk down at Aaron's side.

✝

CHAPTER NINE

"I'm used to taking point," Titus said as he caught his breath. He was shoulder to shoulder with Corban, their backs to a crumbled wall that had once been a residence. The wall now bordered a crater.

Titus had settled into the rhythm of sprinting and waiting through the haunted streets of Gaza. He was careful to use his rifle's night vision scope to study the darkest corners of bombed buildings where an enemy could be hiding. The fires and distant explosions lit up the night only so much.

"I used to be that way about life." Corban poked his head over the wall, Titus with him, to see a small unit of IDF soldiers lingering at a crossroads. "But I let God take point now. Goes much smoother. If we're not yielding to Him, we're living without Him."

"I'm talking about taking point through this war zone, and you relate it to your faith?" Titus shook his head. "Don't make me run out there into an IDF hail of gunfire just to shut you up."

"Let them move on. They're friendly, but we don't want them slowing us up with a bunch of questions, even if you are being a Good Samaritan at the moment."

"Hey, I do plenty of good things for people!" Titus shifted his pack. Corban had given him the heavier pack, the one with all the Bibles for the Palestinian people, instead of the insulin and medical supplies. He guessed that was probably one of the Bibles digging into his spine between his shoulder blades. But he dared not complain or Corban would give him another lesson, probably about self-sacrifice or bearing another's burdens. "I'm just saying I'm used to taking point. Usually, I'm the one in charge, risking everything to get what I want or go where I want."

"I understand your discomfort. It's humbling. Now you're risking everything to give others what they need."

"I swear, Corban, if you give me one more Bible lesson, I'll drop this pack right here and return to Oleg. We may not even make it back in time for the deal now. All this cursed waiting!"

Corban showed him the time on his watch.

"We're doing fine. It's only another few blocks."

"How can you tell where one block ends and another begins? Look at this devastation!"

"War is ugly, but no uglier than the hearts of the men who hate this much to go to war."

"The Palestinians are always the bad guys with you."

"No, not true. Israel isn't faultless. I know that. But I'm also a student of history. As a people, the Jews have been blessed, and they work hard against all odds. Many Palestinians claim to be victimized and want everything for free. Their immigrant parents and grandparents temporarily abandoned the land so Israel could be wiped out during their first few wars for survival. Later, when Israel won their conflicts, those Palestinians returned and expected their property back. The Bible talks about how God will never abandon His Chosen

People, but as individuals, He loves each and every person in this conflict—Israeli, Palestinian, Lebanese, even those instigating Iranians and Syrians."

"You're opinionated, Corban." Titus laughed. "I get what you're saying about God taking point in your life. You even let Him take point of your opinions and advice."

"If that's a Bible lesson you're repeating back to me, then my job here is done." Corban smiled, then flinched as an RPG suddenly exploded near the intersection. "Oh, that didn't sound good."

Both men raised their heads over the wall to see the IDF unit scatter and take cover as Hamas militants fired down on them from rooftops.

"Give them cover fire!" Corban yelled over the noise. "The Israelis are pinned down!"

Titus swung his NL-3 over the rubble and fired on the ambushers above. Corban joined in, and from their angle of covering the IDF soldiers, the Hamas terrorists were caught in the crossfire and forced to move back. The IDF troops took that opportunity to retreat past Corban and Titus. Titus raised his hand to gesture to the friendlies that it was he who had saved their lives, but they kept running down the street, two soldiers in the rear providing additional cover fire.

"They didn't even know we helped them!" Titus loaded a fresh magazine by slamming it home. "We risked our lives and that's the thanks we get?"

"Now you know how God feels." Corban swept his night vision scope from side to side, still watching the rooftops. "You'd think people would show a little gratitude for all that God does for them."

"It looks clear. Are you ready to go?"

"I'm ready." Corban nodded. "You still want to take point?"

"I don't know where I'm going."

"Exactly my point—in more ways than one."

Corban rose from behind the wall and crouched as he ran across the street, his muzzle aimed upward. Titus watched the older man dart down the street to the intersection and pause to sweep the area. Titus felt the Bible against his spine. He looked back the way they'd come, wondering if he could be back at Oleg's side in an hour if he left now. But Corban was right: Titus' conscience needed to clear itself by helping the helpless. And he hated sitting around doing nothing, waiting for his client. One of the things on his conscience had nothing to do with shooting Aaron or selling a weapon to evil people. It had to do with Annette. A clothing model in this carnage? He hadn't comforted her or gone out of his way to make her feel safe. Sure, she seemed brave, but what had become of his life when he was holding frightened people as prisoners?

"My conscience isn't stronger than my greed, though," Titus mumbled and rose to his full height to check the street behind him. He didn't mind helping the helpless as long as it didn't interfere with his pocketbook.

Two hundred yards later, Titus knelt next to a withered cypress tree and searched the shadows for Corban. Titus briefly fought panic as he imagined traveling alone in Gaza City. He had plenty of NL ammo now, but the enemy had live rounds. Without a partner to offer cover fire, his chances were slim. That's why he'd brought Oleg—to watch his back.

A chickadee whistled to his right. Titus peered across the front dirt yard of a three-story apartment complex. Through his night scope, he could see fifty-caliber bullet depressions in the structure's walls. Corban waved from the second story railing.

Titus climbed rickety stairs and knelt next to Corban outside the metal door.

"Is this it?"

"Remember the man who lay dead with these packs?"

"Sure. You called him Jachin."

"This is Jachin's home. His wife and two kids are inside. They're still expecting him."

"I don't do well with mourners."

"Your friend, Luc Lannoy, is the one who killed Jachin. The least you could do is comfort the widow. Her name is Leah."

Corban tapped lightly on the metal door, waited, then knocked twice more.

Titus shook his head.

"Nobody's home. Let's go. We can still—"

"They have to be home. There's nowhere else to go. They're Palenstinian Christians, and their neighbors shun them. They have no one."

"Why do they have Hebrew names? Leah, and you said the diabetic girl is Huldah?"

"And the boy is Levi. They renamed themselves when they accepted Christ into their lives. That's how much their faith means to these people, but their neighbors saw them only as Palestinians who were disowning their heritage by taking Hebrew names. Jachin's life was full of trials, but he was happy. He knew God's love was real."

"He was insane." Titus scoffed.

The padlock finally jiggled inside and the door cracked open. A bearded man's face appeared. Titus stuck his muzzle in the face that Corban didn't seem to recognize.

"Let us in." Corban ordered in Arabic. "We have insulin for Huldah. Jachin sent us."

"Where is Jachin? He was expected back yesterday."

"Titus, push through the door," Corban said in German. "Something's wrong."

Taking a step back, Titus kicked above the door handle. The bearded man stumbled backwards, and Titus plowed through the door with a heavy shoulder. Corban followed after Titus and shut the door. The room was dark until Titus flicked a lighter. He lit a lamp on a paneled countertop to illuminate the bearded man lying on his back on the floor, in the midst of six children and two women.

As Corban used the lamp to study the faces of the frightened people, Titus kept his gun on the bearded man. Corban motioned to a woman in her sixties.

"Where is Leah and her children?" he asked in Arabic. "Jachin sent me with insulin for Huldah."

The woman remained silent and pulled one of the younger children closer.

"I am Nuri, Jachin's friend," the bearded man said. "When Jachin didn't return yesterday, Leah brought the children to my home where many of us had gathered for prayer. A gang of men rushed in as you have done, and they took many of our people, including Leah, Huldah, and Levi. We didn't know where else to go but here. What news do you have of Jachin?"

"He's with his Lord in heaven," Corban said.

"You're all Christians?" Titus lowered his rifle and shrugged out of his heavy pack. "What do you want to do, Corban?"

"Watch out the window. If anyone comes for these people, I'll gladly disappoint them." Titus moved to the window and peeled back a corner of the shatter-proofing tape to watch the street, but he kept an eye on Corban as well. Corban pulled Nuri to his feet and kissed the man on both cheeks. "My name is Chris. I am also a Christian. I am Jachin's friend and supplier from America. He has told me much about the church here, but we thought it safest if I dealt only with Jachin." Corban unzipped the pack that Titus had carried. Bibles, vitamin packs, and bundles of Israeli shekels tumbled out. "We brought all we could. I wish it were more."

Corban set aside his rifles and pack to offer the children chocolate candies. The children didn't hesitate to become chocolate messes in their glee.

"So, can we call this mission accomplished?" Titus asked in German. "It took us two hours to get here from the factory and it's already after midnight."

"Nuri, can you tell me who took Leah and the others?"

"They were Palestinian men—I'm certain, but I didn't see which division." He smiled as one of his children crawled into his lap and pushed candy into his mouth. "We haven't had sweets for months."

"Nuri, I know you don't want to endanger your family, but I need to know why Hamas took Leah."

"We're Christians, but we're also Palestinians. Leah and the others will become human shields, or they'll be killed to make Israel look like war criminals."

"Where would they be taken? Does Hamas have a base you know of?"

"The mosque!" The older woman blurted. She held a child on her hip. "Nuri, tell him about the mosque."

"My mother-in-law," Nuri said. "There's a Crac Hassad gang who's been hiding in Ibn Uthman Mosque in Shuja'iyya. The Israelis destroyed it last year, but it has been rebuilt. Crac Hassad keeps part of his army there because the Israelis now know there are many civilians being housed there as well."

"Human shields," Titus said with a growl, but then he shut his mouth. It was those same animals to whom he was about to sell a biological weapon.

"Then Leah and the others are at this mosque?" Corban picked up his rifles. "You're certain?"

"It makes sense." Nuri shrugged. "There's a school building farther east where other women and children are forced to live, but the mosque is closer. The military uses Christians when they can, because we're now outcasts. When we're not available because we're all dead, Hamas will use their own families."

"Titus, how's the street?"

"All clear at the moment."

"Shuja'iyya is on a hill east of here." Corban reloaded his weapons. "How will we recognize this mosque?"

Titus tried to listen as Nuri gave Corban directions to the mosque, but one of Nuri's children had wrapped herself around Titus' leg. She stared up at him with large eyes, a toothy smile on her face that begged for more candy.

"Are you a superhero?" she asked.

"No, I'm the villain." Titus gestured at Corban. "He's the

superhero." Titus stepped away from the window and out of the girl's embrace. He drew Corban aside and spoke in German. "There's no way we can get back to Oleg in time for the meet if we go farther east. If you want to help every suffering Christian in Gaza, you'll do it alone."

"We're going together, Titus. Leave everything here but your canteen, ammo, and weapons. We'll be traveling fast and light with—"

"No!" Titus gripped the front of Corban's shirt and shoved him against the wall. "None of these people are worth it! Even if you did help them tonight, what about next week? They have a death wish to live here. Their own people want nothing to do with them. They're Christians!"

"They stay here out of love for their people," Corban stated calmly, even as Titus breathed in his face. "They risk their lives to show Christ's love to the people who hate them. The least we can do is help them for one night. They aren't afraid of dying like you are."

"Then you're on your own, and you'll die like the fool you are if you think you can make a difference here."

"I'd die a hundred times for these people."

Titus released Corban and backed away.

"These aren't your people, Corban. All they do is kill one another. How can you care so much?"

"I'm obligated if I can help. God has given me the desire, resources, and a few meager skills. I wasted most of my life serving myself and stashing funds from spy networks that no country dared to take for fear of reprisals. Money that was meant for evil was left in unclaimed accounts, and all I had to do was direct those funds for good. That's why I do this—

because I can. For God. And because He did it for me. That was a much more costly price than a few spy resources."

"Shut up. I'm not spending my fortune, even if you are, on the likes of these." Titus adjusted his weapons and prepared to leave. "I have to get back to the factory. Oleg needs me."

"You don't get it, do you?" Corban chuckled. "So careful, yet so blinded by greed. You really think I'd risk my life to help a few here if there was a biological weapon threatening thousands?"

"What? What are you saying?" Titus felt the blood drain from his face. "That's the second time you've said something like that! What are you talking about?"

"There won't be a deal for whatever canister you have."

"Why not? Did Israel get Crac Hassad?"

"As far as I know, Crac Hassad's alive. The deal will fail because there's no biological weapon."

"You're crazy. I witnessed a demonstration myself in Pakistan. I saw what it can do."

"In Pakistan? And your little case has never left your sight?" Corban walked forward and placed a hand on Titus' shoulder. "No, friend. An Interpol agent wouldn't allow such a chemical to fall into Crac Hassad's hands. It was just a matter of time before you found out. Now seems like the right time, because I need you focused on something other than what you've already lost."

"Interpol? How?" Titus felt sick. He turned away to lean against the wall. "You're lying. I've been too careful. I haven't let anyone close to me for weeks."

"I recognized him the minute you guys entered the factory to talk to Luc Lannoy. I've been out of the game for a few years, but I still recognize some of the older guys in deep cover."

"No. No, Oleg Saratov is . . ."

"He's Interpol, Titus. As soon as I saw him, I knew he must've switched out the weapon before it ever arrived in Gaza. His superiors would've arrested you days ago, otherwise. The IDF probably knows all about you."

"Then why haven't I been arrested? Why let me come this far?"

"I can guess," Corban said. "They're after Crac Hassad. He's Iranian by birth. You probably know more than me what he's done, the people he's killed to gain status, even his own family, the news has said, before he came from Iran."

"Oleg!" Titus started for the door. "I'll kill him myself!"

Moving quickly, Corban planted his foot in front of the door. When Titus grabbed for Corban's shirt front this time, Corban twisted Titus' hand sideways and slammed Titus' face against the covered window. Corban kept hard pressure on Titus' hand behind his back.

"Just think for a minute, Titus! This is your chance to do the right thing. Give Crac Hassad to Interpol and to Israel. You can walk away. The Serval can put on a new face. There's no deal tonight. Help me go to the mosque, and then we can go help Oleg take down Crac Hassad, if there's still time."

"You don't know what you're saying! Crac will have an army with him. They're probably already on their way to the factory with Luc Lannoy."

Corban released Titus and let him turn around. Titus rubbed his shoulder, hating the feel of defeat, but Corban was talking more and more sense. Over the last weeks, Titus had left the canister alone with Oleg enough for it to be swapped out. It was possible the old man was telling the truth.

"Then it's a good thing we're armed for an army." Corban touched the NL-X1 strapped to his back. "At the right angle, this thing can take out three to five targets with one shot."

"I can't switch sides just like that!" Titus hung his head. "I've been hunted by too many countries for too long to turn around and help people now."

"Forget those countries and start helping the people. You know who I am. I can help you start over. I've done it for others."

"I don't need you to do it. I have my own resources." Titus rested his hands on his hips. His eyes went to Nuri and his wide-eyed family. They didn't seem to understand English, but their faces showed concern for him. "If Oleg is who you say he is, he's supposed to take down Crac Hassad, right? Single-handedly?"

"Well, he probably didn't take into account Israel's blanket communications jam. He was probably hoping to have support at hand when Crac Hassad arrives at the factory by three o'clock."

"If the canister doesn't have anything real in it, Crac will kill Oleg," Titus said. "Then he'll take Annette and just kill the wounded Israeli kid. But first, Oleg will probably try to put the deal off, once Crac Hassad arrives, until I'm there to back him up in some way. He knows I'd back him up through anything. I can't believe he's Interpol!"

"Oleg won't be able to move with Aaron since he's injured. We need to get to that mosque, bring Leah and the others back here, and run to back up Oleg."

"That phone call you made to your contact, it was about all this?"

"It was. They know I'm with the one who brought in the supposed bio-weapon. They seem to know everything except where Crac Hassad is. And they want to secure whatever may be in that canister, just in case."

"I can't believe this." Titus took a deep breath. "I was going to get millions for that thing. Whatever. Okay, we have two hours to do everything. If I help you, you better get me out of the mix when the IDF closes in. The Mossad would love to get their hands on me."

"The Lord would love to get his hands on you, too, but you're too slippery. Something we'll have to pray more about." Corban nodded at Nuri. "We won't be long. Stay here with the lights out."

Nuri put out the lamp before Titus opened the door for Corban to take the lead down the stairs and into the street.

Titus looked back at the family. He felt like he was doing a lot of looking back lately, and he blamed Corban. But it felt good to be doing the right thing for a change, even if it cost him everything. His brother and sister back in Arkansas wouldn't recognize him now.

†

CHAPTER TEN

SOUTHWEST GAZA CITY, DISTRICT OF TEL AL-HAWA

Luigi Putelli crouched behind the burnt skeleton of a semi-trailer. Chewing a mouthful of bubble gum, he hoped his chomping didn't make any sound to alert the unit of men he was trailing. They were deep in Gaza City, somewhere west of the Old City. No one had suspected he was a stranger when he used the Israeli forces to infiltrate the secure border. He'd abandoned the IDF troops three miles north of the city and tossed the IDF uniform.

Now, Luigi wore black dress boots with black slacks and a crimson silk shirt—the same clothes he'd worn on the plane from New York. The toxic belt buckle and nylon belt around his waist topped off his wardrobe. It was his only weapon, but he knew it well.

Israeli Saraph gunships hovered nearby. They were staying parallel with the Hamas unit, watching the heavily-armed militants as they marched south. When the Hamas unit far ahead passed burning buildings, Luigi glimpsed at least a dozen Hamas radicals who carried RPG tubes. If the gunships moved any closer to the militants, Luigi guessed they'd fire a grenade at the choppers. The Hamas army was over fifty-strong here, a force armed too heavily and moving too rapidly for even organized ground units like the Israelis to intercept.

Fifty Hamas soldiers! Luigi was tempted to jump one of the masked men and infiltrate their forces as well. If masked, he could move freely instead of in hiding. But it would take just one Hamas militant to ask him a question in Arabic, and his cover would be blown.

Regardless of the Hamas soldiers' discipline, they didn't seem too concerned about their back trail, where Luigi lurked from building to building, occasionally darting across the street for better cover. He wanted only to find Corban, and from what he'd heard from Colonel Kalil Yasof at Forward Command, following this weaponized unit of killers was a potential track to his friend.

Unfortunately, Luigi didn't know the city, but he had maintained his compass points. When the Hamas militants turned east, Luigi also moved east, a block north of the soldiers. A helicopter thumped above him as he ran east to get ahead of the soldiers. The gunship may have noticed him, but they seemed preoccupied with remaining parallel to the enemy. Luigi glanced to the right as he dashed across a street. He was ahead of them now, but where were the militants going?

A factory building loomed ahead of Luigi. Using the safety of the building to continue moving east, he stepped through broken glass and was pleased to find a wide corridor still heading the right direction. At least for a moment, he wouldn't have to worry about the choppers above disintegrating him into ash.

The dark corridor forked and Luigi crept to the right. He passed a purring critter against a wall and heard voices ahead. Slowing, he hoped they were merely refugees from the devastating bombing. He moved forward and was surprised to hear English. *English in Gaza?*

". . . Just try not to move," a woman's voice said. "You're lucky he got that bullet out without bleeding you dry. It was pretty deep."

A man coughed and Luigi used the noise to mask his footsteps. He eased closer and peered through a tangle of clothing racks. It took Luigi a moment to focus on the objects around a single flashlight twenty paces away. At the corner ahead, he saw a woman lean over an injured man with bloody bandages on his chest.

"Thirty minutes until the meet," another man said with a Russian accent, somewhere out of Luigi's view to the right. "You two should move down the hall and out of sight before Luc Lannoy and Crac Hassad arrive."

"Aaron's in no shape to move or be moved," the woman said. There was disdain in her voice. "Just keep your terrorist pals on that side of the wall, huh?"

There was no answer. Luigi reflected on what he'd learned with Chloe: there was a missing American woman and an Israeli soldier. He looked back down the corridor. The Crac Hassad soldiers had been zigzagging through the city, but they'd been heading in this general direction. Both prisoners would make powerful hostages in the right hands. Luigi had a decision to make since Corban wasn't here. Corban would want him to help the captives, but Luigi wanted only to help Corban.

Quietly unwrapping another piece of gum, Luigi slipped it into his already stuffed mouth. Like Chloe had told the colonel, Corban would be in the vicinity if he knew such hostages were local. And the odds against Corban wouldn't stop the old spy.

Sighing, Luigi decided he would stick around. If Corban were any other man, it would be unlikely he'd be in the area. But with Luigi near, Corban's chance of success, whatever he was up to, was better. And instead of leaping into a situation he didn't understand, Luigi waited and listened, ever aware that dozens of Crac Hassad militants were closing on the factory.

"If You're up there, God," he prayed, which felt awkward since he wasn't a praying man, "take care of Corban, and get us home to our girls."

Luigi touched his breast pocket, then remembered he'd removed Heather Oakes' photo before leaving the States. But her face was in his memory. He hoped to see her again. Maybe someday he would view the world and the reason for life the way she did. Maybe someday he would become a Christian, but not yet. It was still easier to live by his own willpower.

...†...

EAST GAZA CITY, SHUJA'IYYA DISTRICT

"They're your friends," Titus said as he lay on his belly next to Corban. "Why don't you go in there instead of me? Let me cover you from here with the sniper rifle."

"Refresh my memory. It's been a while since I read your file. You're a trained marksman?" Corban kept his eye on the night scope trained on a courtyard a half-mile away. From their vantage point on top of a half-demolished office building, Titus could see the Ibn Uthman Mosque's interior.

Scaffolding stood against several walls, as if the mosque were still under reconstruction since the last bombing. "No, Titus, just look at that courtyard. All you have to do is get through the front door, and I'll be able to cover you everywhere inside."

"Yeah. Easy." Titus counted eight armed men at the double doors in the front. "I'll be shooting my way in and out."

"Draw the enemy into the courtyard and I'll put them to sleep for an hour."

"I can't believe I let you talk me into this!" Titus gathered his NL-2 and NL-3 weapons and rose to his knees. He checked his watch. In less than twenty minutes, Oleg would be hosting the buy-sell meet with a phony biological weapon. Oleg had betrayed him, yet Titus couldn't help but be flattered by Interpol's attention. He understood Oleg was doing what he'd been trained to do: stop the bad guys. And that meant Titus' bank account wouldn't increase now, if Corban was telling the truth, and Titus believed he was. His accounts had actually decreased by the funds he'd spent on the real weapon before Oleg had apparently swapped it out, leaving Titus five million Euros fewer. Whatever the cost, Titus felt drawn to assist Oleg in catching Crac Hassad. The two had been partners for months, though he realized now, each with different objectives. "Just come get me if they get the upper hand."

"Roger." Corban gave Titus a thumbs up without looking. "Do what you do, Serval."

Titus descended four flights of stairs through shrapnel-strewn walls. Once outside, he jogged along a street of closed shops toward the mosque. Before turning a corner, he looked back at Corban's building. He couldn't see Corban, but he trusted he was there. In fact, he had more confidence in Corban than most partners he'd had over the years. Corban had that selfless air about him, something that made Titus feel important and secure. And a little envious.

The mosque was before him. The eight doormen still stood as they had been ten minutes earlier. Titus took a deep breath and walked toward them, the NL-2 machine pistol in his left hand, the NL-3 carbine strapped and cradled in his right.

"*Salam alaykum!*" Titus greeted in Arabic as he approached. He counted the paces to the men, about twenty left. "We've been blessed with a beautiful night, brothers. Have you seen the sky?"

The eight seemed tense, probably expecting an Israeli gunship at any moment, but a single man talking about the night wouldn't seem like much of a threat, and Titus marched closer, directly at them. Two men stepped forward to inspect Titus. The city was densely populated, but Titus guessed the worst of Hassad's men knew one another. An approaching stranger would be a threat.

Titus leveled the machine pistol when a gunshot echoed through the night behind him. An instant later, three of the eight in front of the mosque grabbed their chests and fell over. Dropping to one knee, Titus peppered the five remaining with pellets from both guns. Far behind him, Corban fired once more with the sniper rifle and took down the last two militants.

Taking stock, Titus realized not one of the eight had managed to fire a single shot. And Corban's suppressed rifle shot was a half-mile away, alerting no one in the mosque that a foe lurked nearby. The whole assault had lasted no longer than ten seconds. The soldiers had seemed both confused and frightened by the pellets. They probably believed they were being hit with live rounds, grabbing at their assumed wounds rather than returning fire.

Stepping over the snoozing bodies, Titus opened the right side of the mosque entrance. Though he expected to find a passage full of killers relaxing in the safety of the mosque's porches, Titus discovered an empty hall all the way to the courtyard. Knowing Corban was covering him, Titus passed through the door and ran silently to the edge of the courtyard. The yard under construction was surrounded by short pillars. He weaved his way through the pillars to a wooden door on the far side.

"It ain't easy being the Serval," Titus mumbled, then threw the door open. He was now out of Corban's sight, but as long as Corban kept the street and the courtyard clear, Titus guessed he could manage the rest.

Before him, on the right side of the corridor, loomed two arched doorways that led into rooms with dimmed lamps. He grit his teeth and stepped into the nearest one. Two men on floor mats and one at a table all looked up to receive pellets in their throats. A breath later, they tumbled over. The clicking of Titus' weapons drew a giant Palestinian with bushy brows from the second room. Titus fired too quickly and his pellets slapped the man's waist before Titus was punched firmly on the jaw. He bounced off the doorjamb and backed into the first room, but Bushy Brows continued his assault, kicking and punching with battering blows.

Titus dropped his firearms to hang at his sides from their straps and clenched his fists as he parried a punch meant for his nose. He ducked under a wild swing and threw a solid punch into the man's solar plexus, making the larger man back up to catch his breath.

"You got in a couple good ones," Titus admitted in Arabic. He spit blood from a cut lip. "Nobody told you I'm working with the Christians now, did they? Things aren't looking so good for you, pal. Come on. Just like junior high back in Arkansas."

In a martial arts stance, Titus raised his mitts and waved the man closer. The Palestinian's scarless face showed he wasn't accustomed to challengers, especially from those he'd already struck a few times.

Bushy Brows faked a jab and kicked at the side of Titus' knee. Titus raised his leg and took the blow on the side of his shin. Harmless.

"That's all you get," Titus said.

With a flurry of elbows, knees, and hands, Titus drove the Palestinian back into the hallway. He glanced a blow off the man's ear so hard, the giant shook his head. Titus gave him space, and both caught their breaths.

"Where are the Christians?" Titus demanded. "You have no hope to win tonight."

"You will never get out of here alive," Bushy Brows said with a growl and rushed, arms wide.

But Titus was ready this time. He pulled the trigger of the NL-2 and swung it up, pelting the big man with rounds from his knees to his oversized forehead. The man did succeed in tackling Titus, but he was unconscious moments later. Titus rolled him off and struggled to his knees in the hallway. Looking up, he saw an older Palestinian in glasses watching from the entrance of the second room.

Suddenly, the man lunged back out of sight into the room. A chill coursed through Titus' body, and he dashed forward, hoping he could get to the man before he could get his hands on a gun. Titus entered the room and froze.

"Come closer . . . American Satan," the man said in halting English, "and everyone go boom!"

Titus' eyes strayed from the detonator in the terrorist's hand to a black box with a blinking red light. Attached to the black box was a set of wires trailing to an explosive charge wrapped in black tape and plastered to a rafter on the ceiling. Directly below the charge were ten women and children, their hands bound and their mouths covered with tape.

"Stupid," Titus said aloud to himself. He knew now he should've cleared this room before the other. His choices were affecting others' lives, and he wasn't used to recognizing the responsibility of taking care of others.

"You, American Satan, give me gun!"

"No." Titus swallowed hard. "The mosque is surrounded. Give me the detonator. You don't want to kill innocent women and children, right?"

"Yes, if I am surrounded." The Palestinian snarled and Titus saw the crazed look on the suicidal man's face. "It is Allah's will."

"God, help us," Titus whispered and took a step back, but there was no escaping, not from a charge that size. Titus realized in an instant he would meet his Maker. It wasn't a pleasant realization. The Palestinian squeezed his detonator, a surrendered look on his face . . . but nothing happened. He frowned at the device in his hand and pumped the trigger again. Shaking the shock from his brain, Titus shot the man with five tranqs in the chest. The detonator fell from his hands and he collapsed.

Titus stared at the detonator, then gasped in surprise for several breaths. No meeting his Maker yet. The explosive had failed!

"Nuri sent me," he said to the captives, using a knife to cut their binds. "Which of you is Leah?"

"I am Leah," a young Palestinian woman said after she peeled the tape off her mouth. Her eye was swollen, and several of the children around her had lacerations on their faces.

"Corban is outside. Help me get the others back to your house."

"Where is my husband? Where is Jachin?"

"He is . . ." Titus checked the hallway as he stalled for the right words. He remembered his brief thought of God before the detonator malfunctioned. "He's with God. Quickly, everyone."

Titus gathered them at the door. Then, as the international arms dealer he was, he easily identified and plucked off the faulty wire in the explosive device. Instead of disarming it completely, he twisted the wire around a connector to complete the circuit which had been the bomb maker's problem. Before he led the way down the hall, he slid the detonator trigger into his breast pocket.

In the hallway, he stood against the wall and rushed everyone toward the courtyard.

"Run outside! Stay together!"

Waiting until everyone had exited the room, Titus then stepped into the hallway to bring up the rear. Something zipped through the skin on his neck and slammed him into the wall. Stunned to see his blood spattered on the opposite wall, he slid down the marble tile to sit on the floor. He heard voices. They were coming for him from the depths of the mosque.

He could no longer see the women and children. They'd moved beyond the courtyard where the door would lead them into Corban's view.

Titus touched his neck. It was wet with blood. Lots of blood. His vision swam. His hand felt the detonator in his breast pocket. Men with assault rifles crowded the hall. They shouted at him as they advanced. He thought of the wicked life he'd led, and his family with whom he'd never reconciled. The fires of hell seemed his destiny, and he hadn't cared until this night.

"God, remember that I saved Your people . . ."

Titus pumped the detonator trigger twice. This time, the device in the room just a few feet away exploded.

†

CHAPTER ELEVEN

EAST GAZA CITY, SHUJA'IYYA DISTRICT

Corban felt his heart sink when the mosque's central dome and nearby minaret tower exploded in a flash, then crumbled onto itself. But an instant later, he watched through his sniper scope as several children stumbled through the front door, dust billowing around them. He counted ten women and children, but no Titus. Since Corban was a half-mile away, he couldn't signal Leah to flee southwest toward her home. He watched her gather the children in the street, and then they turned to look at something to the north.

Swinging his rifle, Corban spotted three Hamas soldiers approaching the mosque at a run, AK-47s leveled on the women and children. Corban pulled the trigger, working the bolt action quickly, and fired again even as the first tranq darts struck home. The three gunmen slumped to the street.

Leah gazed south. In the dark city, she couldn't possibly see him so far away, yet she waved in his direction, anyway. Titus must've told her he was outside, Corban guessed. He checked the mosque rubble again for some sign of Titus—the one who had saved them. But he didn't emerge.

Now, with some sense of direction, Leah led the children and other women out of the street on a southern route toward Corban.

Still, Corban watched the mosque for several more

minutes, praying he would see the blond man from Arkansas, but instead, he saw only smoke and concrete ruins.

When he noticed Leah and her people below his four-story building, Corban peered over the edge.

"Leah!"

"Corban! Praise His Name! You're here!"

"Go west for—"

"I know where I am, Corban. Is it safe to go home?"

"Yes, Nuri and his family are waiting for you. Where's the man who rescued you?"

"There was a bomb in our room. He stayed behind. I pray he is well, Corban."

"Go, Leah. Huldah, are you there?"

"Yes, I'm here."

"There's insulin at your house, enough for several months. Stay against the buildings as you move down the street. I'll watch over you until you get back to Zeitoun."

"You're an angel from God, Corban!" Leah praised, then hustled everyone west.

Corban used his scope to watch the streets ahead of Leah, but Hamas militants seemed drawn to the mosque now, as were a few Israeli helicopters. At the moment, Hamas wasn't hunting Christians; they were instead grieving over their demolished religious site and hideout—demolished by their own ordnance.

By the time Leah passed beyond Corban's one thousand yard range, she was a couple blocks from her apartment. He relaxed and prayed they would be safe for the night. They would have to relocate, perhaps to a refugee camp on the coast, since they would be targeted civilians from now on.

Other Christians in Gaza would hopefully help hide them. Corban would check on them again in a few months.

As he walked to the stairs, Corban strapped the NL-X1 to his back and swung the NL-2 and NL-3 into position for closer combat. If Crac Hassad and his terrorists were on schedule, they were meeting with Oleg at that moment. Aaron Adar and Annette Sheffield would be taken as hostages, Corban guessed, unless Oleg had something up his sleeve.

And somewhere out there, Chloe had said Luigi was lurking. Luigi was always lurking.

When Corban reached the street, he checked his sat-phone. Israel was still jamming communications. He stowed the phone then jogged northwest toward the factory.

Though he couldn't pray for Titus' soul now that he was gone, Corban hoped the international crook had repented before God as he sacrificed his life for ten strangers.

...✝...

SOUTH GAZA CITY, ZEITOUN DISTRICT

Oleg Saratov was nervous. It was after three o'clock in the morning. Titus and Corban hadn't returned, and Luc Lannoy and Crac Hassad were overdue. He knew his assignment well: to arrest Crac Hassad once Titus Caspertein led him to the terrorist, then arrest Titus. But now Oleg was torn between his assignment and saving the lives of Annette and Aaron. Oleg had been in dire circumstances before. He could put a gun to Crac Hassad's head and walk out of the factory and find the nearest Israeli patrol. That was one way to save himself, no matter the odds. But he wasn't sure he could save Annette from the likes of Luc Lannoy or Aaron Adar from the likes of Crac Hassad's murderous men.

"Corban, where are you?" Oleg whispered in Russian as he eyed the street from the factory window. His Beretta pistol hadn't left his hand for hours. He had nine rounds remaining—not enough to face an army and protect two innocents.

It'd been fifteen years since Oleg had first met Corban Dowler at a Washington DC seminar on post-Cold War relations. Everyone had heard rumors of Corban's stealth in restricted countries and across closed borders. The man was a low-profile legend, nothing like the flashy arrogance Oleg was forced to tolerate in Titus. Even if Corban had moved from the government to the private humanitarian sector, the man was obviously in top form. Pinned down in the factory with foes on every side, Oleg had been comforted by the idea that Corban was on the side of good. With Corban, Oleg had hoped to take down Crac Hassad, Luc Lannoy, Titus, and maybe a dozen Hassad terrorists at the same time. But not alone without an ally, and with dependents under his care.

"We need to move Aaron," Oleg said to Annette as he stalked back into the room. "Titus and Corban won't be back in time to help me deal with this." Oleg tapped the canister strapped to his shoulder. He'd swapped the bio-weapon out with a canister of cheap perfume in Athens—with the help of a team of Interpol agents. Titus had been asleep and hadn't suspected a thing. "We need to build a stretcher to carry him, at least deeper into the building."

"You know he's in no shape to move!" Annette said from Aaron's side. "Why are you doing this now?"

Annette rose to her feet as Oleg dumped the contents of the medical packs onto the ground. Since he had maintained his brutal terrorist cover, he knew she didn't trust him, but things were about to get desperate.

"I have to rig up something to carry him. There are things I cannot explain, but without Corban and Titus here, I'm not willing to meet Crac Hassad. Take off Aaron's boot laces and tie it all—"

"Excuse me. Did you say Corban?" a voice said from the dark corridor. Oleg turned his pistol on the stranger as Annette used the flashlight to illuminate a tall, gaunt man. He chewed a wad of gum and didn't flinch from the light. "I assume you speak of Corban Dowler?"

"Who are you?" shifting to his right, Oleg could see the stranger wasn't armed. "Speak!"

"I'm a friend of Corban's. He's a friend of mine. I've been listening and watching you from back there. You must be expecting the soldiers down the street, yes?"

"They're here?" Oleg wanted to go to the window, but not with this character at his back. His accent sounded possibly Italian. "You're with Crac Hassad?"

"No. I'm not with Crac Hassad, the terrorist. And neither are you, so why do you expect to meet them?"

"He's an arms dealer!" Annette backed away. "Look at that thing on his shoulder."

"Shut up!" Oleg felt exposed, tired, and isolated. As an Interpol agent, a wrong move now could cost him his life. "Things are not as they seem. I'm not really with Titus. I'm Interpol. If you're really a friend of Corban's, then you'll help me. I'm also a friend of Corban's though it's been many years."

"He's lying!" Annette shook her fist at him. "Oleg, what are you doing? You don't need us! Let Aaron and me go with this guy and you can do whatever you want with Hassad. We won't say a thing!"

"I'm not taking anyone anywhere," the stranger said. "I want only Corban Dowler. Where is he?"

"He left hours ago to deliver insulin to a child southeast of here," Oleg said. "Since he's not back, I can only assume Hassad militants got him."

"Then Hassad is who I shall meet. I am Francis Malvao." Francis seemed to ignore Oleg's gun as he walked over to Aaron to inspect his wound. "These stitches are secure. If you move him gently, they won't tear." Francis faced Oleg. "You fixed his bullet wound?"

"Yes." Oleg relaxed a little. Someone else who could share the burdens of the moment eased the pressure.

"If you're really a friend of Corban's then you won't let these two fall into the hands of Hassad's soldiers."

"You don't understand. I'm obligated to catch Crac Hassad, but not with civilians in the way." Oleg surveyed the man's appearance again. "You're not armed, but if you can take these two, I can slow down Hassad's men so you can get away."

"I'm not here for that. You take them. Leave Crac Hassad to me. He'll regret ever laying eyes on Corban Dowler."

"You can't be serious!" Annette moved the flashlight between Oleg and Francis. "You're really Interpol? And you're really going to face those terrorists alone?"

"They're close." Francis moved to the window. "Go out the back. It leads west. Signal an Israeli chopper. You can hear them everywhere."

"What will you do with Crac Hassad?" Oleg asked. He didn't want to run away, but he could leverage another meet since he still had the canister, once he had a plan and backup. "You have no weapons and apparently no sanity. You need to come with us!"

"As you said, things are not as they seem . . ." Francis hooked his right thumb over his belt buckle. "Go before they come inside. And pray I find Corban soon, or Gaza will become a greater zone of destruction."

Tucking his pistol into his belt, Oleg bent down to fashion a stretcher for Aaron. He was relieved someone else was about to face Crac Hassad, to slow him down if nothing else. Oleg wasn't willing to die just yet.

...✝...

UN escort and Belgian national Luc Lannoy led Crac Hassad's men from the south toward the dark factory. They were late, but Luc was happy they had made it at all. The many RPG launchers amongst the Hassad men had kept the Saraph gunships at bay, but Luc was surprised an F-16 hadn't dropped a smart bomb on the street, blowing them all to bits. His only guess was that Israel didn't know what these guys were up to. And that worked for Luc. If he could arrange the weapon sale, and take his share and disappear, then Hamas and Israel could do whatever they wanted to each other. Chances were, once Hamas had the bio-weapon, Israel would pay dearly.

And there was the matter of Annette Sheffield. Luc licked his lips, thinking of her beauty. If he could satisfy both parties—Titus Caspertein and Crac Hassad—Luc hoped he would get Annette as a bonus.

"Stop," a man at Luc's shoulder whispered in English. The Hassad men called him Petra. He was a young, sly man from Jordan, a trustworthy stone-faced man who Crac Hassad had sent in his stead. Crac had stayed farther to the east with his nephew in a school building. It was too dangerous for him to move, and far too risky to enter a potential trap where the biological weapon was concerned. Petra spoke Arabic to his men behind. "Stay here. We'll go ahead. If you hear gunfire, come to us." He nudged Luc with his rifle barrel. "Go first, Luc. I don't trust you."

"Fine." Luc edged into the factory, stepped over a broken door, and peered ahead for a glimpse of light where he'd left Titus, Oleg, Annette, Aaron, and Corban. Luc squeezed his pistol grip, uncertain about having only five rounds left. "Titus! Oleg! I've returned!"

"No one is here," Petra said. An explosive flashed somewhere in the city and lit up the room. The tall, still figure of a man shimmered for an instant on the wall. Petra swept his rifle toward the window. Though the lighting was bad, Luc saw a slim hand grasp the assault rifle muzzle and rip it out of Petra's hands.

"Don't move," a deep, calm voice ordered in English. "Drop your gun."

A lone man stood before Luc and Petra. Luc glanced down at the pistol in his own hand, but it was aimed at the ground. He saw no way to win against this assailant whose voice he didn't know. Were other guns aimed at them as well? Luc dropped his pistol. He hadn't anticipated an ambush. Oleg and Titus must have been double-crossed somehow. This sale had been too important to them to leave without a fight.

"You don't know me," Petra said, "but I come in Crac Hassad's name. You interfere with his destiny!"

"Crac Hassad didn't come himself? Move back." Luc and Petra took three steps back. The lone man scooped up Luc's pistol. "Are you the traitor known as Luc Lannoy?"

Luc gasped. *Traitor?* No one was supposed to know he was facilitating a bio-weapon purchase. If UN authorities knew, then Luc would have a complicated escape from Gaza. He certainly couldn't continue as a UN worker. Living as a fugitive would be expensive. When he found Titus again, he would demand a larger cut for the deal.

"Take your traitor and walk away," Petra said. "I have fifty men outside. If I call for them, you'll die."

"I'm not afraid to die, but I won't die. The God of Corban Dowler watches over me. Now, tell me where I may find Corban Dowler."

"Who's Corban Dowler?" Petra asked.

"You're a Christian?" Luc relaxed and sneered at the lone man. "Then you won't hurt us."

Luc dared to take a step forward, glad at the chance to show Petra his courage, but he was met by his own pistol in his face.

"Don't mistake me for a Christian just because I'm loyal to Corban Dowler. I don't care what you do tonight. I don't want anything but to know where Corban is."

"Honestly, I don't know." Luc took a step back, but his pistol was still aimed at his forehead. "I left him here. That was at sundown. Titus sent me to bring Crac Hassad."

"Where's the weapon?" Petra asked Luc. "If the weapon isn't here, then I'm leaving."

The stranger didn't speak for a moment. With one hand, he unwrapped something and popped it into his mouth. Luc's stomach growled. He hadn't eaten in hours. Where was Titus with the weapon? Luc's life depended on that weapon sale!

"If Hassad has Corban Dowler," the stranger said, "I will come for Crac Hassad to collect him."

"You threaten a merciless servant of Allah, a man you don't know?" Petra asked. "What is your name?"

"I'm Francis Malvao. I'll stop at nothing to find Corban Dowler."

"This Corban Dowler I don't know."

"He's a Christian who goes by Christopher Cagon," Luc said. "He's a friend of the Jews."

"Ah, then I hope Crac Hassad has this Zionist. I would take pleasure in killing him for Allah and for Crac Hassad. And when you come, we'll kill you as well, Francis Malvao."

Too fast for Petra to avoid, Francis Malvao whipped off his belt and swung the buckle across Petra's cheek. Luc stumbled backward as the buckle snapped next at him. Beside him, Petra fell against the wall, then collapsed, unconscious. Luc knew the effects of poison when he saw them. He moved to the side as Francis Malvao continued his assault, whipping the belt at Luc.

"Help!" Luc screamed, and didn't wait to see what happened next. Turning, he ran down the dark corridor. It merged with another hallway. He continued running, a barrage of gunfire echoing down the hall behind him.

Luc emerged from the factory building on the west side and collided with two Hassad soldiers who had posted themselves at that exit, but they were unprepared for Luc's sudden arrival. Rather than explain his presence, Luc wrenched one of the guns away and smashed both men in the faces with the rifle stock until they were still. He stole their ammunition and a canteen, then dashed across the street to the west. An Israeli chopper thumped overhead, cruising south. Luc hid against a building, then ran north.

He didn't know where to go, only to run. Turning east, he slowed to a walk. Checking his back trail, he guessed the bold man with the poisoned belt had been killed. But Luc wondered if the man had somehow escaped Crac Hassad's troops. It was unlikely, but still, Luc could live happily the rest of his life if he never again had to face the committed man in search for his friend. He suddenly wished he were far away from Gaza, far away from Francis Malvao, and even farther away from Crac Hassad. If the brutal Hamas leader hadn't gotten his weapon as promised, he would blame Luc.

Jogging, Luc approached a sanitation building where three water towers loomed behind it. The towers were tall enough to keep the gunships away. He took a moment to collect his wits and laugh aloud at his fear. It wasn't like him to be so scared.

Luc had been leaking information to Hassad and other Hamas leaders for years. As a UN security officer based outside Gaza, he'd been privy to Israeli intelligence briefings. When Hassad had asked him to bring him a weapon, Luc had contacted Titus Caspertein, a known thief and arms dealer. In the months leading up to the weapon's delivery, Luc had felt anticipation. He'd been in control, fully aware he was about to become very wealthy. But now he was out of control, frightened, and without the prospects of wealth.

"What? Who's there?" Luc called in Arabic. He aimed his stolen AK-47 at the sanitation building. A noise had come from a smelly pile of garbage. A soiled mattress shifted.

Cautiously, Luc approached, licking his lips. Since he hadn't delivered the weapons as Crac Hassad had wanted, everyone in the Hassad army was an enemy. If he killed the right people, he could steal an identity and sneak out of Gaza. There were ways, tunnels, cracks in the perimeter. He had to survive now, to think of himself, and that meant he would do anything to stay alive.

He heard the distinct click of a gun hammer. Luc dove to his right, then rolled to his feet as he sprayed bullets into the heaping garbage. A muzzle flashed twice in his direction, and Luc focused his gunfire. He heard a man grunt and a woman cry out. A woman! Luc rushed toward the garbage as someone crawled through the filth in the semi-darkness. He lunged over a broken crate and caught at the shirt tail of a struggling man.

"No!" the man screamed in English. But it wasn't a man!

Luc threw Annette onto her back amongst the rotten debris and clasped his hand around her throat.

"Hold still!" Luc growled. He glanced over his shoulder. "You're not here alone! Where is Titus? Where is Oleg? Who's out here with you?"

Annette continued to struggle. Luc punched her twice before she was still. Only then did he realize that on Annette's shoulder was the canister. He had the weapon!

Suddenly, Luc felt no fear. He felt in control. And he once again sensed riches on the horizon. He didn't need Titus or Oleg. This was a game he would win himself!

✝

SOUTH GAZA CITY, ZEITOUN DISTRICT

Corban arrived at the factory where he'd left Aaron and Annette at the instant a man inside called for help. The line of Hassad militants didn't see him as they surged into the southern factory entrance. Corban's primary weapon was already sighting on them. Even without Titus, he'd hoped to reach the factory by the time the Crac Hassad meeting took place. In the least, he hoped to save Annette and Aaron's lives, and if things went right, he could help Oleg capture Crac Hassad as well. However, the dozens of Hamas men were an obstacle to be surmounted.

No matter the numbers, Corban was well-armed. He crouched behind rubble in the street, near Jachin's still body, and fired his NL weapon into the factory window. Since the CO_2 cartridge produced no muzzle flash, the soldiers inside couldn't locate him immediately to return accurate fire. Nevertheless, a few did try to return fire, and in doing so, they killed each other. Corban hadn't intended further bloodshed, especially since Annette and Aaron were still inside!

He counted nine Hassad men left standing when his machine pistol clicked on empty. The nine exited to the south and ran west up the street, three of them wounded. The dead and unconscious lay everywhere, and Corban was reminded of Gideon's torchlight and pottery assault on the camp of Midian. A Saraph gunship swooped down on the fleeing nine, now two blocks away. A second chopper descended from the sky, and the nine raised their arms in the air, a spotlight illuminating them on the street.

Without waiting to see if the IDF had noticed him, Corban climbed through the factory window. He reloaded his pistol, and kept the NL-3 within reach on its sling, with the NL-X1 still on his back. He stepped through the tangle of bodies, searching desperately for Oleg, Annette, or Aaron. Since his primary objective had been completed—delivering the insulin—he was ready to focus on the additional lives now under his care. But in the darkness, amongst the blood and cries of several wounded, he seemed to be too late.

"You've saved my life again, Corban," a familiar voice said from the far wall. "Some of them believed they were caught in an ambush. They killed each other."

"I didn't wish for their deaths." Corban could hear the strain in Luigi Putelli's voice, and knew his old friend was in bad shape. "I believe in a God who can take even a bad situation and use it for His glory. Perhaps when the others wake up, they'll consider their lives that have been spared. Maybe some will change their lives toward a peaceful existence for their Creator."

"I believe you are right, Corban, because you said those same words to me once in Lebanon, and your God has been close ever since."

Corban reached the far wall and found Luigi slumped to the side. He was bleeding from a bullet wound to the gut. Another bullet had pierced his leg.

"How are you, old friend?" Corban sat down next to him and lifted Luigi's head onto his lap. "I've seen you survive more than this. You hear the helicopters? IDF ground troops are probably on their way to investigate what's happened here."

Luigi struggled to breathe. He closed his eyes at Corban's touch.

"I fear I've wasted my life, Corban. Heather won't be pleased that I've come here to die without calling her." Luigi choked on a sob. Crimson was seeping from his gut wound. "You're the first to bring meaning to my life."

"It was God who brought us together that day in Lebanon."

"Yes, I know. I've known since then. I once thought you weren't human. You scared me, Corban. But I know God has been on your side. He's always watched over you."

"God could be on your side, too, old friend. You have only to accept the gift of His payment for your sins. Yield to Him, Luigi."

"Sins. Oh, Corban, I have many sins."

"You don't have long, Luigi. Talk to God."

Luigi tensed and shuddered. He reached one hand up and grasped Corban's hand. Corban bowed his head. First Jachin, then Titus, and now Luigi. Somehow, he had to find Aaron and Annette and get them all out of Gaza.

"God, I'm a stupid man," Luigi said, his voice weak. "I've made many problems in my life. I've taken lives, many lives. I'm selfish, not like this man you sent to save me from evil. I believe, God, that You paid for my sins, even though that's a shameful thing. I know the story of the Cross. I believe it's real because Corban has told me it is. Because of him, God, I've seen lives change, and because of You, I know You have loved even me."

Then, Luigi spoke in Italian, his voice drifting off. But he continued to squeeze Corban's hand. As desperate as Corban was to leave, he wouldn't go until his friend had passed.

Suddenly, Luigi lifted his head and pointed away.

"That man is Petra. See? He's an emissary for Crac Hassad. I sent Oleg Saratov away with Annette Sheffield and the wounded Israeli. Do you see Luc Lannoy?"

"No." Corban studied the scene by two flashlights that had been dropped and left on. "He's not here."

"Then he fled into the factory, Corban. Find him. You must!"

"Relax, my friend. Oleg is Interpol. He'll keep Annette safe. Israeli soldiers are probably rescuing them right now. They'll live because of you."

Luigi began to tremble uncontrollably.

"I'll not be afraid," he whispered through grit teeth. "I'm a Christian now. Tell Heather, will you? Tell her I became a Christian, finally."

"I'll tell her. I'll tell everyone. Praise God," Corban whispered, his eyes full of tears. "I'll shout it from the mountaintop!"

Corban held Luigi's head until the old assassin exhaled one last time, and was still.

"He's Yours now, Lord."

Taking a deep breath, Corban squeezed his eyes shut, his tears falling on Luigi's head. He left him there, his head resting on a crumbled rock, and went to the man Luigi had called Petra. The man's pulse was strong, and he had no apparent wounds except a familiar scratch across his cheek, surely from Luigi's belt buckle. Though bone-tired, Corban managed to lift Petra onto his left shoulder, keeping his right hand free to access his NL pistol.

"I'd like to hang around and meet your friends when they wake up, Petra, but Israeli commanders will want to talk to you right away."

Corban was halfway down the corridor when he heard movement and a man grunt behind him. He paused and looked back at near darkness where the two flashlights shined in the room of dead or unconscious men. Someone was still alive back there, but he couldn't stop to rescue anyone now. For an instant, he wondered if he should've checked Luigi's pulse to make sure . . .

Outside the west factory doorway, Corban carried Petra toward a wide street intersection where a chopper could make a safe landing. Not far to his right, a rifle barked. Its thunder echoed around three tall water towers, and Corban was reminded he was still in great danger, regardless of the Hassad soldiers he had incapacitated temporarily. There were hundreds more in Gaza.

In the center of the intersection, Corban laid Petra on the ground. He knelt next to the terrorist and was still wondering how he would manage a safe extraction when a gunship illuminated him in its spotlight. Exhausted and feeling his chest wound now more than he had earlier, Corban lay on his belly in surrender fashion, arms and legs outstretched. The chopper's rotors beat the air over him.

Moments later, a heavy boot kicked Corban's NL-3 from

his hand, and then he was stripped of his other weapons.

"My name is Corban Dowler!" he yelled over the rotor wash. Other soldiers secured the perimeter at four points around the intersection. Someone jerked him to his knees to face a man in an IDF uniform. He wore a black beret of the IDF armored corps. "This man's name is Petra. Francis Malvao captured him. Petra is close to Crac Hassad."

"I'm Colonel Yasof, Mr. Dowler. I've known about you for several years. Chloe's back at headquarters. Where is Francis Malvao?"

"He's dead. There's about thirty unconscious Hassad men in that factory there, the south side." Corban paused as Yasof yelled an order in Hebrew to a man with a radio. He then waved Corban toward the chopper.

"Chloe said you'd try to help. Did you come across the biological weapon?"

"Oleg Saratov has it secured. You haven't found him yet? He has Aaron Adar and Annette Sheffield."

"No sign of them yet." The colonel recalled his men to the chopper, two of them dragging Petra into the hold. Yasof gestured to a reclining figure behind the pilot's seat. "This guy won't give us a name. He says he's a friend of yours. Do you know him, Mr. Dowler?"

Corban sat amongst the IDF soldiers. He squinted through the green and red light from the cockpit that illuminated the cabin. He barely recognized the dusty heap of Titus Caspertein who gazed back at him.

"Yeah. He saved civilian lives tonight. He's a friend of mine."

...✝...

"Are you alive?"

Aaron weakly opened his eyes. Darkness surrounded him, but the feel of cold night air on his cheek told him he was still alive. He reached a hand out and touched a shadow next to him. Someone grasped his hand.

"Oleg?"

"Yes, it's me."

"Someone took Annette." Aaron heard his own wheezing breath and knew he was barely alive. "Are you hurt?"

"Luc Lannoy took Annette, but not before he put a bullet in me. Broke my hip. I can't walk."

"Annette can't be far. Please." Aaron clawed at Oleg. "She saved my life. She kept me alive!"

"I know, but I can't walk, Aaron! Maybe if . . . Yes, I hear helicopters near. I'll take you."

Aaron gritted his teeth as Oleg used one leg to crawl through the garbage, then dragged Aaron ahead a few inches. All Aaron could see were the water towers above. He focused on their height and tried not to feel the agony every time Oleg dragged him toward the street. To make matters worse, the stench of garbage made them both gag constantly.

Finally in the street, Oleg collapsed next to Aaron's head. Aaron placed a hand on Oleg's arm.

"I'm sorry for believing you were a criminal. Without you, I would be dead already."

"Don't thank me yet. We're on a street known for its traffic of Hassad's militants."

"Annette is gone." Aaron wept. His own safety seemed less important now without the American woman. "How will we find Annette?"

Oleg didn't respond, but Aaron could hear the man breathing, even though the tough Russian was unconscious.

Aaron knew he would be dead if it weren't for the kindness of several foreigners he'd met over the last day and night. Oleg and Annette had worked on him, and Corban and Titus had risked their lives to fetch medical gear from somewhere—and Titus was the one who had shot him! The crook was probably dead by now, but Aaron no longer despised the man.

"I'm not a man who has thought much about You, God, but I believe You had a hand in keeping me alive. Corban said he works for You. Wherever he is, and wherever Annette is, please help them. I—"

Frantically, Aaron waved one arm as a helicopter flew up the street, hunting for targets. Its searchlight swept over Aaron and Oleg, then moved on. Gasping, Aaron dropped his arm next to Oleg's still body.

"Another may pass soon," Aaron told Oleg. He felt a warm wetness leaking from Oleg's wound onto the cracked pavement. "Don't die, Oleg. We're almost home."

The chopper that had passed circled and investigated Aaron again. Aaron was certain he was unrecognizable as the IDF soldier he was, but the chopper descended cautiously to the street.

"Oleg! Oleg, we're saved! I will see my Elizabeth again!"

Forty-eight hours later, Corban stood with his hands in his pockets and watched two grave diggers lower Luigi Putelli's casket into the ground. Behind him stood Chloe Azmaveth with Titus Caspertein, his arm in a sling. Oleg leaned hard on a cane and stepped up next to Corban.

"You should be in the hospital still, Oleg," Corban said without taking his eyes off the casket. After having Luigi in the shadows for so many years, it was hard to believe the man was actually gone. He would miss him.

"You knew this man well? The colonel said by the time they tried to retrieve his body, a stray Hamas missile had blown up the factory. The recovery team did their best, I guess." Oleg nodded at the grave. "Was his name even Francis Malvao?"

"It doesn't matter now. He's with his Lord and Savior."

"For what it's worth, Aaron and I would be dead right now if it wasn't for Francis. He let us escape as he faced Crac Hassad's people alone. Without you or Titus, I couldn't face Hassad without backup."

"Francis was always trying to redeem himself for the evils he'd done in his youth." Corban smiled at Chloe. "In the end, he received redemption, but it didn't come from anything he did. It came from God. He became a believer in those last moments."

"Maybe we're all trying to find redemption," Oleg said.

"Maybe we're all trying, but only Jesus Christ can deliver us from the sin we've committed. It's not about trying to be better or to be improved people. It's about trusting Christ to make us new." Corban looked Oleg in the eyes. "Did Colonel Yasof debrief you?"

"He did." Oleg glanced at Titus, who was just out of hearing range. "I kept Titus' name out of my official report, like you asked, but I'm obligated to explain the situation to my boss, at least. We at Interpol are primarily after Crac Hassad. I hope you know what you're doing. I've lived undercover with Titus for months. He thinks only about his own desires."

"We're all that way until we're changed by God. I know I was that way."

"What about Annette? She's still somewhere in Gaza with Luc Lannoy."

Corban's shoulders slumped a little. He didn't like leaving anyone behind. Not only was it against his training, it was against his conscience. All he could do was pray that Annette remembered their few words about faith, and he hoped she trusted in the God of compassion, even when circumstances and evil seemed to oppress. Hamas militants wouldn't be kind to an American woman, if Luc had handed her over to them.

"I'll talk to the Israelis. They're better equipped to find her at this point."

"I never heard," Oleg said. "Did you ever get that insulin to the Palestinian girl?"

"Yes, with Titus' help."

"Well, at least something good happened this week."

"Yes, good things did happen."

"If Titus strays again, I'll come for him, Corban. There's still a warrant with his name on it."

"He knows that."

"Well, goodbye."

Oleg Saratov turned and hobbled away to a waiting car. Titus and Chloe took his place at Corban's side.

"How mad is he that he's not taking me away in cuffs?" Titus asked.

"He could take you away if he really pushed for it. Hustling guns for mercenaries is one thing, but this time you were arming Palestinian Muslims who were willing to commit mass murder."

"So why didn't he take me? It's his job as an Interpol agent, right?"

"I asked him to leave you to me, for now," Corban said. "Or maybe he believes there's hope for you yet."

"Okay." Titus chuckled nervously. "What are your plans for me?"

"That depends." Corban turned to Chloe. "Chloe, what do you have for us?"

"It's not an easy mission. It's something Colonel Yasof is trusting me with. The Mossad has intel on a family member of Crac Hassad who's actually a Christian. You sure you two are up for another op so soon?" She held up a file, a taunting smile on her face. "Colonel Yasof is still pretty angry with you for going into Gaza illegally, even if it was to take insulin to a little girl, but this might help patch things up for us."

Corban took the file and studied it, then handed the papers back to Chloe.

"That's not going to be easy," Corban said. "But it's something I believe God must have arranged." He took a deep breath and made note of the location of Luigi's gravesite in relation to the other graves. Someday, Heather and Anna would probably want to visit the place, too. "Let's get to the airport, Titus. We have some planning to do. Lord willing, this will lead to getting Annette Sheffield back home as well."

As Corban climbed into his rental car to drive to the airport, he moved aside a piece of paper with a smear of blood on it. Then, before Titus climbed into the passenger seat, Corban stuffed the paper into his pocket. It'd been left for him and him alone, even if it defied the odds of a man's survival. No one could know about it. This was an opportunity for a fresh start, and Corban had no doubt he'd eventually hear the details of how this was even possible. When it was time, they would talk again. It had to be him. Who else would leave a bloody gum wrapper for him to find?

†

CHAPTER THIRTEEN

SOUTHEAST YEMEN

Nathan "Eagle Eyes" Isaacson stood on the edge of a desert cistern and stared down at the bodies. The magnitude of death was wearing on him. It was all he seemed to find nowadays—dead Christians, broken lives, lost souls. The soft glow of the rising sun over the sand dunes did nothing to brighten his embittered heart.

Closing his eyes, Nathan prayed for strength to maintain—spiritually, physically, and mentally. He willingly served God as a COIL agent, but ever since he'd been deployed as a lone operative, he'd struggled with depression and loneliness. Only rarely did he work with his fiancée, Chen Li, or other COIL operatives.

Each life-threatening mission distracted him from his loneliness, but afterward, his depression returned. Instead of dwelling on Christ to comfort him spiritually, he dwelled on his longing for Chen Li. His faith was waning, and this was partly due to the inability to have a Bible in many of the countries he frequented.

Tested. That's what came to him at that instant. His faith was being tested. When he'd been on the Special Forces team he'd led for COIL, his faith had been supported by other believers. Now alone, his spiritual needs were most visible.

Movement from inside the cistern drew Nathan's

attention. He'd been sent to extract the Yemeni Christians by way of the coast. He was too late. They'd all been slaughtered. But someone or something down there stirred. Was it an animal?

A gust of wind caught Nathan's white *thobe* robe, but also brought the sound of a motorized engine to his ears. His beard and sun-darkened skin had helped to disguise him in a Kawkaban market, but here in the desert, if authorities detained him, his identity would be scrutinized. Though he spoke fluent Arabic, he couldn't explain why he was on the edge of the baked desert, standing over a mass grave of Christians.

The cry of a child sounded from below. Now there was no doubt; someone had survived the massacre! Ignoring the approaching vehicle—and pushing aside his own distress—Nathan leaped from the top of the cistern wall and landed ten feet below on a rock platform. Where water had once pooled, Nathan reached his hand into the stinking dead bodies and pulled out a squirming boy of about two years old.

Crying even louder, the boy clung to Nathan as he bounded up the stairs carved out of the cistern wall. If the boy was found now, he would be killed or forced into Islamic submission. His parents were dead, but Nathan was meant to rescue them. He would honor the wishes of the dead. The boy had to live!

A call in Arabic made Nathan pause at the top of the cistern. For a moment, he stared at three Yemeni soldiers. One stepped from a jeep and waved at the other two.

Nathan glanced toward the sun, then the beach. It was a mile, maybe a little more, to the coast. He could run for the raft on the beach or try diplomacy. If things got sticky, he was liable to hurt someone, and as a Christian now, that wasn't an option. The giant curved *jambiya* on his decorated belt was simply part of his costume. Every man wore the dagger in that part of Yemen, but he would never use it on anyone. He was no longer the heartless soldier he'd once been before coming to Christ.

Before he'd fully decided what to do, Nathan was running eastward. His heavy *thobe* would protect him from the wind and sand, but it wasn't aiding his flight. The heavy fabric strangled his knees as he sprinted up the first dune, causing him to fall twice before he reached the crest. Thankfully, he managed to avoid falling on the toddler.

The boy smelled like blood. He may have been wounded, but Nathan didn't have time to check for injuries. The three men behind opened fire with their AK-47s, and tiny sand explosions puffed all around him.

Finally, Nathan dove over the crest of the dune. The sunlight glistened off the shoreline an unreachable distance away. Setting the child roughly on the sand, Nathan tore off his belt and *thobe*. Keeping the *jambiya* blade, he grabbed the boy by the back of his shirt—the child's only covering. Now in only shorts, a T-shirt, and boots, Nathan ran with a swiftness that reflected the disciplined Christian mercenary he'd become. And as a reminder of past struggles, his left knee brace squeaked with each step as sand filled the joint.

Regardless of the respite from gunfire, Nathan didn't hesitate to charge down one dune and up another. The impossible distance to the coast was possible by faith, he reasoned. Perhaps this was what he needed. Faith without testing could wane, and by placing him in a situation of impossible circumstances, Nathan could see God's hand. It was all he had now.

Adrenalin pumped through his veins. His dark mood floated away, and he regretted his unchristian-like attitude. This was what serving Christ was all about: seeking God to do the impossible as he put himself on the line for others. God brought life out of death, and the boy was evidence of this spiritual lesson.

The child stopped screaming and seemed to will him faster. Nathan's breathing settled into a heart-pounding rhythm and he even smiled at the boy.

"God is with us," he said in Arabic, then focused on the plain of sand before them. The dunes were past, and only a flat expanse stretched before the water.

The jeep roared over a dune and into sight to the north, two hundred yards away. The soldiers wildly fired their rifles.

As trusting as he'd been, Nathan's heart sank once more when he realized his little raft was nowhere in sight. The inflatable he'd left on the shore had been carried out to sea during high tide. He chastised himself. *Amateur mistake!*

Nathan turned straight toward the surf. The ocean was only a temporary escape since he had no boat now, but he forced himself to trust God. His God indeed knew his plight.

Bullets zipped past his head. There was nowhere to hide but in the waves. Nathan stepped high, leaping over the first few waves, then dove into the rolling sea. Water filled his mouth and eyes, and he lost his hold on the boy.

Surfacing, he found the boy, now gasping and crying, and Nathan drew the child to himself. The plopping of bullets punched the water around them. A wave hid them from the gunmen for an instant, then the barrage continued. Steadily, Nathan clawed with one arm as he swam straight away from the shoreline.

He didn't dare submerge with the boy in his arms. The way the little arms were wrapped around Nathan's neck, he was certain the child was too young to hold his breath through his fear.

The gunfire stopped. Nathan drifted in an offshore current and faced the shore. The jeep and men were a safe distance away. They seemed to be arguing, but their voices were indiscernible over the water. From whatever Muslim faction these soldiers came, they were definitely hostile toward Christians—as was the rest of the country. If only Nathan had been one day earlier, he could've saved the whole lot of believers!

The struggle of treading water with dead weight around his neck now concerned Nathan. The leg brace wasn't helping, either. A degree of fear swept over him at the prospect of dying an unknown death. Most at COIL, except Corban, Chloe, and Chen Li, thought he was already dead. And Nathan still wanted to marry Chen Li, raise a family, and—

He scoffed at himself. God had just protected him from countless bullets. His raft was gone, but he was alive and uninjured. Sure, a military patrol boat was probably on the way, and Nathan guessed he couldn't tread water for more than a few hours with the boy. But God was a big God! And a big God had the capability of doing big miracles.

Nathan held the boy against his chest and leaned his head

back to rest his arms, while he continued kicking to stay afloat. His boots were too heavy to swim with. Sacrifice for survival, he thought, and drew the *jambiya*. He managed to slice away the laces and kick off his boots. Lastly, he let go of the curved blade.

Completely dependent on God, Nathan began to pray, and even to rejoice, in a Savior so loving and kind. After all, Nathan and his little companion were potentially hours from standing before Him.

CHAPTER FOURTEEN

<u>*UZBEKISTAN*</u>

Corban Dowler used his fingers to press the face mask against his temples. The epoxy was sticking everywhere but there, where he was sweating the most. If only the mask would hold for one more hour.

This wasn't the first time Corban had been in an Uzbekistan prison, but last time, twenty-five years ago, he'd been a political prisoner under the guise of the KGB. Now, he was disguised as a guard in the Southern Kysyl Kum Rehabilitation Facility. After one week of surveillance, he and Titus Caspertein had identified two different prison guards they could impersonate to infiltrate the prison.

Though identities had been tactically acquired, and entrance through the guard house had been accomplished, Corban had no idea what his responsibilities should be as a guard inside the facility.

He turned a dimly-lit corner in a basement level and bumped into a tall guard wearing a dark green uniform. The crescent moon emblem on the breast pocket of the guard reminded Corban if he were caught now, he'd be at the mercy of Islamists who had an inclination toward inhumane interrogations.

"Relax, Corban," the tall guard whispered in English. "It's me. What're you doing down here?"

Corban glanced down the corridor. It was quiet except for the occasional echo of dripping water.

"I'm hiding so I don't have to speak to anyone—same as you." He checked his watch. "Less than an hour. No problems coming in?"

"No problems." Titus touched his neck. Corban admired the Arkansas man's expertise at applying his mask. Even his blond hair was now a dark brown to match the man he'd replaced. "My Russian is better than my Uzbek, apparently. Some sergeant upstairs didn't even understand when I asked for the bathroom."

"We didn't have the luxury of more preparation time." Corban shoved Titus back as a gate closed nearby. Together, they peered around the corner to see a maintenance worker push a laundry cart in the opposite direction. "Just trust God and stay sharp."

"Hey, I'm in my element. You're the one with his face falling off." Titus gripped Corban's head and pressed hard on the mask that was detaching. "Honestly? I'm wondering if we were safer a week ago running around Gaza with Israeli gunships and Hamas killers targeting us."

"Serving Christ on the frontlines has its risks, no matter where we are."

Titus rolled his eyes and said nothing. Corban had been praying for the international criminal for the last week. Both men still bore marks of the Gaza conflict, but Titus wasn't seeing that their spared lives were gifts from God. At least, not yet.

"Going after Crac Hassad's brother still doesn't seem wise," Titus complained for the hundredth time that week. "We should be out hunting Crac, not busting his brother out of prison!"

"You have a tendency to get into trouble when you do things your way," Corban said. "If you go back to your old contacts, you're liable to get arrested by Interpol, so we do things my way. This is Israel's plan, anyway, so let's follow through."

"I'm liable to get killed doing things your way. Look at us!"

Corban scoffed, sensing the sarcasm in Titus' voice. Titus was enjoying himself. Being true to his character, the Serval was an adrenalin junky.

But Titus wasn't the only one who was restless about their plan that morning. Corban didn't like the idea of Crac Hassad, Hamas terrorist, still on the loose. Only by Interpol agent Oleg Saratov's careful genius had the biological weapon been swapped for a fake. But Crac Hassad was surely not detoured from his plan to destroy Israel. And if that weren't bad enough, Annette Sheffield was still missing. Her family had been on the news, offering a reward, pleading for her return. And somewhere out there, Luc Lannoy was hiding.

Annette wasn't the only American who was wanted at home. Corban had called home twice to talk to his wife, Janice. She hadn't pleaded for his return, but he heard it in her voice, in her soft goodbye. This had been a lengthy deployment. Usually, a week was to be expected for a well-planned operation. But it had been over three weeks since he'd held Janice, and eaten breakfast with Jenna, his adopted daughter, who was about to enter high school a year early.

"You're not dragging me along on any more of these missions for Jesus," Titus stated brusquely. "I know what you're doing. You can't change me, Corban. Others have tried. My parents used to preach to me all the time. My brother and sister drove me crazy asking me to come to Bible studies with them."

"I'm not trying to change you, Titus." Corban smiled, his mask wrinkling slightly. "God doesn't need my help to do that. I'm confident He'll do it when He wants."

Titus cursed and looked away. For nearly an hour, Titus' remarks continued, but Corban batted them aside. This wasn't the first time he'd adopted a cantankerous fugitive to show him Christ's love and sacrifice for others. In an instant, Corban could call Interpol's Oleg Saratov and have Titus picked up for numerous offences, the worst being the trafficking of biological material.

"It's time," Titus insisted, and pushed past Corban, but Corban held him back. "What now, old man?"

"We can't do this without God watching our backs." Corban placed a hand on Titus' shoulder, and for once, Titus didn't argue as Corban prayed in a low whisper for safety for themselves, for the guards, and for Rasht Hassad, the name of the prisoner they'd come for.

Corban and Titus climbed two flights of stairs to reach ground level. Since they walked together, and seemed to be about some assignment, the guards they happened across didn't pay them any mind. For certain, the stations their Uzbek doubles usually filled were waiting for them. Supervisors would be asking questions soon. Duties were being neglected, and neither Corban nor Titus knew what exact duties those might be.

Titus gestured down one wing of cell doors, and Corban

stopped in the corridor. They would've continued down the prison wing, except four guards were extracting a man in ankle chains from his cell. The prisoner was Rasht Hassad.

The five passed by Corban and Titus as they moved aside. Corban hoped to make eye contact with the prisoner to check his identity. Because of a childhood accident, Rasht's right eye was white with blindness, but Rasht's eyes remained on the floor in front of him. Forty-eight-year-old Rasht looked thin and old, his collar bones showing through his threadbare inmate clothing. Once Rasht and his escort were past, the two imposters fell in step not far behind them.

Titus nodded at Corban, and Corban was reminded he wasn't working with a Christian, but a veteran of the underworld. Except, instead of stealing a banned shipment of munitions, Titus was this time abducting a Christian prisoner in order to catch his evil brother.

A crash gate buzzed open, then a heavy metal door was opened with a key. A nearby guard asked Corban a question he thought was, "Where do you think you two are going?" Corban frowned at the man and pointed at the prisoner, who was just stepping into the sunlight of a cement courtyard. Two guards with batons were waiting to begin what looked like a painful interrogation.

But to the right, Titus opened another door, accessed by a key he'd gotten from the guard he was impersonating. This steel door opened to the parking alley beside the prison. Fresh air wafted in. Corban desperately wanted to be outside in the sunlight, but instead, he turned his back to the door and hustled to catch up to Rasht, who was being strapped to the wall for his session. Glancing back, Corban saw Titus coming up quickly, the door to the alley left open for their escape. Lord willing, the transport van was still parked where they'd seen it that morning.

This was where Corban's plan ended, and he hoped Titus didn't improvise with violence. There was still a high fence and gate that caged them inside the facility perimeter, even if they could make it to the van. If they made a wrong move, they'd be trapped by the gunner in the high tower outside the prison, who could see everything that happened outside.

The guards with Rasht exchanged a few words as Corban advanced. Six guards, two with drawn batons. The odds were unlikely, but there was only one right way Corban was exiting this prison—that was with Rasht Hassad in tow.

Before Corban had rehearsed his moves to systematically engage the six guards, Titus passed him on the left. Corban thrust his hand in his pocket, then edged to his right. Three guards for Titus, and three for Corban.

From his pocket, Corban drew a pen-like device. He clicked it once, and a stubby needle sprang to attention, glistening with tranquilizer venom. As Corban whirled to attack the nearest guard on his right, he glimpsed Titus draw his own tranq-pen from his sleeve.

After a stab in the first guard's thigh muscle, Corban clicked the pen twice to wet the needle again. In a flash, he spun toward the next guard and tranqed him as well. When he turned to inject his third, he realized Titus had already reached him. One guard raised a whistle to his lips as he fell to his knees, but then he collapsed. Corban checked the others, feeling his age a little since Titus had gotten four in the amount of time it had taken Corban to take out his two.

Without taking time to gloat, Titus reached above Rasht and unstrapped the prisoner's hands. Corban grabbed one guard's ankles and dragged him through the door out of sight of the corridor.

"What's happening?" Rasht asked in Russian.

"Quiet, and do what we say," Corban said, and placed Rasht's wrists back into the cuffs the guards had removed from him earlier.

Titus shoved Corban toward the corridor, and Corban moved ahead to secure their exit to the parking alley as Titus, like an official guard, escorted Rasht. Behind him, Titus closed the door to the six unconscious men, and Corban waved at him to proceed into the corridor and to the outside door. Since they weren't rushing about frantically, the few guards in view hadn't noticed the outside door was still open, and the prisoner was being led out.

Corban lingered in the corridor a few seconds after Titus led Rasht outside. All seemed quiet, but he knew they weren't safe yet.

Rasht stood with Titus at the back of the white transport van. Corban did his best to glance casually up at the tower over his right shoulder. The gunner was up there, about thirty feet above the alley. Though the guard was facing them, he seemed to be wiping at something on the front of his uniform with a handkerchief.

The back of the van was open. Corban reached the vehicle as he heard a grunt, and Rasht slumped over in a back seat meant for transporting prisoners.

"You tranqed him?" Corban asked.

"I thought it'd go smoother." Titus shrugged and tossed

Corban the van keys. He grinned. "It's not easy thinking of everything, old man."

Corban caught the keys and climbed into the driver's seat. The gunner was apparently watching them now, because as Corban started the engine, the massive gate began to open. Before them was the highway that led through the Kyzyl Kum Desert.

Titus waved out the window as Corban drove the truck forward.

"*Hvala puno, rostilj!*" Titus called to the gunner.

Corban shook his head and steered toward the highway.

"You're losing your edge, Titus. You just called that guy a barbeque and thanked him in Serbian."

"Huh." Titus frowned. "No wonder they didn't understand me when I came through the entrance this morning."

†

CHAPTER FIFTEEN

GAZA CITY

Annette Sheffield woke with a shudder. Were they coming for her again? No, it was just a door slamming somewhere out there. Gaza. A woman—one who'd beaten her—had told her she was still in Gaza.

Almost two weeks, she calculated. A lifetime ago, she'd been dragged from a Gazan street by Luc Lannoy and marched through the night by Hamas militants.

She touched her lip. It was bleeding again. That angered her, and though most of her anger was focused on her abusers, she was mad at herself, too. Expecting to be accosted by men, her captors had surprised her by being women—four women of hatred and violence. The anger she had for herself was related to her being so naive about a simple trip to Gaza and Israel. The Palestinian conflict was no small matter, and her intent on a few good deeds for the camera and a bathing suit shoot seemed like the most ridiculous idea now.

Crac Hassad. That's who controlled her now, though she hadn't seen the dark quiet man since the first night. The best Annette could guess was that she'd been handed over to Crac Hassad's wives. Two of them looked like Arab sisters. Their English was excellent, so their accusations against her weren't lost in translation.

They accused her of being a Zionist and a Christian.

Under the weight of their brutality, Annette couldn't help but cry out to God. If she hadn't been a Christian before Gaza—which she doubted she had been—she was one now. She hadn't read the Bible since she was a youth at camp, but she knew enough about Jesus to know that He'd died for her, and she needed Him for the forgiveness of her sins. Corban Dowler had reminded her of all this—of her need for a Savior.

With disgust, she reflected on the years she'd wasted pretending to be a humanitarian, when in truth she just enjoyed the publicity. Because of her family's connections in California, and her career as a clothing model, being famous, wealthy, and spoiled seemed like the best of what life had to offer. But Gaza had shown her a major part of her life had been spent in ignorance, even blindness. The recent torment had caused her own sin to become very apparent, as if her suffering were a purifying agent.

Thus, she was angry at herself for being ignorant and naive, but also because she wasn't fighting back. The four women who kept her locked in the humid room were smaller than she was. Annette guessed she could fight and win against two of them, but not when three or all four came for her. She'd been waiting for her chance, to catch them with their guard down, but they were too careful. And now the beatings were taking a devastating toll.

Bruises covered her arms, back, and ribs. Usually, she was able to protect her head, but not when they held her down. And for what? Because they thought she was a Christian? Well, she was now! Their torture had backfired! No one could cry out for Jesus' comfort and deliverance as much as she had and not be a believer.

Annette rose to her feet and limped to the metal door that blocked her escape. Tapping her broken fingernails on it, she could tell it wasn't very thick. A few strong kicks might break it down, or crack the jamb. But such noise would surely bring her tormentors back. Maybe the occasional explosions outside would cover the noise of her escape. If she lived that long.

Or maybe there would be a time when two or more of the women weren't in the house. Yes! Finally, hope rose in her heart as a plan came together. If she learned to read the sounds of the house better, she might be able to determine how many were in there at any given time.

She looked down at her bare feet. She would need something on at least one foot to protect her heel from injury. Once she started kicking at that door, she wasn't going to stop. And whoever tried to catch her once she was free had better be able to run fifteen hundred meters under five minutes—which was her college track team record.

"Thank You, Lord," Annette prayed, certain the plan had come from God. Even if the plan didn't work, she decided it was still God helping her focus on something besides beatings and hatred.

Hatred? Limping, she turned from the door and began to pace the floor of the small bare room. No, it wasn't really hatred. It couldn't be. It was pity. She was a Christian now. If the Spirit of Jesus Christ was in her, then that's what she must feel—anger and fury at evil and injustice, but not hatred. The women who'd beaten her were bound in their own way. And she was bound in her own way—the Lord's way. Corban Dowler's non-lethal tactics had taught her something about a Christian's response to evil in the world.

Kneeling, she picked up her plate and fingered the last of the stale bread crumbs into her mouth. It was almost time for another meal to be brought to her, accompanied by one cup of tepid water. But a beating would precede the bland meal. A beating and a meal. It reminded her of a horror movie she'd once auditioned for. She hadn't gotten the part in the movie, but she was the lead actress in this mess!

VIENNA, AUSTRIA

Titus Caspertein stood outside the Cafe Sperl in downtown Vienna and looked up Gumpendorfer Street. Now was his time to run, if he were going to. Sure, the CIA had seized his accounts and Interpol knew a few of his old haunts, but Titus still had a hundred caches of cash and weapons no one knew about.

"Hey, Titus!" Corban called from a public phone a few yards away. The old spy pointed at the patio table. Titus fetched a napkin for Corban to write on. Whoever Corban was speaking to, it was in a mixture of German, English, and Hebrew. Knowing only English and fair German, Titus couldn't follow the conversation, and he was reminded the old spy could outsmart him any time he wanted to.

Looking northwest, Titus imagined the Danube Canal about twenty twisting blocks away. He could run that far and steal a boat when he reached the canal. A few years back, he and a partner had stolen a few paintings and escaped on the canal. He could do it again, and Corban would never find him.

But things weren't that easy. Sure, escaping was easy. Titus had given government agents the slip before, but Corban wasn't exactly an agent anymore. He'd shown Titus kindness when Titus hadn't expected or deserved it. Instead of sending him to rot in a foreign prison, Corban was treating him like a partner. The Uzbek operation had been daring and potentially deadly, but Corban hadn't hesitated to put his life on the line for Rasht Hassad, who waited for them at the airport. It was the second time Titus had risked his life for someone else. The first time had been for the Palestinian Christians. Both times, Corban had been involved, but Titus knew it wasn't Corban who was influencing him. He suspected God was chopping away at his hard heart, and he didn't like it.

Titus inhaled the aromas of Naschmarkt two blocks away, where both local and foreign exotic merchandise and spices were on display. He glanced at Corban, still speaking cryptically on the phone. The man was a rock. He prayed to God as often as he breathed. So connected internationally, and yet he was alone here with Titus.

Death had haunted Corban, Titus knew. Corban's family had been harassed for years by the US government. He'd shared some of this with Titus in the last two weeks of laying low while Rasht healed before they returned to Gaza for the final stage of the operation. Just because people were close to Corban didn't mean they were invincible, though. Luigi Putelli had died saving Aaron Adar and Oleg.

Oleg Saratov. The man caused Titus to reconsider his thoughts of running away to live underground again. Titus had learned a little more about the Interpol man who'd seemed at home as a criminal by his side for months. The man had only wanted to disrupt the bio-weapon sale and try to arrest the criminals involved. It was just a matter of time before Oleg would be back on his trail if Titus ran now. He'd have to look over his shoulder the rest of his life, and be especially careful since Oleg knew best how Titus' own network operated now. Corban was the only man keeping Titus out of prison. That meant Titus was dependent on the old man.

Outside of Vienna, a giant Ilyushin 76 cargo plane sat in a field near the Hungarian border. The flying tank from the Soviet era was Corban's remote base of operations. The monstrous machine with a forty-meter wingspan made Titus scoff at his own private jet he sometimes used to smuggle small shipments of contraband over foreign borders. Corban could carry sixty tons of rice into the heart of Africa—and that didn't count the fifteen extra tons of Bibles the plane could carry in the phantom cargo space beneath the main hold. The full-time pilot Corban used had once been an outlaw aviator from Uganda. If Titus hadn't spent the last two weeks with Corban, witnessing his uncompromising commitment to Jesus Christ, he would never have believed someone could be so selfless for their God.

"Good news," Corban said as he approached. He was clothed in khaki shorts and a Hawaiian shirt. A camera hung around his neck, playing the part of a tourist. "Luc Lannoy was spotted in Pakistan. Seems he's trying to acquire another weapon, maybe a dirty bomb this time on such short notice. I wish I could've seen Crac Hassad's face when he realized the canister they had wasn't the real thing."

"Luc could lead us to Annette." Titus watched Corban's face. "We can't forget about her, Corban. I know people in Islamabad and Karachi. If we could pick up Luc's trail—"

"No." Corban sat down at one of the patio tables. "It's too far out of our way now. Our responsibility is Rasht. Besides, Luc wouldn't be traveling with Annette. He probably left her in Gaza. We have a better chance at getting both Crac Hassad and Annette if we stay the course."

"But Luc is a direct link to Crac! How can you take a chance like that? You said he could be after a dirty bomb."

"I'm not saying Luc's not being looked into. Relax, Titus. Others are on it, but we're not."

"We can't risk it. Corban, we have to go to Pakistan. Hand Rasht off to someone else. I know Luc Lannoy. Trust me. He's not that smart, but he's smart enough to lay down contingencies if he knows we're onto him. Others won't know to be that careful."

"Titus, they're not even sure it's him in Pakistan. But the people that need to be are on it. If it's real, they'll get the bomb before it can be sold. Even if Luc's watching his tail, it won't be anything these agents can't handle."

"Who is it? Mossad still giving you orders, like they did with Rasht?" Titus joined him at the table. "Luc hired me to get the last weapon for him. I don't trust any government policy-makers to nab him. You shouldn't, either. We need to get him ourselves."

"That's not how this works, Titus. We have functional unity with other agencies, other operatives intent on the same objective. We're a team, to a degree. My people will keep us informed on Luc's movements and when he's been picked up. Right now, Rasht is healthy, so we're headed back to Gaza. Israel is waiting for us."

"So I don't even get a vote?" Titus asked with more bite to

his words than he wanted to express, but Corban had a way of seeming stubborn. The first time they'd met under fire in the Gaza factory, Corban had been immovable and bull-headed about completing his own mission. He was still just as unyielding.

"No, you don't get a vote. If you haven't figured it out yet, you're in my custody. You have a lot to answer for, Titus. You sold your freedom with that stunt in Gaza. The only vote you do have is between being in my company, or in Interpol's. I hear they still have wanted posters with your face on them. Oleg wouldn't mind seeing you again, I'm sure."

Titus gritted his teeth and looked down the street. He had too much pride and skill to be treated like this. He was the Serval! For a moment, Titus had thought seriously about sticking around, but not now. Nobody kept the shackles on him like this. He could call in his own favors. After all, he was the American exile who the US couldn't afford to prosecute because of his resources.

Thrusting his right hand into his pocket, Titus felt the tranq-pen. He was nobody's prisoner, and he definitely wasn't trusting a police force to bring in Luc Lannoy. Titus would get him himself, and even find out what he'd done with Annette Sheffield. He'd show them all he wasn't just an arms smuggler. They weren't better than him!

When Corban rose to his feet, Titus was an instant behind him. He drew the pen. Titus was taller and stronger than the older man, but Corban still blocked the thrusting motion of the pen.

Titus didn't retreat. He even ignored several pedestrians who cried out and pointed at the two men locked in the struggle. Little by little, Titus strained against Corban's strength. The pen moved closer to Corban's chest. It punctured his shirt, then his skin.

Slowly, Corban went limp, but didn't go unconscious immediately. Titus eased him into the nearest patio chair.

"This is a . . . mistake," Corban said, his voice shallow.

"Yeah? Why?" Titus searched Corban's pockets until he found the napkin. Sure enough, there was a Karachi address written on it.

"I'm one of God's servants, Titus. The Lord is my shield and my . . ."

Titus' nostrils flared. *What was he becoming? Where was the honor in doing this?* Shaking his head at himself, Titus pushed his way out of a gathering circle of observers. Several Austrians tried to grab him, probably to hold him until the police arrived, but Titus shook them off.

He was a fugitive again, but at least he wasn't anyone's prisoner.

...†...

GULF OF ADEN

Nathan Isaacson fought against the hypnotizing roll of the ocean as he floated on his back in the Gulf of Aden. Night had come and gone, and now the sun was baking them alive.

Beside him, sleeping softly now, was the child Nathan had saved from the Yemeni soldiers. Nathan cradled the boy's head in the crook of his arm, supporting him amidst the gentle waves. His lips were cracked, but Nathan was helpless to do anything. They had drifted too far out to sea. Part of him wanted to live, but the rest of his being had resigned to drift into the afterlife. He was ready to go, and his prayers through the night had reflected as much.

He'd lived a full life as a man of war in the Middle East, and then a Special Forces operative for COIL. Dozens of times, he'd escaped death by bullets, and even a series of poisonings in Germany. Had God saved him from all that only to die some obscure death at sea?

There were worse deaths, he decided. If only he could save the boy. Whatever language he spoke, it wasn't Arabic, and Nathan didn't know any of the Yemeni tribal dialects, so he couldn't communicate God's love to him. No, that wasn't true. He was communicating God's love perfectly—so said the cramp in his right arm from holding the boy as he slept, keeping his face above the surface of the water.

A muffled chiming reached Nathan's ears. It sounded like his satellite phone, but it wasn't possible. He was miles from shore. His sat-phone had been lost when his raft had drifted from the shore. Under other survival extremes, he'd had similar hallucinations. Now he knew he was close to dying; he was losing his mind.

Nevertheless, Nathan righted himself to tread water for a moment, careful to continue supporting the boy. He stared at a black mass ten feet away before he realized it truly was his raft. Gasping a sob, he kicked sluggishly toward that which had to be an apparition. But the sat-phone continued to ring.

He lifted the boy into the raft first, then climbed halfway in before he reached for the phone.

"Yeah?"

"Nathan, it's Corban. Can you talk?"

"Sure." Nathan squeezed his eyes shut, allowing several

tears to slip out. "You called right on time, Boss."

"I need you in Colombo by tomorrow. Can you make it? Are you finished in Yemen yet? Chloe said you haven't called in."

"Uh . . ." Nathan opened his eyes to check the raft. The boy had found the water container and was struggling with the cap. "Yeah, I'm just finishing up here. Another one to chalk up to God's touch, let me tell you!"

"Okay, I look forward to hearing about it. Here are the coordinates where I need you to meet me . . ."

Nathan stored the GPS coordinates in the phone, then hung up. With a final kick, he dragged the rest of his exhausted body into the raft. The inflatable was equipped for eight people and had enough fuel to reach Somalia.

After helping the boy drink a little water, Nathan gazed northward before he took a sip. He confessed his previous feelings of despair. Too quickly, he'd stopped believing that God was watching over him, in control of even the ocean currents.

Not only had the phone rang at precisely the right moment, but at no other time since Nathan had gone solo did he crave company more. The Lord was moving the world to take care of him, Nathan thought with a smile. Whatever Corban needed from him in Sri Lanka's western capital, this recent lesson of faith and trust had to be applied!

All he could think about now was sharing everything with Chen Li.

CHAPTER SIXTEEN

SRI LANKA

Corban Dowler stood beside a crumbled cement wall. Villagers from a dozen towns had gathered to rebuild the ruined church. Those picking through the rubble weren't disheartened—they were the true Christians. It brought tears of joy to Corban's eyes to be in the presence of such faith. And though the persecution in Sri Lanka was vicious, these people had already prayed to forgive their tormenters.

The road into the hill country six hours north of Colombo was rutted and muddy this time of year. Corban had parked his Land Rover and walked the last few miles. Humidity caused his clothing to cling to him, and the mosquitos seemed to sense he wasn't a native and attacked his exposed skin.

A translator had helped Corban communicate upon arrival, but since he didn't speak Sinhala, he remained separate. His work was done here: delivering supplies, flannel graph materials, and other Sunday School items to this persecuted body of believers.

"Couldn't you have picked a more remote meeting place, Boss?"

Corban smiled as he turned.

"Nathan!" He embraced the young man in khakis and safari hat, then stepped back and grimaced. "Yeman was that tough, huh?"

"I about beat you to my mansion in the sky." Nathan chuckled, touching his bushy beard and cracked lips. "But you shouldn't talk." He frowned and pointed at Corban's chest.

"Oh . . ." Corban felt his shirt to find his collar open, exposing the bandage on his upper chest. "That Titus Caspertein used a tranq-pen on me. It didn't faze me other than to tear my skin and bruise me up a bit. You were right: that tetradetoxin works against our tranquilizer toxin."

"Bet Titus was surprised when you didn't pass out." Nathan slapped his thigh. "Wish I could've seen that!"

"Actually, I let him think it worked. I'm not as young as I used to be, Nathan. Titus is just too strong for me. He might've gotten violent if I didn't go away."

Corban saw the anger pass across Nathan's sunburned face. The ex-Marine was protective of his friends.

"Well, I can't say I'm sorry it didn't work out with him, Boss. It hasn't been easy the last few months." Nathan's broad shoulders sagged.

"Working alone takes a special calling. You've made a phenomenal impact for Christ."

"Here I am blabbering. This is the first time I've seen you in person since the Caribbean. How're Janice and Jenna?"

"They're in the Lord's hands. Jenna is almost as tall as me now." Corban turned to the debris of the church. "We can hardly build churches fast enough to stay ahead of the Tamil separatist destruction—if that's who did this."

"Do we need to pay someone a little visit?" Nathan's shoulders lifted again with boldness. "It's been a while since I took the offensive. You have a couple NL carbines in the country?"

"The COIL plane is all loaded, but we're headed back to Gaza. I had hoped to use Titus for backup, but since he's on the run, I can't risk going in alone. As you know, two are better than one. You ready?"

"Just tell me what you want me to do."

"Gaza's a total war zone. Let's get back to the plane. I want you to meet Rasht Hassad. Somehow, we have to perform a bait and switch, and get everyone out of Gaza alive."

✝

CHAPTER SEVENTEEN

GAZA STRIP

Crac Hassad was about to lose his composure. Everything in Gaza seemed to be imploding. The tunnels from Egypt had caved in, except for three. That meant Hamas weapons from the Muslim Brotherhood had slowed to a minimum. Without a steady flow of rockets and weapons, how could he arm his freedom fighters? Allah demanded the lives of the infidel, and Hassad was not fulfilling that duty!

The two towns in Northern Gaza, Beit Lahia and Beit Hanoun, from where many of the rockets were fired, had been hammered so terribly by IDF war planes that Hassad had to pull his launch platforms back to Gaza City. Two of his missile teams had retreated as far south as Khan Younis.

Hassad, on the second floor of a school building in the Gaza Strip, peeked through a glassless window. The school hadn't been bombed, but nearby homes and other weapons caches had been, which had blown out the windowpanes. No, Hassad had been careful to protect the school from the Israeli bombers. The UN had been influential with that, making sure Israel didn't bomb the documented civilian building. Now, Hassad allowed no more than one Hamas freedom fighter to approach or depart from the school at a time. That way, Zionist drones couldn't say conclusively that the school was being used as an attack center, which, of course, it was.

If the Israelis ever did bomb the school, it would be to Israel's shame, since Hassad had turned the first level of the building into an orphanage for the many parentless children. Yes, bombing the school would incur a massive body count. The world would scream at Israel, as the media often encouraged, and Hassad would simply find another command center. After all, he had killed his own family to make it appear the Mossad had killed them in Iran. Fighting for Allah required many sacrifices.

Killing Jews for a living required patience as well, Hassad considered, and with his soul, he reached out to Allah for strength each day. So many setbacks, but not all was lost. Sure, the biological weapon two weeks earlier had been fumbled by Luc Lannoy, but Luc had called from Pakistan. Another weapon was being purchased and would be flown into Gaza within the week.

For every tunnel Israel bombed, Hassad recruited another dozen freedom fighters to the cause. Each tunnel entrance was hidden inside someone's residence or shop, and each bombing destroyed a residence. The survivors had nowhere to turn but to come to Hassad for help. He gained many recruits this way. And he'd become very wealthy from Western charity organizations giving to what they thought were Palestinian aid efforts. Thus, Hassad didn't mind the bombings. With every bomb, he grew richer and his fighters multiplied.

"We are invincible!" Hassad whispered at the window, gazing out at the fires of the city. "Well, at least *I* am invincible . . ."

For months, he'd moved unscathed throughout the Gaza Strip. The Israeli Air Force bombed and their ground forces invaded, but Hassad believed Allah was protecting him for a special task. There were still enough weapons caches to continue the fight for two more months. By then, he imagined a cease fire would be organized so he could smuggle in more weapons to re-arm his men.

Even Fatah, the political party within the Palestinian Authority, had joined the rocket firing. When they had run out of their short-range Qassam rockets, Hassad had given them Grad and M-75 rockets. Beersheba and Tel Aviv, home to thousands of Jewish civilians, were under constant alert. The Iron Dome, Israel's missile defense system, could barely keep up with Hassad's heightened attacks.

Luc Lannoy, his Belgium ally, had failed as yet to provide the lethal material for his warheads, but Luc had gifted him in another way. The American celebrity, Annette Sheffield, would serve a purpose he was only now beginning to embrace. Soon, the whole world would believe Israel had killed her. It would be the final element to drive a wedge between America and Israel. Without America, Hassad believed Israel would crumble. Without America, Hassad's plans would be unleashed upon Israel, and—Allah be praised— all of Palestine would be his!

"Uncle?"

Hassad turned from the window to face his nephew, Sohayb. He was a worm of a man, barely thirty, but as loyal as a soldier could be to Allah. No one had sent out more suicide bombers than Sohayb. The man was a genius with TNT, and had wired young enthusiasts himself in order to kill the enemy. Yes, *jihad* was alive and well in the heart of his right hand, Sohayb, who was more important to him since Petra had been captured by Israel.

"Yes, my nephew?"

"The drone is complete." Sohayb's face beamed. "We are ready to move it into place."

"The controller?"

"I have sent him through the tunnel. The Israelis may look for him in Gaza, but he will be on the Israeli side of the border in our safe house."

"Allah be praised."

"When the controller is killed, the drone is programmed to slam into the Dome of the Rock." Sohayb adjusted his shoulder holster and sidearm. "The IDF will be condemned after that. No Muslim in the world will be able to restrain himself. No Jew in the world will be left alive, not after an Israeli drone destroys one of our holiest sites."

"I told you I was a genius." Hassad raised his chin. "When I rule, you will rule with me from Jerusalem, my nephew!"

"Praise Allah. I only wish Father were here to witness our triumph."

Sohayb's joy seemed to wane, and Hassad considered a lie to keep the young man's zeal afloat.

"Your father would be proud of you, as I am." Hassad embraced his nephew. "Your father is at Muhammad's side, looking down with pride upon you as you carry on Allah's work. Tell me: what of the tunnel expansion? Everything relies upon the development. The drone must get through to Israel, Sohayb. All of Gaza is relying on you. If you fail me, I swear—"

"Perhaps two days, Uncle, if we do not stop digging."

"Send word to the launch sites. They must not stop firing, even if it costs more lives. We cannot risk the Israelis finding us here. The rockets are our shield."

"Yes, Uncle. I'll tell them. One last thing: you said you wanted to arm at least one of the six drone missiles with a germ or chemical. You must give that to me soon, or we'll have to launch the drone without it."

"I'm waiting for the delivery to arrive. Focus on the tunnel as you're told, Nephew, and I'll pray Allah provides a weapon worthy of his name."

Sohayb returned to the school basement where he needed to supervise the labor on the tunnel. Hassad didn't join him. He hated tunnels himself. Cave-ins were a constant threat. The risk of leaving Hamas without a spiritual leader was too great. Besides, Sohayb had accomplished more than anyone else under Hassad's command.

Hassad wasn't really a commander, though. The men needed little urging. They only needed direction, purpose, and some training. Their hatred drove them, parallel to his own hatred.

As long as Sohayb never discovered the truth about his father, everything would remain perfect. Even as loyal as Sohayb was, Hassad still hated his brother's son. After their strategies were implemented against Israel, Hassad planned to silence his brother's prodigy once and for all.

"May Allah speed Luc Lannoy safely to us!"

✝

CHAPTER EIGHTEEN

Interpol Agent Oleg Saratov was in a sour mood. For months, he'd accompanied Titus Caspertein, acting as his partner, all for the chance to arrest Crac Hassad, Luc Lannoy, and eventually Titus himself. But when the moment had come, Hassad had evaded him, Lannoy had escaped, and Titus had been adopted by Corban Dowler, who everyone knew still had deep CIA ties.

The pile of reports Oleg had to complete for the head office of Interpol in Lyon, France, had provided good healing time for his bullet wound, but his hip was still sore. He wanted retribution, and the looks from others in the office made the Russian agent feel as if he'd failed the whole world. Three dangerous criminals were still on the loose, free to endanger countless civilians with weapons carelessly bought and sold.

Titus was as dangerous as anyone on his list, Oleg thought. Sure, Hassad was an extremist in Gaza and wanted to kill just about everyone for his god. And Lannoy was corrupt and had selfish motives. But Titus was smart enough to have built a smuggling network underground. He had the wits and the funds to purchase, transport, and deliver the deadliest weapons on earth. And his carelessness made him scoff at risk. The man had lost all concern for any moral cause and for

171

purposes that weren't for his own gain. When a man no longer cared, he could do any evil thing. A man with brains and resources who had stopped caring—that man had to be put down.

But Oleg's dark mood evaporated when he received the email from Corban. Titus Caspertein was on the run again, and probably in Karachi, Pakistan, chasing Luc Lannoy. At that news, Oleg sneered. If Lannoy was involved, a profit was meant to be had, and where there was money and risk, Titus would also be attracted.

Grabbing his cane, Oleg hobbled out of his third floor office and down the hallway to the director of foreign assignments, which was a diplomatic name for covert operations. Oleg knocked twice, then barged in on Director Harcoff, an aged man originally from Iceland.

"Saratov? Why don't you come in?" The blond director gestured to a black soft chair, then frowned. "Did you sleep in your clothes again? Oleg, I don't want more complaints about you."

Oleg set his cane aside and tucked his shirt tail into his slacks, then tried to smooth down his uncombed hair. In the field, his appearance as a slob was an asset, but in the office, some of the women upstairs had actually complained, saying a homeless man was prowling through the cafeteria. He'd just been in search of a sandwich!

"Director Harcoff, you know I haven't been here in months. I don't have a home in Lyons."

"There are hotels, Oleg, and clothing called pajamas. Please, make an effort. We represent the best our nations have to offer."

"Yes, sir." Oleg seated himself, flinching from the pain in his hip, but then his grimace became a grin. "Titus Caspertein is on the run. The CIA and IDF contact, Corban Dowler, has informed us if we want him, he's in Karachi. He sent us an address."

"They won't interfere? I'm worried less about Pakistan than the Mossad or CIA." Harcoff glanced at his corner cabinet. "Few international criminals have a file as thick as Caspertein's. It would mean much to this office if he were brought to justice. But look at you. You're barely able to walk."

"I can manage. This isn't a mission. This is an arrest. And it's two for the price of one. Luc Lannoy, the Belgian UN observer is there. Dowler said he's trying to buy another weapon to sell to Hamas militants. You've read my briefings?"

"You trust this Corban Dowler? He's the one who harbored Caspertein two weeks ago."

"We have different goals, but his intel is always true. His man, who we now know was the spy, Luigi Putelli, is the one who saved my life by buying me time to escape with the American girl and Israeli soldier. Differing goals or not, Corban Dowler and his people can be trusted. They're on the side of right in ways I cannot exaggerate."

Harcoff stood and gazed out the window at the ships on the Rhone River in the distance. Oleg wondered if he missed being in the field. Rumors were that he'd been an Icelandic Special Forces commando in his youth. Now, nearly seventy years old, the man who was still all shoulders and chest, operated vicariously through the next generation of operatives.

"How many will you need?"

"Give me four. We can surveil for two days, then move in. I believe we could be back in a week."

"Put it together." Harcoff faced Oleg. "A dozen countries want Caspertein, and Belgium is embarrassed by this Luc Lannoy. Bring them in, Oleg."

"Yes, sir." He rose and took up his cane.

"And Oleg? Dead or alive will do."

"I understand."

As Oleg packed and filed emergency requisition orders, he reviewed Titus' tactics. They didn't call him the Serval for nothing. The man was downright sneaky. If anyone could avoid the net Oleg had planned, Titus could.

Betrayal. The word had continued to play on Oleg's conscience. He and Titus had truly become friends. Titus was a likeable man, to a degree. To develop trust, Oleg had joined Titus on several smuggling and buy-sell arrangements. They'd risked their lives and stared death in its hollow eyes— together. Could Oleg really shoot the Serval? He might have to, if Titus gave him no choice.

Sixteen hours later, Oleg flew over the Hindu Kush Mountain Range and landed in Karachi at the nation's largest airport. The strife in the region, especially in the northwest, had destabilized the city. It had become a melting pot of criminal contacts, extremist ideals, and underground cargo— human and otherwise. The capture and death of Osama bin Laden years earlier in Abbottabad was an exception to the lack of law and order in the struggling country. Police action wouldn't interfere with the transactions in Karachi. Wealth was prized more than the compromise of religion. And if the police did make a show of force, money had a way of dissolving national allegiances.

All this Oleg considered, with teeth clenched, as he carried his bag through the airport, leaning on his cane along the corridor. Two of the four-person Interpol team he'd requested waited outside the airport for him. They'd flown in hours earlier to secure equipment and firearms, and to confirm the address of Luc Lannoy.

Oleg and his men didn't speak as they took his bag and he climbed into the waiting car. Titus Caspertein was near, Oleg sensed, and there would be no escaping this time. Deep down, Oleg knew he would shoot and kill Titus, given the chance. He simply didn't want someone like the Serval alive to get revenge if he didn't kill him. No, Titus Caspertein had to die.

✝

CHAPTER NINETEEN

"May I have everyone's attention?" Israeli Colonel Kalil Yasof called the Forward Command briefing room to order. "For our American guests, I will speak English this morning. Is that acceptable? Good."

Corban stood against the cement wall of the sparsely furnished room. A table and a few chairs had been provided for the Israeli commanders and coordinators. Nathan Isaacson stood against the opposite wall, and Chloe sat in one of the chairs amongst the IDF officials. They were busy taking notes and logging data into their laptops as Colonel Yasof used a digital projector to draw his orders on the wall for each contingency of the pending operation.

The only civilian in the room was Rasht Hassad—the ultimate pawn in this most recent Gazan conflict. Corban had rescued the Christian from the Uzbek prison and brought him back to the Israelis to be used to capture his brother, Hamas terrorist Crac Hassad. Rasht had been tortured in Uzbekistan for his faith in Jesus Christ, though few had believed Corban when he'd reported that Crac Hassad's own brother was truly a devout Christian missionary. For years, the man had been a refugee from Iran, but even while homeless, he'd become a pastor in Uzbekistan, preaching over the radio airwaves when it was too dangerous to share Christ any other way. Now, the nearly fifty-year-old man was to be the IDF's key to a cease fire. Corban had his doubts. Crac Hassad was a radical Muslim. Why would he care about his brother who was now a Christian? And just because Corban had brought the terrorist's brother to Israel didn't mean he'd allow the IDF to place Rasht in unnecessary danger.

Yasof continued his briefing as he revealed his tactics. Corban glanced at the wall occasionally to memorize the features of the colonel's plans. Otherwise, he was prayerful and watchful over the room occupants. He was indeed Israel's ally, but the IDF was in a desperate state. The whole world was pressuring Israel to end the conflict, though the world didn't quite grasp the danger Palestinian extremists presented, particularly their leader, Crac Hassad. There were others in influential positions in Gaza, both political and religious, but at the present, Hassad was the one with a bull's eye.

Since Corban's interests were spiritual in nature, and not political or militaristic, he prayed for the eyes to discern the difference. Israel would have to rely on something other than worldly means to end the conflict in Gaza. Corban had a spiritual vision where people—Jews and Palestinians alike—could be reconciled to God through Jesus Christ alone. His secondary ambition, and his only other purpose to remain in Israel, was to recover Annette Sheffield. The US State Department had authorized Corban to act on behalf of the president to broker her release. No American civilian was in Israel who knew more about the situation to pursue Annette's interests.

Acting as diplomat or not, Corban was in operative mode and would allow Chloe to speak for him since their ideals were the same. Looking across the room, he could tell Nathan was in operative mode as well. They both wore the standard COIL gear: a desert tan-colored parka with a zip-out fleece for cold nights; battle dress uniform pants with pockets, buttons, and zippers resistant to tearing; tactical all-weather boots; uniform rappel belt with a front clip for quick action; and a black assault pack with three days of supplies and gear. Their COIL weaponry—the NL-X1 sniper rifle and NL-3 rifle—leaned within reach of each of them, which had drawn no special attention since everyone but Chloe and Rasht were also armed with state-of-the-art weaponry. And since a biological or chemical attack seemed imminent, a modern gas mask and germ warfare kit had been provided to everyone in the room.

Nathan nodded at Corban, as if to say, *"Just like we prayed last night, I'm ready for anything. I've got your back, and God's got us all in the palm of His mighty hand. I'm just glad to be here."* Corban smiled and nodded back. A lot could be said through a nod. Operative mode was like that: not much needed to be said since the senses were alert and the body was tense for action.

"This is Operation Wolf Hunt," Colonel Yasof explained, his presence commanding silence. "Crac Hassad is the wolf, and we are the hunters. Our latest intel puts Hassad east of Gaza City, so we'll breach the Strip's perimeter north and south of Karni Crossing—two teams. Each team will be supported by two Merkava battle tanks, equipped for urban fighting. Two Saraph helicopters will also escort each team into Gaza, and I'm committing a drone for each team with instant intel piped through. We've been tasked with one Sufa warplane for laser or coordinate smart-bombing. Personnel will be transported in and out in Namer heavy armored carriers. No one else dies during Operation Wolf Hunt.

"Many of you have been introduced to our American . . . observers. They'll be accompanying each team. This is Nathan Isaacson and that's Corban Dowler. During Operation Wolf Hunt, they'll provide support for our secondary priority and that is to locate and recover American civilian Annette Sheffield. She's presumed a hostage. You each have her photograph.

"Don't anyone think our American observers are passive participants. Aaron Adar fell into the enemy's hands two weeks ago. Corban Dowler and Annette Sheffield kept Aaron alive and got him home. The mutual care we have for one another will unite us and keep us safe.

"Our latest intel says Crac Hassad is attempting to acquire another biological weapon. This cannot happen. If it does, or if a weapon has already been smuggled into Gaza from the Mediterranean, we have to get it back, whatever it is, at all costs to prevent a biological attack against Israel. While Operation Wolf Hunt is under way, airstrikes against tunnels and militants will continue. Hamas has intensified their own firing, which may indicate cover for something ugly on the horizon. All IDF ground forces have been pulled back from eastern Gaza City, al-Qubbah specifically. The only people you'll see in Gaza will be one or another of the factions that are trying to destroy every man, woman, and child of Israel. We cannot afford to lose this battle, my friends. The world is watching. Be aware, there may be civilians on the streets, but at night, they'll mostly be inside. Let's never forget our code,

Ru'ah Tzahal: 'Defend the State, its citizens and residents; love the homeland and remain loyal to the country; and maintain human dignity.' We move out in two hours. We breach Gaza at sundown. You have your orders. You are dismissed."

As the officers filed out of the room, Corban signaled Chloe to intercept Colonel Yasof. Corban was aware the two had known each other during Chloe's Mossad days. Approaching the colonel a step behind Chloe, Corban appreciated that Nathan remained wary against the wall.

"Colonel Yasof, what about Rasht Hassad?" Chloe asked. At the mention of his name, the dark-eyed man rose from his chair and stepped forward. "COIL has unofficial custody of him, having rescued him from imprisonment in Uzbekistan. We acted on your intel—that Crac Hassad had a brother. We're responsible for him."

"Of course." The colonel scratched at his left hand, and Corban noticed the veteran was missing his pinky finger. "The world may not have connected an Uzbekistan prison escape with a Hamas leader, but the Palestinian Authority knows us too well. They know we have Rasht. They filed an official warrant for his arrest, saying he killed several women and children in Khan Younis."

"But I have never been to Gaza," the quiet man said. "And I have never killed anyone."

"We know it's a lie," Yasof said, "but . . ."

"Yasof!" Chloe guffawed. "You can't be seriously thinking about giving him to the PA! His brother is behind this. They'll kill him just because he's a Christian!"

"I know. They want him badly. Rasht, we need to somehow use your brother's hatred to our advantage." Yasof sighed and looked at the floor. "Israel is desperate. Offering you to them may draw your brother out. We may even find out where Annette Sheffield is, or trade you for her, Rasht."

No one spoke for a few moments. Corban began to formulate a plan. Rasht was their leverage against Crac Hassad. His idea was risky, but it could work.

"I am not a soldier, or even a member of the nations at war here," Rasht said. His face displayed sadness, his resignation apparent. "But if it ends this conflict and helps this missing woman, I will offer myself as an exchange."

"I fully object to that!" Chloe protested. "Yasof, how manipulative of you to place that upon his conscience!"

Corban stepped aside as Chloe continued to dismantle the colonel's best intentions, though the colonel maintained his idea as the only possible way to draw Hassad into the open, if the conflict came down to negotiations overnight.

Nathan approached Corban and set a hand on the shoulder of his shorter boss. Their heads came together to speak quietly in German.

"I've got a plan, Nathan." Corban glanced back at Yasof, who watched them closely, but he was out of hearing range. "It'll change Yasof's plans, and it'll put us in the path of death. I just don't see Operation Wolf Hunt really working. Men like Crac Hassad are experts at evading the Israelis. And this idea to offer up Rasht will just get him killed."

"What's your plan? You know I'm up for just about anything, Boss."

"I know, but I still want your permission." Corban calculated a dozen moves. He needed to bring in other COIL resources, but most of them couldn't be there by nightfall.

"Okay, I was going to keep it a surprise, but . . . Chen Li's on her way here to meet you."

"What?" Nathan grinned. "You ol' softy, Boss! Janice is really turning you into a romantic, isn't she? Wait. What permission do you need from me?"

"I figured you and Chen Li could enjoy a little of Israel while we waited for word on Annette. But now, I'm thinking we should just go get Annette ourselves. For my plan—you, me, Chloe, Rasht, and Chen Li—we'll all be in danger. But we need to go in tonight while Operation Wolf Hunt keeps most of Hamas busy."

Nathan stared at Corban, their eyes locked. Corban knew it was a lot to ask, and Nathan certainly couldn't make decisions about his fiancée's life, but Corban couldn't proceed without Nathan's permission.

"Can you team her with me?"

"No, you'll be teamed with me. We can't risk our women around Muslim fundamentalists. I want Chloe and Chen Li to handle our over-watch. We'll pair them as a sniper team as you and I deliver Rasht."

"Flush Crac Hassad out?" Nathan rubbed his jaw, still bearded from his Yemeni mission. "It's risky, especially if you want to do this without the IDF."

"No one can know. Not even Yasof. Or we're dead when we get in front of Crac Hassad. We may be dead anyway, if we run into an Israeli F-16 missile. I have in mind to arrange additional COIL backup, but nothing that can be set up tonight."

"Let's do it. May God help us. I'm in." Nathan chuckled, which Corban thought was a good sign. Eagle Eyes was starting to sound like his old confident self again. He'd just needed a little friendly company and fellowship. "Chen Li is well-trained. She and Chloe will make a good team, but I don't think Chen Li is sniper-trained."

"That's okay." Corban winked. "Chloe is."

†

CHAPTER TWENTY

ISRAEL / GAZA

Annette listened past her own whimpering to the noises of the house. Her cheek was split open and she felt a few loose teeth from her last beating from Crac Hassad's four wives. Since she was beaten every time a meal was delivered, she had decided to use that time to speak boldly for Christ.

When the door had opened that morning, she'd stood in the corner and said, "I know you're about to beat me. But let this be known: you are beating me because I'm a child of God, a believer in Jesus Christ. I don't hate you for what you must do."

Then, as their fists and feet had rained down on her, through gritted teeth, she had recited John 3:16. She felt bad she hadn't been a Christian earlier, or that she had no other Scriptures to rely on from memory, but it seemed an appropriate verse, something God had helped her remember from her selfish youth.

There was a sense of joy she couldn't identify, just knowing she wasn't being beaten without a reason—but she was being beaten because of her faith in Christ. The abuse had seemed to intensify the last few days since she'd become bolder, but somehow, it seemed worthwhile.

The house was quiet. Could it really be empty? Once in a

while, she heard distant explosions, vehicles outside, and war planes above—but the house seemed to be unattended now.

She stood in front of the door, her left foot wrapped in a torn strip of blanket. Her right leg was normally stronger than her left, but her right knee was swollen nearly twice its normal size, thanks to one of her tormentor's heels. Permanent damage didn't trouble Annette; she just wanted to be free. If she stayed much longer, her four Palestinian friends were liable to kill her.

Annette's first kick cracked the door frame. Sure enough, they had underestimated her, and overestimated the security of their hostage room.

If someone was in the house, Annette wasn't about to wait for them to stop her. She gasped and cried out, kicking the door up high, where she believed the dead bolt was fastened.

When the door finally gave way, the frame didn't just splinter. It burst open on dry hinges. For an instant, Annette stared into the unveiled face of one of her captors, a young woman no older than Annette. Muslim women didn't have to wear veils at home in the company of other women, so Annette had wondered why the four wives had worn full coverings when they'd beaten and fed her. Now, Annette no longer wondered. The poor woman's face was swollen and bruised, apparently from beatings she'd received either from Crac Hassad or his other wives.

Annette stepped through the door, and the wife backed away. She didn't dare attack Annette without her cohorts, but Annette remained ready to defend herself. Glancing to the right, she saw a window and a flight of stairs that descended to what she guessed was the street level.

"Come with me," Annette said. "You don't need to live like this any longer."

The woman blinked, and opened and closed her mouth several times. Finally, she turned toward the stairs.

"Follow me."

Annette didn't have to be told twice. She limped hurriedly after the woman. At the ground level, they heard men's voices speaking Arabic. The wife gestured at Annette, and the two retreated up the stairs then beyond the hostage room, into the recesses of a hallway that smelled like damp earth.

Suddenly, a masked figure stood in front of them. The wife attacked him instantly, silently, and Annette joined her. She had to get free. Who knew what America and Israel were being forced to concede to the terrorists because of her!

The masked man was armed with a rifle. While the wife entangled his arms, Annette stepped behind the man and kicked him low in the back. Under the woman's weight, the two crumbled onto the floor. He must've hit his head hard enough, because he lay still an instant later. Annette ripped the man's mask off and drew a knife from a sheath on his belt.

"Come!" the woman urged, moving toward the dank smell. "Others are coming!"

Annette cut the laces on the man's combat boots and tugged them off. She couldn't run away barefoot! Snatching up the rifle, she rushed after the wife.

The hallway sloped down to a wide garage, empty, but large enough for three trucks. The floor was of dirt. One of the three garage doors started to open. The wife darted to the left where light bulbs lit up the back of the garage. There it narrowed into a tunnel, sloping down into the earth.

Containers and oil drums crowded the tunnel mouth. The wife hid between two drums, and Annette crowded beside her as voices rose from the garage. The unconscious man had evidently been found.

A Toyota truck was driven into the garage and the large door began to close. Outside the door, the day was turning to dusk. To Annette, approaching darkness seemed the perfect time of day to escape on foot.

"Let's go!" the woman whispered, and emerged from her hiding place.

Annette reached to pull her back, but the woman was already gone, running for the closing garage door. Helplessly, Annette watched as she sprinted past the Toyota. Her timing was completely off. The wife squirmed under the door as it closed on her waist. The chain above ground to a halt. The wife screamed and twisted in fright, halfway outside the garage, drawing everyone who hadn't already seen her try to escape. Gunmen rushed to the door and raised it while pinning the woman to the floor.

"Run!" the woman yelled, her voice outside echoing back through the garage. "Run!"

But Annette didn't move. The terrorists now assembling clearly believed Annette had already escaped through the door. Two men with handguns exited the garage. One went left, the other right. A tall skinny youth wearing a shoulder holster gave orders in Arabic, then stepped over the woman, who seemed injured from the garage door. With chills running up her spine, Annette realized the woman wasn't wearing her veil, as required by Sharia Law.

The skinny man drew his sidearm and aimed it at the

disobedient wife's head. Annette looked down at the rifle in her hands. Was it loaded? Was the safety on? She felt inclined to help the battered wife, but how? A dozen armed men now surrounded the woman on the floor.

The gunshot, even thirty yards away, hurt Annette's ears. She slid farther back behind the drums, panting, trying to control her breathing and shock. The youth had just executed one of Crac Hassad's wives! That meant he had authority— merciless authority.

Settling her gasps, Annette gazed at the smelly black boots in her lap. Removing the shredded laces, she shoved her bare feet into the footwear. Since she was six feet tall, the boots were close to her size, though wide. Using a couple of lace scraps, she tied the top boot eyes together and pulled the mask over her head. From the earthen floor, she gathered dirt, spit on it, rubbed her hands in the mud, then smeared it underneath her mask. The holes in the mask now wouldn't show her pale skin around her eyes and lips. She smeared more mud over her hands and arms.

The men in the garage remained standing over the woman's body, discussing something. Annette gazed into the darkness of the tunnel. There were more voices coming from in there, and activity, like digging. It seemed to be the only escape from the garage. If she didn't move soon, she'd be captured again, and the skinny leader with the shoulder holster didn't seem like he was in the mood to show mercy to a woman.

Annette prayed for help and silenced a sob as she started to cry. Corban Dowler. He had to be near. She'd settle for Oleg Saratov, or even Titus Caspertein at this point. Just not

Crac Hassad or Luc Lannoy! Shuddering at the thought of capture again, she rose to her full height in the shadows of the tunnel mouth. Air wafted down into the tunnel. A draft meant an exit, somewhere. Did that mean they had tunneled into Israel? Of course. Why else would Crac Hassad dig a tunnel? The thought of freedom in Israel made her dizzy.

There was nowhere else to go. She squared her shoulders, held the rifle across her chest, and entered the tunnel.

†

CHAPTER TWENTY-ONE

KARACHI, PAKISTAN

Titus Caspertein's conscience bothered him, and he blamed Corban Dowler. For years, Titus had suppressed the good morals of his youth so he could commit unspeakable criminal acts. Every inclination his flesh had, he fed it. Weapons brokers loved the ex-American's rebellious attitude, and loose women loved his rough but handsome features, topped off by a head of blond hair, almost the color of wheat. What he didn't steal or enjoy for free, he bought with his riches.

Nothing in his criminal career helped him make sense of his pursuit of Luc Lannoy into Karachi, Pakistan. For years, Titus had called himself one of the good guys, just with his own set of rules. No one could blame him for looking out for number one, right? It wasn't like he actually fired the missiles he sold, or pulled the pin on grenades he smuggled to militants. But living next to Corban Dowler for just a few hours in Gaza, had intimidated his version of self-righteousness into the dark recesses of his heart—the darkness he liked to pretend wasn't really there.

"I'll show you!" Titus spat as he stood in an alley of a slum neighborhood of Karachi. He wore no disguise and made no apologies for his Western appearance. As the smuggler who was called the Serval, he would capture Luc Lannoy and

190

prove to Corban Dowler he was as good as anyone else.

But deep down, Titus knew Corban would never buy an act of justice for a change of heart. True Christians—men like Corban—didn't judge matters by appearances, but by the standard of Jesus Christ. And that left everyone wanting and at God's mercy for any righteousness at all.

Across the street, Luc Lannoy, the tall Belgian from Gaza, poked his head out of a doorway that Titus himself had frequented over the years. Lannoy looked up and down the crowded street, then hopped over a drainage gutter of raw sewage. Four armed men followed Lannoy, their rifles held ready for use. They seemed determined in their local uniforms, their gait hurried enough to send several civilians scattering out of their path.

Titus didn't care to spend much effort capturing Lannoy. The traitor to UN policies was going down. Lannoy was like all the other men Titus had done jobs for over the years—too corrupt to realize they were being used for darkness.

After flexing his gun hand for action, Titus drew a cell phone from his pocket and gazed after Lannoy's party. Titus didn't want to kill Lannoy, just wound him enough to capture him. The explosive charge he'd placed down the street was small, but adequate. His Glock 18 handgun would take care of whatever the explosive didn't. They were just about in place, now. . .

"Don't move, Caspertein!"

The booming voice of Interpol's Oleg Saratov was unmistakable. The English words themselves caused bystanders within earshot to pause and stare. The only Americans bold enough to be in that district were criminals, and even then they usually didn't speak English openly. Westerners were disliked by the general Pakistani public, but truly hated by militant extremists in Karachi. An English speaker was considered fair game for robbers and murderers, or *jihadists*, which were often one and the same.

"It ain't easy being caught in the middle," Titus mumbled dryly to himself as he guessed he was about to die.

Lannoy looked back at Titus, their eyes meeting. With visible panic on his face, Lannoy spotted Oleg. Titus turned to see Oleg coming up the street behind him. He wasn't alone. There were at least three others with him—surely Interpol officials.

Screaming at his four armed escorts, Lannoy pointed at Oleg's party. Titus stepped deeper into the alley and dove to the ground as gunfire thundered past him, catching the Interpol agents unsuspecting. Trapped between two groups with weapons, Titus drew his Glock and pressed SEND on his cell phone. As quick as the signal could relay to the pirated cell tower two blocks away and bounce back to the explosive down the street, the detonation shook the dust from the concrete and deafened the neighborhood. Visibility was lost for a few minutes as the dust settled.

Lunging to his feet, Titus scrambled into the cloud. Lannoy was still his target, regardless of Oleg's presence. With a little luck, he could have Lannoy gagged and hogtied for a private plane ride back to the Middle East. Corban would eat his uppity words, and Israel would honor him with a dinner and a weekend in Eilat.

But the dust was thicker than Titus anticipated, and though the wounded were scattered across the street, Lannoy and his people weren't among them. Titus cursed as he approached the injured to see that the explosive had turned part of a building into a thousand pieces of concrete shrapnel. Two dozen were wounded and bleeding, yet everyone seemed able to walk under their own power to receive help.

Gunfire started again between the Oleg and Lannoy parties. Since Titus valued his own skin over the value of Lannoy's capture, he thought it best to abandon his pursuit of him. Titus had lived an aimless and careless life, but that didn't mean he wanted to die or risk it needlessly.

One street away, Titus slowed to a walk and searched for a taxi. Emergency personnel rushed past him. If he hurried to the airport, he could be over Eastern Europe by midnight. Forget proving himself to Corban. He had other things to do. If Lannoy was still alive, he could hunt him down after Oleg and Interpol cooled off.

Suddenly, Titus stopped in the street and listened to the gunfire. The battle was raging on. Now he felt guilty for running away. He'd never liked Lannoy, but Oleg had been his friend, even if the man had been an undercover agent. Sure, the only reason Oleg was even there had to be because Corban had notified him that Titus had escaped. But Titus couldn't just run away, not this time. His blood boiled at the thought of the likes of Lannoy killing a dedicated man like Oleg.

Growling to himself, Titus turned around and jogged toward the haze where dust still settled.

"If you get me killed, Oleg," he said with clenched teeth, "I'll never risk my life for you again!"

When he reached the street, he knelt next to the corner of

a shop to study the situation. Clearly, Lannoy's goons had been better armed and had overwhelmed Oleg's team, who had probably expected to face only Titus. Oleg's men had been killed in the street, and Oleg was pinned down in the doorway of a second-hand store, his leg outstretched and bleeding.

Lannoy appeared uninjured. He signaled to two of his men still standing, but they responded with gestures that showed they were out of ammunition. Oleg fired two shots desperately down the street, then he clicked on empty as well. Cursing, he threw his gun down, certainly knowing his end had come.

Laughing triumphantly, Lannoy walked confidently down the street, his sidearm aimed at Oleg. In French, he shouted the horrible things he would do to Oleg before he killed him. The words made Titus grimace.

"Luc Lannoy!" Titus called.

Lannoy pivoted and fired his gun automatically. His bullet struck the corner of the building above Titus' head.

"Titus! I thought you were gone." Lannoy looked down at his weapon, and Titus walked toward him, his own gun at his side. "I didn't mean to shoot at you, Titus. Just these Interpol guys."

"Throw down your firearm, or die, now!" Titus raised his weapon and aimed. Lannoy hesitated and started to speak, then pointed with his pistol down the street at Oleg. Firing, Titus' bullet hit the shoulder of Lannoy's gun arm.

No longer laughing, and now knocked to the ground, Lannoy tried to crawl to his weapon that had clattered into the drainage ditch. Titus moved into the street and fired several wide shots at Lannoy's remaining men. With their guns empty and their boss down, they didn't dare stay on the scene. They fled in two different directions.

"Titus!" Lannoy gasped and tried to sit up. "Seriously, I thought you died in Gaza. I wish you had, now. Setting me up like that with Crac Hassad. I was lucky he let me live after he discovered that weapon was a fake. Even bringing Interpol into the deal. How could you not know Saratov was Interpol? You owe me!"

Standing over Lannoy, Titus fingered his gun trigger.

"How about I don't kill you," he said, "and we call it even?"

"I could live with that. Okay, we're even."

"Under one condition: Annette Sheffield. What did you do with her?"

"Come on, Titus!" Panting, Lannoy's face reddened. With his shoulder bone shattered, he held his head awkwardly. "Okay, okay. When the weapon wasn't real, I had to give Crac Hassad something. She was collateral. He said I could have her back if I returned with the real weapon within three weeks."

"So you left an American female model with a Muslim fanatic and his boys who are bent on the destruction of Israel and all things Western?" Titus holstered his Glock, but drew out the tranquilizer pen he'd used on Corban. "I have dirt on you, Luc, and I'm going to make sure Interpol gets it all."

Titus stabbed the pen into Lannoy's thigh. The Belgian fell to the street, unconscious, his shoulder leaking blood. The emergency responders worked their way down the street, pausing to see to the bystanders as they drew closer to where Titus was.

Moving toward Oleg, Titus picked up a sturdy cane off the ground.

"Lose something, Oleg?" Titus twirled the cane like a baton. "Seems you just got shot by that fool a couple weeks ago. You should still be in the hospital, not out here on vacation. The coffee's great, sure, but the gunfire really smarts."

"Maybe I missed playing Dodge-the-Bullet." Oleg yanked the cane out of Titus' hand as Titus sat down next to his old partner. "My whole team is dead. I'll be on desk duty until I retire."

"If you would've waited five minutes, I would've had Lannoy, then you could've gotten us both."

"I could still get you both." Oleg's face wrinkled in pain as he applied pressure to his leg wound. "You would've killed me already if you were going to. You didn't have to come back for me."

"I'm not especially fond of being taken into custody." Titus chuckled. "Not that you could, though. There are advantages to being the Serval in a third world country, even if Pakistan is becoming more modernized. You shouldn't have come, Oleg."

"So, what now?" Oleg spit into the gutter. "It's not like you to hunt down someone like Lannoy. You trying for another weapon for the Palestinians? Was Lannoy stepping on your turf?"

Titus watched the paramedics attend to the unconscious Lannoy.

"I guess I was wondering if I could live up to Corban Dowler's standards."

"Thinking of going Christian?" Oleg elbowed Titus. "The world would never believe it. The Serval's a killer, a thief, and a dishonorable scoundrel. And those are the nice things from your file!"

"Then maybe it's time I shock the world in a new way." Titus stood and stepped aside as a medic cut away Oleg's pant leg to examine the wound. "After all, you turned on me, and I already forgave you. Maybe there's something good in me yet, huh?"

"That's different." Oleg smirked.

"How so?"

"You didn't want to kill the only man in the world uglier than you. That'd make you the ugliest man in the world."

Titus smiled. He would miss his old partner.

"You got Lannoy from here? I'm on the move."

"Take off. I'll catch you later, Serval."

"Not likely, Oleg Saratov. Not likely."

†

CHAPTER TWENTY-TWO

GAZA / ISRAEL

Corban sat with Chloe Azmaveth in the front seat of a rented tour bus. Rasht Hassad rested in a seat three back from the front, and Nathan Isaacson and Chen Li sat in two seats in the very back. The couple leaned across the aisle toward each other, their heads touching in prayer.

"It's nearly dark," Corban said softly to Chloe, not wanting to wake Rasht before it was time to move out. The Iranian missionary wasn't in the best physical condition; prison hadn't been kind to him. "We need to beat Colonel Yasof's ground incursion into Gaza if this is going to work right."

"Look at them." Chloe nodded her head toward Nathan and Chen Li. "They don't see each other for months, and now they spend their first minutes together praying."

"It says something about God's love in a relationship," Corban said. "Janice and I could've been spared a lot of heartache if we'd married with Christ at the center."

"The Lord brought you two around when it was His time." Chloe lifted the NL-X1 sniper rifle from the bus seat and settled it on her lap. She was dressed like a Gazan rebel: a checkered headdress, faded parka, and worn jeans. "I'd feel better about this if we had more COIL backup."

"I've got some calls in but we can't wait to see who shows up. India has drawn two COIL teams into the fray, and we

198

have three others in Indonesia, Angola, and Turkey. Like always, God's people are spread thin so we trust on Him more and more."

Chloe stood, her battle gear—pack, canteen and NL-3—strapped tightly for combat. Chen Li, the Hong Kong native and COIL agent of a dozen missions, was dressed identically to Chloe, though armed with a spotting scope instead of a weapon.

"Chen Li, we need to move. It's time. Sorry, Nate."

"No harm done." Nathan led Chen Li up the aisle. "Just make sure we get a honeymoon on the Med, Boss."

"Let's bring Annette Sheffield home, then we'll see what the Lord has in store for you two, huh? Rasht, can you pray for us?"

Nathan and Chloe each held a hand of Corban's. Rasht's English was rough as he completed the circle between Chloe and Chen Li, but his words to God were full of praise and trust. Now was a time to stand on His power and Lordship over all, even over the bullets that might soon be zipping at their heels.

With their prayer of dedication finished, Chloe and Chen Li stepped off the bus and jogged over to a ladder that lay at the foot of the Gazan perimeter wall. Together, the two women leaned the ladder against the wall and climbed up. They'd already shot out the nearest lights, and dusk hid them enough from the many aerial patrols. Besides, the IDF seemed more concerned about people leaving Gaza than entering.

When Chloe reached the top of the wall, she used a grapnel hook and rope to slide out of sight. A few seconds later, Chen Li disappeared after her.

Corban and Nathan checked their watches simultaneously. The plan was to give the women a five minute head start, to find an elevated position near where Crac Hassad was hiding.

"You're sure he'll be there?" Nathan asked for the third time that evening. "I mean, Chloe was Mossad. Israel is her stomping grounds. I'd guess she'd be the one with the inside intel on this crook."

"Chloe's irreplaceable, no doubt." Corban used the bus side mirror to apply a heavy beard that reached down to his chest, and thick-rimmed glasses under fake bushy eyebrows. "But she's not Muhammad ibn Affal. Crac Hassad's contacts in Syria and Iran have been acquainted with ibn Affal for twenty years. It was just a matter of setting up the meet. Hassad's men told me exactly where to meet them, and under this much Israeli pressure, I'd guess Hassad isn't moving around too much."

"And you're sure that stuff will pass the test?" With his toe, Nathan nudged a blue canister on the floor next to Corban's foot.

"It'll pass. Hassad's zeal to kill Israelis has blinded him to certain threats. Between what's in this canister and Rasht, we should be able to get Annette Sheffield back. You ready, Rasht?"

"Ready." The aging missionary stood before Corban. "You look like the Ayatollah in Iran. My brother is a devout follower. May God blind him from the good we are about to do."

"Amen. Let's move."

Nathan led the way up the wall, then Corban brought up the rear after Rasht. For now, Corban and Nathan were both armed with NL-2 machine pistols under their clothing.

Once inside Gaza, Corban caught sight of Nathan, who was a much more adept urban warrior. Corban jogged after him and Rasht. They were quickly among the buildings of the border city of al-Qubbah, which was slowly being consumed by Gaza City to the west.

Corban looked to the sky. Saraph choppers were beginning to patrol closer to the street level, but they were farther south. He hadn't felt it necessary to tell Colonel Yasof where Crac Hassad wanted to meet, and why Corban and his people were opting out of the IDF incursion. After all, it had been agreed that Corban was there for the American Annette Sheffield. She was Corban's priority. Later, if there was room to take Crac Hassad, or to inform the Israelis of his true whereabouts, then he would do his part—if Corban was still alive to do so. The secrecy used against the IDF was to protect the ibn Affal identity, not to spite Israel. The identity had secured many Christians' safety in the past, and Corban prayed for one more successful Muhammad ibn Affal mission.

†

CHAPTER TWENTY-THREE

EASTERN GAZA

A nnette stood in the shadows of the tunnel as long as she dared, then she stepped into the lamplight. She cradled the rifle in front of her and kept her black mask pulled down all the way. With purpose, she walked past shirtless men who hacked with shovels and picks at the tunnel walls. It was then she discovered these men were not digging the tunnel anew, for it went on and on. Rather, they were widening it. *But why?*

The working men seemed to ignore her as she moved beyond the excavation to a part of the tunnel already widened. Several of the diggers had left their packs there. Annette picked up one and found a green army jacket. Tugging it on, she felt more the terrorist part. She also found packaged food and water, which she gulped down before anyone came around to discover her. A meal without a beating for a change!

A man up the tunnel yelled in Arabic, and she dropped the provisions. He gestured and was obviously hailing her. Annette looked back the way she'd come. She had to cross over to Israel. It was her only chance to live. No one even knew where she was, or if she was still alive. Only when she was in Israel could she relax.

But first, she had to do nothing suspicious. It began with

this middle-aged man calling to her. Lowering her voice, she mumbled incoherently and approached him. The tunnel dipped down, and when it sloped up again, Annette realized why she'd been hailed. Seven men were using a makeshift cart to wheel an aerial drone up the tunnel! It was clearly marked as a drone belonging to the Israeli Air Force.

The man who'd hailed her took her rifle and gave her orders to do something with the cart. Though she didn't understand, she could guess. He leaned her rifle against the tunnel wall, and Annette joined the men to move the cart wheels over the soft ground. The widened tunnel now made sense. The drone's wingspan was about fifteen feet wide.

Annette did her best to anticipate what the others were doing to move the drone forward, but she still received a whack on the side of the head and a volley of Arabic when she didn't lift her side of the cart over a section of rock. Though the size of a man, she lacked the brute strength necessary, and eventually she was pulled from her cart position and hooted toward the front. In front, she was given a shovel. After more instructions in unknown Arabic, she grunted a low response, then went ahead to dig away last minute chunks of earth for the wings. Thus far, and by some miracle, she'd escaped discovery.

Going back the way she'd come was unnerving, but she didn't dare throw the shovel down and run down the tunnel. Instead, she dug at the walls where the others ahead had miss-judged the wingspan. The militants who belonged to Crac Hassad had obviously captured an Israeli drone, and the snub-nosed rockets under each wing had Hebrew writing on them. Hassad was up to no good, and Annette didn't like the idea that she was helping them transport the drone under what she guessed was the Gaza-Israeli border.

After an hour of work, they caught up to the main excavation crew Annette had first encountered. Another thirty yards, and they would reach the garage.

A man she recognized from the garage tromped down the tunnel, so Annette made an effort to show she was an aggressive digger, requiring no more interaction. Two of the men who pushed the cart with the drone wore masks still, and others had wrapped their faces against the fine soil that settled on everything, falling constantly from the ceiling. The dirt glittered in the lighting from the hanging bulbs.

Falling back some, she knelt to untie her barely tied laces, and made a dramatic show of dumping dirt out of one boot. But no one seemed to be watching. Now was her chance. She preferred to hide rather than be forced into another job.

Tightening her laces, she rose and walked briskly away from the drone. She would've sabotaged it if she could have, but not with so many enemies around her. She had to get to the freedom of Israel! As she reached where her rifle leaned, she prayed for continued safety. Sure, her whole body was one big bruise from the beatings, and her knee hurt like hot iron, but she was alive!

When she came to the tunnel end, instead of daylight, she found a dimly lit basement. Listening for anyone nearby, her boots stepped onto cement. Since she was in Israel now, she was tempted to run for the nearest exit, but she had to resist, at least until she knew no more militants were lurking.

The building she was in was massive, and the basement level housed steam pipes and utility cabinets that spanned one hundred yards. Pausing, she heard explosions and even gunfire that seemed closer and louder than when imprisoned in the house across the border.

Finally, near an ancient furnace, she found a set of stairs. She heard voices now. They sounded like children's voices! There shouldn't have been children in a Muslim stronghold in Israel! With her rifle aimed upward, she ascended the stairs.

Already, she imagined what she would tell the media—about the ambush against UN vehicles, and Luc Lannoy's betrayal of his post. What would she say about Corban Dowler, Titus Casptertein, and Oleg Saratov? Maybe nothing. Those men had disappeared during the end, and she guessed Oleg was dead from Lannoy's frantic gunfire. And then there was the tall, gaunt gentleman who had stood his ground in the factory as she, Aaron, and Oleg had escaped. Had that man survived? Even now, she recalled the gunshots that early morning, and her own capture by Lannoy. It seemed unlikely that anyone good could survive in a place with so much evil.

For certain, she would never be the same. The horrors she had witnessed—against others and herself—had caused her to cry out to God for salvation. That had become a faith she couldn't give back—a faith she didn't want to give back. She had changed, and as a new person for Jesus, she knew from now on her life would be lived differently.

She reached the top of the stairs. A few yards away, another stairway continued to a second story, but she sensed this level was the ground level. Israeli commandos could explore the rest of the building once she ran outside and hailed the nearest Israeli civilian. Everyone in Israel carried a cell phone.

A broad room sprawled in front of her, its wall brightly painted with pictures from the hands of children.

Two dozen women and children hardly looked up as she walked softly into the room. Sleeping mats and blankets covered one section of the room, and the rest of the room held chairs, where several veiled women assembled machine parts. Some children colored more pictures, and others dashed about playing tag.

As a masked militant, Annette moved near the women at the table as they bowed to their work more feverishly. In front of each woman was a pile of metal parts, but a small chunk of clay was easily identified by the wrapping paper that read *C-4*. The women were assembling a variety of bombs!

Annette walked past them, avoided two boys wrestling on the floor, and reached an open doorway. Ahead was another room, the same as the last, with more women and children. Now she noticed the chalkboards and what appeared to be a teacher's desk in one corner. It wasn't a weapons factory or a military administration building. It was a school building. In the basement, the militants did what they wanted, while above, all that would be seen through a thermal imaging satellite view would be women and children, supposed displaced persons from the conflict. But how could Israel allow this right under their noses?

The answer came to Annette before she reached the outside door at the end of a broad hallway. She wasn't in Israel; she was in Gaza!

Throwing the door open, she turned her face to sunlight and fresh air, appreciated even through her mask. As her eyes settled on the city scape before her, her fears were confirmed.

It all made sense now, and she turned to face east. Yes, she'd been held in Israel! When she'd escaped captivity, she had fled into Gaza by way of the tunnel. The militants weren't taking the drone into Gaza; they'd moved it from the Gaza school building to the house with the three garage doors. They were about to launch the drone from Israel—to target Israel!

Now, Annette was torn. No way was she returning to the tunnel, even if it were the fastest route back to Israel. And yet, to remain in Gaza meant she had to keep the mask on. Her face, as a woman under the enforced Sharia Law, was to be veiled, so she couldn't take the mask off or the Muslims would kill her. And yet masked, she would be targeted by Israeli troops if they stormed the school building.

A chopper cruised low over the buildings a few hundred yards away. Annette shrank into the cover of garbage piled against the outside of the school. When night came, she had to find any soldier from Israel. Or maybe she could flag down a chopper without getting shot.

"God, I'm afraid . . ."

Her body's muscles and wounds throbbed. She pulled a section of soiled cardboard over her head to hide. Fear paralyzed her as she imagined what she would have to do to reach safety. In the tunnel, she'd shoveled with the militants out of desperation and necessity. The full weight of the nearness of death made her weep.

She prayed for God to send her help. It was unlikely, but she prayed anyway. Without help, she was dead. Danger surrounded her.

"Send me someone, Lord. I don't know what to do!"

CHAPTER TWENTY-FOUR

ETHIOPIA

Titus stepped out of his private Pilatus PC-24 business jet onto the sunbaked red sand of Gonder, Ethiopia. The Swiss-made jet allowed Titus to travel in luxury, and yet still frequent the crude dirt airstrips that his trade demanded. Though the twinjet could seat ten passengers, Titus had removed the rear seats for black market cargo space to be loaded through the rear cargo door.

But on this trip, Titus had no cargo. In fact, he'd canceled all buy-sell arrangements for the foreseeable future. All that was on his radar was Annette Sheffield. He'd captured Luc Lannoy and helped Oleg. The way things were going, he might just be able to right the wrongs he'd caused during his visit to Gaza. If it weren't for him, Annette wouldn't have remained a captive in the factory. But his desire to find her had to do with more than just righting wrongs. She'd been tough, even standing up to him, and no woman besides his sister had ever done that. It also helped that Annette was an attractive model. He'd settle for a simple thanks from her now, unless she wanted to take it further—if he could get her out alive.

The dust from his landing settled, and the animals around the farm returned to their evening activities—grazing or nipping at the scraps Bekele had left them.

Titus sauntered into the yard he'd frequented during other layovers and cargo transports—as often as any other underground airport where the Serval was best known. Every criminal needed a hideout, and Titus had over a dozen with runways, and many more without.

"Bekele!" He nudged a chicken from his path and stepped onto the porch of the rundown colonial-style house. "I know you heard me arrive!"

After walking through the messy house and finding nothing but dusty furniture and bags of animal feed, Titus returned to the porch. Bekele's truck was parked in the shade of the house. The two rickety barns were the only other structures on the fenceless property. Entering the first building, Titus found Bekele's barley brewery hissing through the pressure valve. Two cows and several goats lay nearby.

In the second barn, Titus crouched over Bekele, a fifty-year-old Ethiopian veteran soldier, retired on the war spoils of a dozen African countries. Titus chuckled at the two hens that roosted comfortably in each arm of Bekele as he slept off his recent binge.

"Bekele, I need you. Wake up!" Titus prodded the sleeping man in the ribs. One hen clucked and ruffled her feathers. "Careful, girl. I haven't eaten too well for a few weeks. A little chicken feast would—"

"You!" Bekele sat upright. The hens flapped away. "You owe me money!"

"For what?" Titus waved his hand in front of his nose. "Phew! You've got to stop sleeping with the animals, Bekele."

"You stole my favorite goat last month!" Bekele rolled over and stood shakily. "How much do you owe me?"

"I owe you nothing. I've never taken a goat from you, but I'm willing to pay you for two pigs if you can think straight long enough to give me a price."

"You do not owe me?"

"I'm in a hurry, Bekele. Your sow had piglets recently, right? I want two of them."

"They are not weaned."

"Then charge me extra. Bekele, focus!" Titus snapped his fingers in his face. "Ten minutes, and I'm gone. Pick out two of your best squirmers for me, and put them in a feed sack."

"What do you want piglets for?" Bekele's eyes opened wider. "Murderer! You want to use them for target practice. Never! Test your rifles on someone else!"

"Nine minutes." Titus' satellite phone rang. He tugged it off his belt, answering it as he left the barn. "Yeah?"

"You called for my uncle. I am Sohayb. Are you the Serval?"

Titus clenched his fist. Crac Hassad's nephew! Rumor had it that, after his uncle, he was the second most wanted Hamas leader inside Gaza.

"Luc Lannoy was arrested in Pakistan," Titus stated.

"That is unfortunate. He was bringing my uncle a gift."

"I have the gift for your uncle."

"The same gift? It must be warhead capable or my uncle will not pay."

"I understand. I'll be in Egypt within the hour, alone. I know you want this gift soon. Can I still use the same tunnel?"

"It's the only one not bombed. But my uncle is angry with you. The last gift you brought was a canister of perfume!"

"This time, I'm bringing you two live specimens. You may

use as much of their blood as you want to infect the Israelis."

"What are these specimens?"

Bekele approached with a feed bag and opened it to show Titus two squirming piglets, one month old.

"Send a truck for me by midnight where the tunnel surfaces in Gaza. I'll show you myself. Have my money ready to wire."

Titus shut off his phone and considered what it meant that Sohayb had called him. Gaza communications were jammed. If Sohayb had called him, then he couldn't be in Gaza. The nephew, and maybe even his uncle, had to be in Israel or Egypt. To continue the assault on Israel and maintain the Quran's instruction to kill the Jews, a strong hand needed to remain in Gaza overseeing the militants. Sohayb and his uncle were surely not far from there.

"Do not cheat me!" Bekele shouted as Titus counted out several bills for the farmer.

"Who's cheating who?" Titus shook his head and handed the retired mercenary the money. "Since when does a pair of pigs this size cost one thousand euros?"

"You owed me for the goat last month. My favorite goat!" Bekele left the feed sack for Titus and walked away, counting his money. Suddenly, Bekele stopped and looked back. "What are the piglets for?"

"Backup."

"Backup?"

"I'm going into Gaza. I'll need backup."

"You make no sense, Titus. Muslims have a superstitious fear of swine."

"Yeah, I'm counting on it."

...✝...

ISRAEL

Sohayb Hassad reviewed his phone conversation with Titus Caspertein as he returned to watch his uncle's men widen the tunnel for the drone. There'd been more men helping with the tunnel, he thought, but perhaps they'd been killed. By dawn, they would have the drone in the garage—on the Israeli side of the tunnel. As soon as a biological element could be added to the warheads, they would launch the drone and watch the news. Thousands of Jews would die, climaxing with the destruction of the Dome of the Rock, the Muslim holy site. The rest of the world would finally turn against Israel forever. Palestinian statehood, with Allah as lord over all, was perhaps weeks away, as soon as Israel was at last removed.

At least, that was the plan. But Sohayb's mind was on different matters, even if he was obediently organizing the attack for his uncle. The American woman, Annette Sheffield, had somehow escaped. Perhaps escaped wasn't the right word. She had disappeared. If she'd gone to Israel's authorities, the IDF would've already swarmed the Israeli tunnel side, and the drone would've been discovered. But the woman had vanished without a trace in Israel. Even the media was still reporting her as a missing UN spokesperson.

Uncle Crac had been enraged at her escape, but that wasn't all. Sohayb had shot his youngest wife in the garage. Then his uncle had struck him across the face in front of several men. The humiliation! Sohayb had questioned his own loyalties toward Uncle Crac before, but now he couldn't continue to serve the Hamas leader. How could his uncle not see Sohayb had been devoted to Allah? Was Crac Hassad's religion true if he mistreated with injustice those who were closest? After all, wouldn't Uncle Crac have executed his wife himself if she'd been caught helping the American escape, especially with her head uncovered? Everyone knew he beat his wives, anyway. What was one less wife?

Sohayb tried to excuse his uncle's zeal by considering the pressure he was under, leading Hamas where they'd never been before by watching Israel die under its own drone strikes. But to shame him by slapping him in front of the men was a disgrace Sohayb could not forgive. He sensed his hatred—felt since boyhood, but always focused on Israel—turning toward his uncle. He prayed and hoped he and Uncle Crac were just experiencing the exhaustion from the bombings, hiding, and tunnel digging.

At least His uncle had returned to the school on the Gaza side of the tunnel. Israel had been so condemned internationally the last year over targeting schools and hospitals in Gaza that those venues were now safer than ever to use as staging areas for launching attacks. Western media was so easily manipulated, and the effects always placed Israel in a place of blame. The Great Satan's own media was destroying the Little Satan. Everything was nearly in place, but Sohayb was having trouble rejoicing with his uncle.

Two more events needed to fall into place, and they both needed to happen in the next few hours of darkness. Weapons dealers around the world had often answered the needs of the Palestinians. Guns, ammo, and explosives were easy to get into Egypt and smuggle into Gaza. The biological weapons were in short supply, however, and the Mossad or CIA seemed to intercept every attempt.

But that night, Crac Hassad was meeting with two weapons dealers. Both were of world renown. The Serval was, after all, an exile from the United States. He wasn't a Muslim, but he had armed Muslim insurgencies for years. Titus Caspertein was greedy, and Sohayb was content to use that greed for the task before them.

The other arms dealer was Muhammad ibn Affal, a true Muslim, dedicated to the cause of Allah for longer than Sohayb had been alive. Sohayb had heard the man's name even as a youth—an Egyptian ghost who moved and sold so covertly, no one had ever actually confirmed a sale. The West hunted him, yet Muhammad ibn Affal disappeared and reappeared without warning. There'd even been a time as a boy when Sohayb had determined to join Muhammad, if he could find him. But then Crac Hassad had required his help. How could he refuse his uncle?

If Muhammad was due in Gaza, Sohayb had to meet him. He'd begged his uncle to let him be at the school building to act as security during the meet. Sohayb didn't care much about Titus Caspertein, but Muhammad was legendary!

"More on the north side!" Sohayb guided as the men excavated the tunnel. They were so close!

He stepped back to give the men more room. Maybe, if he could get close enough to talk to Muhammad privately, Sohayb could arrange a different future for himself. No Hamas leader lived long. Allah was certainly worthy of the Jewish blood that was shed, but there were other ways to exercise *jihad*. Muhammad could be the answer to his renewed restlessness—and to a departure from his uncle. All he had to do was wait a few more hours.

SOUTHERN GAZA

Titus sat in the passenger seat of an ambulance that zoomed north on Rasheed Coastal Road toward Gaza City. The ambulance was the only transportation vehicle the Israelis allowed to operate in the Gaza Strip. He guessed the Israelis probably knew the ambulance transported arms and militants, rather than the Palestinians' own wounded women and children. But hopefully, the IDF didn't send a missile toward him just this once. Annette Sheffield's life depended on it. He looked forward to bartering for her then delivering her safely home, showing Corban Dowler that he'd failed. Titus had to act now, before another night passed.

On the floor between his feet, Titus braced the black travel case that held the two piglets. He'd added holes for breathing and fastened a padlock on the outside of the case, but he had a zipper on the back he could use to loose the animals at the proper instant. Though he wasn't one to offend another man's religious convictions, it wasn't below him to do so to achieve a goal, especially if he believed his offense was morally justified—or a pretty woman's life depended on it. Besides, Israel used guard pigs at their Ofer Military Base to keep Muslim extremists at bay. It worked for them; it should work for him.

✝

CHAPTER TWENTY-FIVE

<u>*EASTERN GAZA*</u>

Corban trudged through Eastern Gaza behind Rasht Hassad, keeping an eye on Nathan, who led the way. Over two weeks earlier, Corban had crept through Gaza City, avoiding Israeli gunships and Palestinian militants. Now, he was worried only about the Israeli drone missiles. Since he had an appointment with Crac Hassad, he didn't mind running into his Hamas troops this time.

His fears of an Israeli drone strike weren't unfounded. Across the street, a rocket smashed into a vacant gas station, pelting Rasht and Corban with pieces of roofing. Nathan was quick to come alongside Rasht and drag him to cover. Corban ran on his own to the nearest building across the street.

"Two more blocks," Nathan said in Arabic to Corban. As a Marine, he'd learned the language fluently from several deployments to the Middle East. They couldn't be caught speaking English in a place like Gaza. "You wounded?"

Corban, still shaken from the near miss of the rocket, checked his limbs. Just a few scratches. He gave Nathan the thumbs-up signal, and they continued. For once, Corban was happy to not take the lead, but rather follow the more agile, cautious soldier through the battle zone that included all of Gaza now.

As they trekked, Corban thought of the risks he'd taken

with his life and the lives of others, for the sake of Christ. For years, he'd escaped serious injury. Scars covered his body, but tonight was different. He wasn't fighting the Janjaweed horsemen in Sudan to protect hungry refugees. Nor was he assaulting a German castle of crazed Nazis to free imprisoned Jews and Christians. This was a mission in God's own ancient land, fighting to protect His Chosen People from a merciless attack. And those same people, the Israelites, were trying to kill him!

Though Chloe and Chen Li were somewhere ahead and above them, they could do nothing against the gunships or warplanes or drones that could fire a volley of rockets from miles away. Their trust was in God, for they had no one else.

Nathan stopped at a street corner with Rasht and waited for Corban. Darting across an alley, Corban caught up to the two and knelt on the cracked pavement. He tried to block out the idea that Israeli spy planes could be watching them right now, ready to blow them off the street because they seemed to be up to something sinister.

"That's the school." Nathan pointed to the east, then took a swallow of water from a canteen. "Look! There . . . and there."

Corban peered intently at the school building. Sentries, under the cover of the building's metal awnings, stood with rifles and RPG launchers.

"Our instructions are to approach the building one at a time so it doesn't appear from the sky that the school is trafficked by militants." Corban drew a pair of handcuffs from his pack. Rasht offered his wrists, and Corban lowered his voice to speak English to the missionary. "Remember, the middle chain is just aluminum. And three links have an intentional crack in them. With a little force, you can break them yourself. Got it?"

"I'm more worried about bullets," Rasht said. "But I will trust you both."

"We're all trusting the Lord, but I thank you for your confidence." Corban glanced at the skyline to the southwest. "And somewhere near, we have a shooter who will secure our escape."

"We're in God's hands." Nathan slapped Corban on the back. "See you inside."

Without further words, Nathan walked calmly into the street toward the school building. The militants under their cover didn't move, since Crac Hassad had surely informed them to expect Muhammad ibn Affal. Corban counted Nathan's footsteps. Israel could fire at anyone they thought was an armed militant. To the west, north, and south, the ground battle had begun. It would be a night of death.

Corban checked the time. Colonel Yasof and his two sweeper teams had been in Gaza for almost four hours. By now, they would've realized their intel was wrong on where Crac Hassad was hiding. Sometime the next day, Corban would stand before Yasof and have to explain why he'd gone in without the Israeli soldiers. And then Corban would expound on what a nonbeliever could never understand, and share the gospel with the colonel: that God intended men to receive life from the hands of those who had life, as messengers for Jesus Christ. Allah's servants were lost men in sin's bondage, and that meant they needed Christ's gracious gift of faith and repentance, not a bullet in the name of justice. Christians didn't look for what was right or wrong, he would tell the colonel, but what was Christ-like. The IDF, in contrast, had one job: to protect its people. Christians had one job: to proclaim the gospel of peace by word and deed.

Nathan reached the school. He looked back and waved, then stepped through a darkened doorway. Since Gaza was in a blackout—its electricity cut off by penetrating bombs—the street was lit by the moon and the flashes of distant explosions.

Rasht, with his wrists bound in front of him, walked into the street. Corban understood the reason they were walking one at a time was to protect the sanctuary of the school, but he would've much rather run across the street as fast as he could. The IDF probably figured soldiers usually moved in groups, not alone. But even crossing the street alone to the school was no guarantee they would be safe, because Israel's methods couldn't always be predicted. They hunted for terrorists, and if Israel was suspicious, they sent a missile.

Once Rasht was across the street and into the same doorway, Corban touched his face. The beard was in place. He checked the blue canister under his shoulder, then the NL-2 under his parka.

"Lord," he prayed, and stepped forward, "do what You do for Your people . . ."

Halfway across the street, Corban stopped and listened to the wind. Looking up, he saw a firebrand flying across the dark sky, the size of a match to the unfocused eye, but growing. By the time his eyes focused on the deadly missile, it was too close for him to do anything but fall to the ground. Covering his head, he lay on his side in a fetal position. Noise, heat, and shrapnel washed over him. The pressure of the blast on his internal organs hurt more initially than the lacerations to his body.

When he lifted his head moments later, one of his ears was bleeding, and he wasn't sure which way to face. For an instant, he forgot where he was as he tried to breathe. When he felt hands on him, helping him, he almost spoke in English, then his senses returned.

He leaned heavily on the thin shoulders of a masked militant, until he recognized Nathan, who picked him up like a child and carried him to the school doorway.

Once inside, Nathan set Corban on the floor. A dozen armed men gave them space, but still lingered in the foyer of the school entrance.

"Please tell me how to assist you, Sheik Muhammad," Nathan offered, kneeling next to him. He spoke loud enough for all to hear, Corban realized, perhaps to remind Corban in his daze to continue his act. Someone brought an LED lamp and held it low as Nathan gave Corban a cursory examination. "Are you hurt badly?"

This time, Corban was hurt badly. Shrapnel had dug into his back and shoulders. One of his legs was numb, but he could still move it adequately. Since he was Muhammad ibn Affal, there was no time for treatment of his wounds. Lives depended on his identity remaining intact, his authority and legend demanding what they had come for—Crac Hassad and Annette Sheffield, if she was still alive.

"Help me stand, my son," Corban requested, appreciating Nathan using the sheik title. A sheik was a man of religious bearing that would parallel the authority of a general amongst Islamists.

Nathan lifted him to his feet, and the thin masked Hamas militant moved up to steady him again. Corban looked into the eyes and recognized a plea for help. It was Annette Sheffield! She carried a rifle in one arm and wore baggy clothes and men's boots, but it was actually her!

"Thank you, my son," he told her in Arabic, knowing she couldn't understand, but it was more for Hassad's men that they understood he affirmed her, as he had Nathan. Holding her close, he nodded at Nathan. "Take me to the meeting. Let us meet this night of death with an end to all of Israel."

The militants seemed to approve, and parted for Nathan and Muhammad. Two men led the way deeper into the school, and Corban looked up at the ceiling. Israel had fired at who they thought was a militant outside the school. It was just a matter of time before they fired at the school itself.

"Corban?" Annette whispered as they passed through a doorway. Somehow she had recognized him from their time together in Western Gaza in the factory.

"That obvious?" he risked in English.

"No, just expected." She touched his cheek, and Corban realized she was pressing his beard onto his face where the adhesive was failing.

"Stay close. You can lose the rifle. You're with me now."

They were shown into a room, and Corban was thankful Nathan anticipated his weakness and provided a chair. Annette helped steady him as he sat, and then stood back. Discreetly, in the dimness behind other LED lamps, she set her rifle against the wall, then returned to his side, her left hand resting on his right shoulder. As other men filed into the room, Corban noticed Nathan give him a concerned look.

Corban fought to think clearly through his pain. If he didn't get a message quickly to Nathan, Nathan could become protective and expose Annette. All it would take was for someone to speak to her in Arabic, and she was finished.

"Thank you, my son," Corban said to Nathan, aware that many others were listening. "Between Ahmen Shofar and yourself—I am preserved by your faithfulness."

Corban saw Nathan silently repeat the name on his lips. *Ahmen Shofar. Annette Sheffield.* Realization replaced his confusion.

"Of course, my sheik." Nathan bowed his head briefly. "May peace and protection be yours by your servants."

Sitting up straight in the chair, Corban browsed the men around him. Someone brought him tea and he sipped it. He felt blood trickle down his spine. A piece of metal was protruding there as well as in his shoulder. With so much requiring his attention, he tried not to think about the permanent damage possibly done by moving around without immediate treatment.

Rasht! Corban spotted the cuffed man held by two sturdy militants at the edge of the light. He appeared calm, like a man resigned to die so another could live. Except, Rasht didn't need to be surrendered now since they already had Annette!

There seemed no time to strategize. A new group of militants entered the room, crowding it even further. Corban recognized cautious bodyguards. One didn't stay alive as a Gazan leader for long without vigilant guards.

The first man of notice, in his early thirties, was a bright-eyed militant with a shoulder holster. If Corban read his face right, the young man was smiling—in a room of Muslim thugs! He had an air about him—pride mixed with anger. A dangerous combination.

The next man of influence was definitely Crac Hassad, Rasht's older brother. They had the same eyes. Corban looked back at the young smiling man. He, too, had Rasht's eyes. The younger one had to be the son of one of them, but which one? And how could Corban leverage it all for their safe exit—with Crac Hassad as their captive?

Corban rose and embraced Crac Hassad, kissing him on both cheeks, and receiving the same, as if they were brothers. A chair was brought for Hassad, and the lanterns were moved closer. The men on the fringes of the light were quiet.

"It is an honor, Muhammad ibn Affal," Hassad said. "Your presence is a gift from Allah."

"And I come bearing gifts." Corban patted the blue canister, bringing a smile to the terrorist leader's face. Otherwise, Hassad's dark eyes were hard to read. "May I introduce my right hand, Dirk Salverskein. He has been with me for many years."

Corban lifted his chin in mock pride. Dirk Salverskein was an alias Nathan had used during other operations, as a ruthless German financier and socialist.

"We are honored by your attention, Dirk Salverskein," Hassad said with a slight nod.

"The honor is mine," Nathan said in perfect Arabic. "May justice from heaven wrap your fate in Allah's embrace."

If he could've covertly done so, Corban would've given Nathan a cautionary glare for his veiled threat, but there were more introductions to be made.

"And Ahmed Shofar." Corban gestured to Annette. "He is

one of my more public voices. Therefore, his face is more important than even my own. He will remain silent on this night for this reason. You understand."

"Of course." Hassad nodded in respect. "I have my own important faces. This is my nephew, Sohayb Hassad, worth ten men. But we are not here to boast of our gifted men. We have long-awaited business to conclude. You have with you our vindication. The Jordan will run red with Jewish blood tomorrow."

"Though we do not all partake of this struggle," Corban said, "the world is watching."

He silently prayed for Rasht. The Christian man hadn't told him his own son was serving in Hamas, or maybe he hadn't known! The fact that he was holding his composure was remarkable, and very well may have been keeping them all alive. Corban didn't want to introduce his fake captive at all, but even with Annette located, Rasht might still play a part in unbalancing Crac Hassad enough for a well-timed capture. Only the shadows kept Rasht hidden from his brother and son.

An explosion shook the building, a missile targeting something or someone a few blocks away. Corban's palms were sweaty.

"Did you bring the chickens?" Corban asked.

Crac Hassad lifted his hand, and Sohayb signaled other men. A square plastic container was brought into the room and set in the middle of the group.

"It is sealed, as you requested." Hassad reached down and tapped the top of the transparent plastic. "Bring the chickens!"

A sliding door on the plastic top was opened and two

grown chickens were placed inside. They flapped their wings in the confined space, then investigated their new house with curious pecking.

"Dirk?" Corban eased the blue canister strap from his shoulder, with Annette's help, and handed it to Nathan. "Please demonstrate for us all."

"Yes, my sheik."

Nathan took the canister and connected it to a one-way valve on the plastic container. The men in the room shuffled closer. With the skill of a professional magician, Nathan inspected every angle of the seal with great care. Finally, he looked up at Corban, who gave a solemn nod. The militants leaned toward the container. Everyone seemed to hold their breath, especially Corban. Several militants covered their mouths and noses, as if that would protect them from lethal nerve gas.

When Nathan turned the canister lid slightly, a brief hissing could be heard as compressed gas escaped, then he closed the valve. Instantly, the two chickens became agitated, and in a few more seconds, fell over still. Nathan disconnected the canister and cradled it delicately, then stepped back to Corban's side.

"Most impressive." Hassad's eyes seemed to twinkle as they gazed longingly at the canister. "The same effect on dogs? Jews specifically?"

"The same, though with a few seconds delay, depending on body mass." Corban was completely fictionalizing now. COIL chemists had produced the compressed tranquilizer at the last minute as requested, but no one knew its exact properties. As long as no one knew how to check a chicken's pulse, the ruse was safe, and no one would know the chickens were merely asleep. "It's a nerve gas with deadly potential. Dispersed properly, this mixture will kill thousands."

"Where's the rest?" Hassad wiggled his fingers as a child anticipating a delicious candy. "You said you had a truckload."

"You and I have not met before," Corban said softly, even warmly, "though we have been active in the same war between good and evil."

"Yes, I sense a kinship with you as well. Allah has given me a peace about you. But the rest of the gas?"

Corban had to buy time. There was no other gas. He already had Annette. Now, he had to think about escaping with Rasht, with Crac Hassad in custody as well.

"The rest of my men came over the wall after us." Corban waved his hand casually. "They will begin to arrive in one hour. We will complete our transaction then."

"More men?" Hassad appeared nervous. "How many more? Israel is always watching."

"Eight men, each with a canister. You asked for six. The others, I give them to you for free. Consider them my gift."

"The IDF may catch them."

"Which is why others have been recruited. They are experts at stealth. Soon, they will arrive. We may wait, yes?"

"Of course. More tea! And remove the chickens."

As Corban intended, the men dispersed at the announcement of the need for more waiting. What they'd come to see had been seen, and their whispered excitement spread all around. Hassad excused himself and left the room. Two men remained to guard Rahst, but no one had given any indication that he'd been recognized as yet. Corban knew it was just a matter of time before he was asked about his cuffed prisoner.

Nathan crossed the room to the doorway, the canister in his arms. He looked back at Corban, perhaps watching for a signal to do something, but Corban didn't signal him. All he'd done was buy them time to think and prepare. Lives depended on Corban's next move. One thing for sure: when he and Nathan did make their move, Crac Hassad needed to be in the room. The terrorist leader was leaving with them whether he liked it or not.

✝

CHAPTER TWENTY SIX

<u>*EASTERN GAZA*</u>

Titus exited the ambulance and the driver drove the vehicle into a garage with no door. Explosions like lightning lit the intersection before him, and Titus walked into the street toward what appeared to be the school building he'd been told to enter for the meeting. He carried the animal travel case in his fist, the two piglets snorting and squealing as they were jostled about.

A few hours hadn't been enough time for Titus to secure an actual biological weapon to use for the purchase of Annette from Crac Hassad. It wouldn't be the first meet he'd entered where he'd have to bluff his way along—maybe with a little persuasion from his Glock in his holster.

At the door of the school building, he was met by two men with rifles.

"I'm Titus Caspertein, the Serval. Crac Hassad sent for me." Titus was poised, perhaps daring them to interfere. Confidence had been his ticket through countless barriers, but now there was more at risk than merely his own life.

In previous weeks, these extremists were merely his latest clients. Now, he felt he'd never had greater enemies. The events over the last few weeks had somehow changed his moral compass. Realizing he wasn't invincible, and not nearly as righteous as he'd believed, was made apparent by the impact certain people were having on his life—such as Corban Dowler, Annette Sheffield, and Oleg Saratov. Though he was only willing to admit it recently, there'd been other genuine Christians in his life he should've been encouraged by, rather than disgusted—people like his brother and sister, Rudy and Wynter. Did they still pray for him? He hoped he lived through the night to find out.

Titus was led through several dark rooms, and eventually arrived at one lit by LED lamps set in the center of the floor.

"Crac Hassad will be here soon. Please wait." His escorts left.

Several Gazan gunmen stood in the room at the edges of the lamp light. A bearded man sat in a chair, and a masked man lurked over his shoulder. Next to Titus, a bearded giant leaned against the wall. This giant held a blue canister protectively—a canister similar to the one Titus had brought to Gaza the first time. So, he wasn't the only one supplying Hassad this night.

"Sounds like popcorn out there," Titus said in Arabic to the bearded man with the canister. "It ain't easy feeling Israel's full wrath, huh?"

But no one said anything, and Titus moved deeper into the room, his piglets restless in his case. They hadn't eaten since they'd been with their sow mother a few hours earlier. As long as they didn't die before he needed them, he knew they'd be just the desired backup, especially in the small room in which he'd been left.

Titus circled the room, then stopped in front of a handcuffed man, a face he knew. It was Rasht Hassad, the very man he and Corban had broken out of the Uzbek prison!

The situation into which he'd stepped suddenly hit Titus full force. He whirled around and studied the bearded man in the chair. Of course! Corban Dowler, though his gaze was averted, was the bearded man in the chair! The giant by the door must've been another of Corban's men, probably a COIL operative who spoke Arabic. He most likely had a weapon under his parka, one of the NL-2 machine pistols Titus had learned to appreciate.

The rest of the gunmen around the room looked to be Hassad's bodyguards. Titus preferred to control the elements of his interactions with clients, but Corban was already on the scene, apparently with a better plan than what Titus had in mind: to loose the pigs and shoot his way to Annette Sheffield, who he guessed had to be close by.

In front of Corban, Titus knelt, as if bowing to a king.

"I did not expect to enter the company of your greatness, my prince of all that is wise." He spoke in Arabic for the sake of Hassad's soldiers. "How may I be of assistance to you this dark night?"

"I am thankful for your presence," Corban replied in Arabic, then switched to German. "Hassad will return any minute. Can you get Rasht and Annette out safely? He and I will take care of Crac." Corban nodded at the bearded giant at the door.

Two men taking on Crac Hassad and all his men? Titus nodded.

"Fine, I'll take Rasht and Annette, whenever you make your move. Where's Annette being held?"

"I believe you know Ahmed Shofar from your factory days."

Titus smiled. His eyes met those of the masked militant—who wasn't a militant at all—standing at Corban's side.

"A masked angel, indeed. Please tell me you have a plan."

"I might now that you're here. What's in your case?"

"Two little pigs that went to Gaza."

"Interesting. Please tell me you haven't laced them with some terrible disease for Hassad."

"Of course not!" Titus sighed. Corban was the only one who could put him in his place. Well, maybe Oleg, too. "Okay, I deserved that. But no, I'm just here for the masked angel."

"I sure wish you were one of God's children, Titus." Corban's voice seemed weaker than normal. "I'd feel better about risking your life for others if I knew you were in His arms rather than a child of wrath in the power of Satan."

"*Power of Satan?*" Titus almost fell over backward. "How dare you!"

"We are either motivated by Christ or influenced by the power of Satan. Why are you here? Try to appease your conscience by your good deeds, Titus, and you'll only grow further from your Creator. Satan's desire is to keep people from dedicating themselves fully to God, which means yielding to His mercy and life-giving death for your sins."

"Really? You're preaching to me right here? We could die in five minutes!"

"Think about that, Titus. You could be standing before God in five minutes. You've broken every holy command of God's law many times over. Do you have a lighter?"

"Yeah, right here." Titus touched his pocket. "What do you need?"

"Spark a flame and hold your hand in the flame."

"You're crazy, old man." Titus moved his hand away from his pocket. "I'm not going to do that!"

"It's not as hot as the place you'll be sent for refusing your Lord and Savior. He died for you, and now you'll be twice condemned. You came here to be a hero, but you're the one who needs to be rescued. Look at your life, Titus. You can't cleanse your sins away. The harder you try, the more of a mess you make."

"I'm not trying to cleanse them!"

"Because God is a just God, He won't even forgive you to welcome you into His presence until you trust in His payment for your sins. Take His side against sin, Titus. You're lost— unless you trust in the value of the cross of Christ, just as God values His death for you."

"Shut up. Just shut up." Titus, still kneeling, pivoted away, then turned back to glare at the man. On the floor beneath Corban's chair was a drop of blood. From Titus' angle, the fresh blood glistened in the lamp light. As he watched, another drop fell from the back of Corban's chair.

Since childhood in Arkansas, Titus had heard the story of the crucifixion. He'd sat through children's church for years, his sister Wynter sitting between Titus and their older brother, Rudy. She'd often been the peacemaker between the two brothers. They'd always been at odds, but now, Titus would do anything to go home, to see one of Wynter's smiles, or gasp through one of Rudy's bear hugs. It was those simple things he missed most.

And here was a man, clearly bleeding to death, telling him about Christ's blood that could erase away the filthy sins of his past, the sins that had driven him from his family, from his country, from a clear conscience, from God's grace.

"How badly are you wounded?" Titus asked.

"Bad enough to need you to follow through tonight." Corban held out his hand. "Can I count on you?"

Titus gazed at that hand. The mighty Corban Dowler, agent of agents, the Ghost of the Cold War, and now founder of COIL—extending his hand of acceptance and need to him, Titus Caspertein, the Serval. Taking that hand, Titus knew, would mean more than just shaking a man's hand. It was a symbol. It was a decision. He felt his whole life was about to change, and it had everything to do with Corban Dowler, and yet, nothing at all.

This was about Jesus Christ.

Taking Corban's hand, Titus gripped it firmly as he rose to his full height. Corban's own grip was feeble, and Titus knew the man was losing more blood than could be seen. His clothes were probably soaking up the blood, and only now they were beginning to drip from saturation. What terrible thing had happened to him that he'd been so wounded?

Leaving Corban, Titus positioned himself against the wall to the bearded giant's left. From that angle, Titus faced Corban and Annette. Rasht was to his left, and the militants were all around.

There seemed to be no hope, but Titus still felt hope. He believed. For the first time in his life, *he believed*. God was no longer far away. God was with him. And he was with God. He was on God's side!

Sohayb Hassad entered the room lit by LED lamps. This

was his opportunity to speak privately to Muhammad ibn Affal before Uncle Crac returned. He passed the rogue Titus Caspertein, who he knew of, but not as well as Muhammad.

"Sheik Muhammad, please receive your humble servant." Sohayb took the legendary *jihadist's* hand and kissed it. "My uncle will return in a few minutes. May we speak confidentially?"

"Of course." Muhammad touched Sohayb's head. "Any relative of Crac Hassad may have my ear."

Sohayb leaned closer to the seated man, hoping none of his uncle's men heard their conversation, though he didn't mind Muhammad's masked man who stood close by.

"Sheik, I have felt Allah may be leading me toward other exploits." Sohayb tested his words as he said them. If Muhammad's loyalty to his uncle was strong, Sohayb could be warranting his own strangling or beheading. But if Muhammad was just another arms dealer . . . "Gaza's burdens have not held my attention as of late."

"I see." Muhammad's face was half-covered by the bushy beard that reached his chest, but Sohayb could see the man watching him closely. "Your uncle may have gone in a direction others do not choose to go."

"Yes." *Yes! A thousand times, yes!* Sohayb could barely contain his relief. This wily man understood the matter perfectly. "Perhaps an apprenticeship under a traveled man of wisdom could teach me much. I was born in Iran, but my whole life, I have lived in Gaza, never leaving."

"There may be a place in my employ for you." Muhammad paused, and Sohayb wanted to shake the man to continue. "I do things much differently than your uncle. In fact, your uncle and I don't share the same vision as many believe."

Sohayb nodded, though he didn't understand completely. Was Muhammad saying he wasn't really in support of the Palestinian uprising, or was there some deeper Islamic principle?

"I have heard of you since I was a small child. How may I walk in your footsteps after this night?"

"Why wait until after this night?" Muhammad placed a gentle hand on Sohayb's shoulder. "Tell me about your father, Rasht Hassad."

"Did you know him in Iran? I did not know, Sheik Muhammad!"

"We first met due to mutual pursuits, and definitely for a common faith."

"My father died when I was young, martyred by Israeli Mossad agents in Iran. They ambushed him after they killed my whole family. My uncle saved me from their same fate. My father is a hero. He's the reason I have remained fighting the Jews, but the people who actually killed him must be very old by now, perhaps already dead themselves. Revenge has evaded me. The Jewish blood I've shed has not appeased my grief."

"What you speak of are lies you've been told." Muhammad leaned closer. "Your father wasn't killed by Israeli agents. Neither was the rest of your family."

"What?" Sohayb rose quickly to his feet and stepped away from the great sheik of Egypt. No one had ever spoken so plainly to him. Suddenly, he was angry at the sheltered life he'd lived. All he knew of the outside world had been filtered by his uncle. If what he knew about his father's death were lies, then Crac Hassad was the liar! "How do you know this? I need proof."

"Your father is a close friend of mine, even today." Muhammad waved him closer, and Sohayb obliged. "We're closer than blood brothers. I would die for your father, Sohayb."

Sohayb felt the weight of the pistol in his shoulder holster. *His father was alive?* And this man would die for him? He felt such confusion. He wanted to kill his uncle for lying to him. A sob rose in his chest. His father was alive!

"Sheik, you've broken apart my whole existence. I don't know what to say or think! Where's my father? Does he know I'm here, alive, in Gaza? Is he still in Iran? I don't have papers to travel to Iran."

"Swear to me you will not harm your uncle." Muhammad looked intently into his eyes. "I can't take you to your father if your uncle's blood is on your hands. Leave him to others who wait for their own moment."

"But my uncle raised me to think—"

"Swear it!"

"I agree. I won't kill him. Where is my father? You must tell me, please!"

"You must follow my instructions exactly. Are you prepared? I'll send you to your father before dawn."

A sob escaped Sohayb's lips. He covered his mouth until he was able to speak again. *Was this really happening?*

"Yes. I'm prepared. Tell me what to do. I'm yours, Sheik Muhammad."

"Your endeavors in Gaza are now over. You'll join me and your father, even if our direction may turn your whole life and belief system upside down. Do you accept, Sohayb?"

"How can I not? If my uncle has taught me what I know, and it's all a lie, then I must choose another way. Tell me what to do."

"I must end your uncle's reign here tonight. Do you have a safe way out of Gaza? You won't need papers. You must only leave Gaza."

Sohayb thought of the drone tunnel. All the work he'd done to set up the attack against Israel—all for his uncle—now seemed inconsequential in light of being reunited with his father again, in the company of this great man. Could it be true?

"Yes. I can be in Israel in twenty minutes."

"Very well. Listen carefully. There's a man over there in handcuffs. Take him now and go to Israel. Are you listening?"

"Yes. I'll take him. What do I do in Israel?"

"Find an IDF man named Colonel Yasof."

"Colonel Yasof? The commander of the invasion?" Sohayb gasped. "Do you want me to kill this colonel?"

"No. He'll keep you safe and under guard until I can reach you."

"But I'm to surrender to the IDF? With this handcuffed man? It's suicide for me! I'm Sohayb Hassad! I've done . . . terrible things against Israel, things this Colonel Yasof surely knows about. He will—"

"Do as I say, Sohayb. Leave now. Don't speak to anyone. Go. Leave this life behind."

"I'll do as you say, but only because of my father."

Sohayb had never been more confused, yet he'd never felt as light as he did this moment. He had not imagined IDF

Colonel Yasof would know someone like Muhammad ibn Affal, but if Muhammad said the colonel could be trusted, then so be it!

Crossing the room, Sohayb approached the bearded man in handcuffs and the men he had known since childhood.

"The prisoner is mine now. I'm taking him to the basement. Stay here. My uncle should return any moment."

The men didn't hesitate to turn over the prisoner. Now, Sohayb wanted desperately to leave the room before his uncle really did return. Crac Hassad was upstairs, conferring with his advisors and organizing threats all over Gaza. There were also many political stratagems to consider in the aftermath of the drone attack on the Dome of the Rock. But none of that seemed possible now, not if Muhammad ibn Affal was against his uncle. And if Sohayb was really leaving it all, maybe it didn't matter to him anymore. All that mattered was finding his father.

†

CHAPTER TWENTY-SEVEN

GAZA

Rasht Hassad glanced at Corban Dowler as the slender gunman took him by the arm and led him out. For nearly an hour, Rasht had stood amongst his brother's militants and listened to the exchanges in Arabic, a language he didn't know. Corban's Muhammad ibn Affal identity had demanded much respect from the Palestinians, but Rasht knew that respect was based on a thin bluff and failing beard epoxy. And if Rasht's eyesight wasn't deceiving him in the lamp light, Corban was bleeding.

Whoever the slim gunman was who Corban had spoken quietly to, Rasht knew he had to submit to him, rather than ask questions that could raise suspicions. Rasht had to trust Corban, a man who had already gone to great lengths to free him from the Uzbek prison.

Reaching a set of stairs, Rasht and his escort descended into the darkness of a basement. At the lower level, his escort flicked on a flashlight and shined it across a large room that smelled like earth. Instead of using the flashlight to light their way, the gunman turned it off and continued leading him forward. Occasionally, he turned the light on to orient himself, then they returned to darkness. By this, Rasht understood they were in danger, and Corban had placed him in the hands of someone who knew a route to safety.

If Rasht had any reason to resist leaving his captive status with Corban, it was because he hadn't yet been traded for the life of the missing woman, Annette Sheffield. Hadn't he entered Gaza to rescue her life? If only he'd learned Arabic, he would've known what had been said in the room. Raised in Iran, Rasht had spoken Persian and read some Arabic from the Quran. When his family had been murdered and he'd run to Uzbekistan, Rasht had learned Uzbek and some Russian. He'd known English since grade school, when Americans had lived in their Tehran neighborhood.

Suddenly, Rasht guessed what was happening. He was being exchanged for Annette still. They must be on the way to her now. Any minute, they would arrive to where she was being held. All the secrecy and caution must have been because Israel was hunting for tunnels and militants.

It had been frightening to see his older brother, Crac, but his brother hadn't seemed to notice him. This was both a relief and a sorrow. He'd known for years that his brother had been instrumental in exposing Rasht's Christianity to the Iranian secret police. With his family in Iran dead, Rasht hadn't remained in Iran to risk further violence from his brother. Instead, Rasht had forgiven Crac, then moved on with his life to share his faith with the Uzbeks. Now, it seemed only a matter of time before he, like his family, would die at Crac's hands.

A few paces into the tunnel, walking side by side, the young gunman turned on the flashlight and left it on, aimed at the earthen floor. His escort spoke a command in Arabic, but Rasht didn't respond. If things got violent, he guessed he could always break the handcuff link and escape somehow, but he didn't want to spoil any plans Corban was using him for. Rasht was more than content with death, for the life of another. He guessed those who wanted to kill simply lacked the love of God in them. After all the deaths Rasht had witnessed in Iran and Uzbekistan, Christ's love in him was still a beacon of bright light against the hatred and violence. As Christ had died for him, Rasht understood love, not hatred, was the only true weapon against the wickedness in these men's hearts. He prayed that in his moment of death, he would represent Christ.

The tunnel sloped down, then up again, and after walking for what seemed like a kilometer, Rasht was stopped by his escort. The flashlight was turned off, and slowly, Rasht's eyes focused on a dim artificial light ahead. It was still night.

The young man spoke to him again. The words were not harsh. More like conversation, or simple information. Rasht didn't see how to continue unless they could communicate openly, but it was unlikely the Gazan gunman knew Uzbek or Russian.

"I don't speak Arabic," Rasht said in English. "Do you speak English or Persian?"

The flashlight shined in his eyes. Rasht nearly broke the cuff link as he raised his hands to shield his face.

"Yes, I speak Persian." The young man stepped closer, the flashlight brighter. "Why am I risking my life for a man Sheik Muhammad ibn Affal told me to take to an Israeli colonel? And why is this man wearing handcuffs?"

"I have many questions as well, but perhaps our friend Muhammad would say it best: things are not as they seem." Rasht laced his fingers together. With more strength than he thought it would take, he broke the cuff chain apart, leaving a cuff bracelet on each wrist. "Should we go now, or discover why we may be the only two men in Gaza who speak Persian?"

"Crac Hassad speaks Persian. He was born in Iran."

"Of course. Crac."

"My uncle."

"Your uncle?" Rasht's initial thought was that their father must've sired other children who had families. But he and Crac had been alone as siblings. If this Palestinian gunman was indeed Crac's nephew, then that made him Rasht's son. But how was that possible? His family had been killed in Iran! "Many years ago, there was a wild boy named Sohayb. His father taught him to swim and run and read. The boy loved his three sisters, proven through his many pranks to make them scream and laugh. Then his mother and sisters would retaliate with pillows—pillow fights that raged until their father returned home. The family would sit and listen to their father's stories of the God of heaven, of Abraham, Isaac, and Jacob, of Samson, David, and Daniel. This boy Sohayb was only five years old, but he learned quickly the truths of God's love, and how God became a Man in the flesh named Jesus, to be the final sacrifice for man. Jesus was resurrected from the dead to prove He was God, triumphant over death, and able to give others eternal life. Are you . . . that boy, Sohayb?"

Rasht glanced at the young man's sidearm, but the gun wasn't drawn, though Rasht had spoken plainly about Jesus Christ and the resurrection—blasphemy according to Islam.

"Muhammad said my father was still alive, that he would take me to him before dawn." Sohayb dropped his flashlight to his side. He bowed his head and no longer seemed to be the fearsome gunman Rasht had witnessed in the room with Crac. "I remember the pillow fights and the stories. The teachings of Jesus—I thought they were a dream, or things I had imagined. My father was a great Muslim, I have been told. A martyr for Allah and his prophet, bless his name."

"No." Rasht shook his head, then took his son by the shoulders. "Your uncle, my brother, is the picture of the perfect Muslim, a man of devotion and bloodshed. Your mother and I were both rescued from Islam's rituals of bondage before you were born. We raised you and your sisters to worship in secrecy the true God, to live in peace and serve our Savior by a life of kindness. Your uncle Crac killed your mother and sisters, and I fled Iran thinking you were dead as well. This is truly a miracle. After all these years! After all the tears I have shed for you. What an amazing God we have! My son is alive!"

"But Muhammad . . ." Sohayb turned his head back in the direction from which he'd come. "Muhammad ibn Affal is a *jihadist* of great courage, slaying the enemies of Allah around the world! How can you say you're a Christian, my own father, allied with Sheik Muhammad?"

"Muhammad ibn Affal's legend convinces many people, and it's mostly perpetuated by what people want to believe. He is a man of dignity who doesn't shed blood, but rather uses his reputation to bring families together, like you and me, and to destroy tyrants of evil and death, like your uncle."

"So you are truly a Christian? My own father?"

"Since before you were born. I'm so sorry you have been alone. If I had known you were alive, I would have tried to rescue you sooner, but even I have been in prison for some years."

"No. No, Uncle Crac would've killed you." Sohayb shrugged off his father's hands and turned away, facing the dirt tunnel wall. "I'm so confused. My whole life, I fought for Allah. I've been the most devoted Muslim, proving my loyalty to Uncle Crac and all who challenge us."

"I know." Rasht sighed. "My son, you've been misled."

"Every Palestinian I know would die for Uncle Crac. He leads men for Allah to eternal paradise."

"Really? You probably know him best. Is he a man of love, of compassion and patience, of tolerance for his enemies, and self-sacrificing for those he leads? These are the attributes of followers of the true God, followers who have the divine nature in themselves. Have I described your Uncle Crac?"

"No. He is none of those things."

"How many times has he told you I am dead?"

"A thousand times. He has even honored your memory for me as a loyal Muslim."

"And here I am, neither dead, nor a Muslim serving a false god. He had to tell you those lies, because he couldn't tell you the truth. He killed the rest of our family. That's the truth. He's the reason I fled from Iran."

"But I have followed him!" Sohayb screamed, still turned away, and Rasht saw his son's shoulders shake as he sobbed. "I have killed for him, Father. I have become a murderer—for him and for Allah, as I was told. I've prayed and cried to Allah for years. No, you don't understand! You can't be my father. My sisters . . ."

Sohayb fell to his knees, the flashlight rolled from his

fingertips, and his head rested against the tunnel wall. Rasht knelt and held his son, sharing the grief they'd each endured for so long while apart. Now they grieved together, the truth releasing them from dark pasts. Father and son were together again.

Several minutes later, they continued their trek, passing three men working on the drone, and exited the garage without anyone stopping them. After all, the young gunman was Crac Hassad's nephew.

...✝...

Chloe hadn't taken her eye from the NL-X1 rifle scope for two hours. The night vision adapter was attached, and every life form—rat, cat, or human—that moved below her position with Chen Li was scrutinized.

"What's taking so long?" Chen Li whispered. The young agent was one foot away, their elbows nearly touching, as they lay prone on the rooftop of a textile shop. Across the intersection below them was the two-story school building. "They've been in there for over an hour."

"These things take time," Chloe said, but she was just as nervous. There should've been some signal by now. The school building was massive. They didn't even know which window Corban, Nathan, and Rasht were nearest, so they couldn't watch for a hasty exit. Corban wouldn't have asked for a sniper over-watch team if he hadn't expected a violent extraction. The NL-X1 wasn't employed except under the gravest of circumstances. "Just pray things move before dawn. You and I can't be caught out here in the daylight. We didn't bring disguises."

To the south, a bomber flew over Gaza. Precision missiles

exploded across a neighborhood. The flashes of light would have blinded Chloe if she hadn't looked away.

"Chloe!"

"What?" Chloe scanned the school building, her heart pounding.

"Movement. One click north. What is that?"

Chloe swung the rifle northward. The heat signature registered bright green through her scope.

"One stealth chopper and a unit of soldiers. They're IDF."

"They're coming straight at us!"

"No." Chloe raised her head and considered the angles. She and Chen Li had seen Corban attacked by an Israeli drone missile the previous hour. "It's got to be a net. Israel must've figured out the school building is active with Hamas terrorists. They're about to surround it and catch everyone they can."

"What about our guys?"

"I don't know."

"What if they're only getting close enough to use a laser targeting device to drop bombs more carefully? We've got to do something!"

"We're doing nothing."

"Nathan would want us to do something!"

"No, he wouldn't."

"We have to hold off the IDF!"

"No, Chen Li. Just relax. Corban's aware of the time crunch out here."

"If he's still alive. You saw him get hurt. If Nathan's in there alone, we need to—"

"Chill out." Chloe settled her eye on the scope. "It's these moments of stress that make or break an op. Lives are saved or lost right here. I've been doing this since before you were in grade school—in this very land. Pray if you feel you need to talk, but panic won't get Nathan out alive. Trust that God is guiding our boys through this storm. They're about to be in the eye of this hurricane in about ten minutes, especially if the IDF starts bombing that school. But we're not breaking cover until we have to."

"God, please . . ." Chen Li prayed and prayed, some words in English, and some in her native Chinese. Chloe didn't ask for a translation; she was busy praying in her native Hebrew.

†

CHAPTER TWENTY-EIGHT

GAZA

A nnette could barely stand the tension in the room, even though nothing was happening. Standing next to Corban was exhausting, and her nerves that had once been taut for action now brought her a great weariness. She didn't understand all the waiting or what was happening. The business with the chickens had been clear enough: a biological weapon was in their presence. If the weapon was to be the payment for her freedom, then why hadn't the bearded one next to the door given the canister to Crac Hassad? And why hadn't Corban left already?

It had been a pure miracle, Annette knew, that she'd been scouting for food and water, and had come upon Corban crossing the intersection outside. While hiding next to the school building, she'd watched him survive the explosion, and had been first at his side. After all, she'd been praying for him to rescue her. And if she hadn't seen Corban in the Gaza factory weeks earlier in that same bearded disguise, she never would've recognized him.

Titus was there as well, waiting with his square box against the wall near the windows. Annette wanted to communicate with him, for deep down she knew he was there for her. She regretted her hard words toward him at the factory. Embarrassed at the memory, she remembered trying to slap him! But here he was, alive, working with Corban, proving he had cared for her all along. They were all there for her. So, why couldn't they leave now?

Crac Hassad. Yes. They weren't there just for her. She was being selfish if she thought she were the only person who mattered that night. If Crac Hassad was left to run Gaza, then Annette wouldn't be the last American or foreigner Hamas held captive. Crac Hassad had to be neutralized.

Her hand trembled on Corban's shoulder, and he shifted under her touch. He turned his head and looked up at her, speaking a couple words in another language, words she didn't understand, but she found them comforting nonetheless. Corban was in control. Titus and the bearded man were with Corban. As soon as Crac Hassad came back into the room, then things would begin to happen.

Thirsty, tired, and hungry, she wasn't sure how much more waiting she could endure. Annette counted the steps she would take to reach Titus. If things got violent, she guessed Titus was the safest one to be near. He was close to the door and she knew he wouldn't be there unless he had some concern for her.

To pass the time, even with her eyes darting from militant, to Titus, to the door, she recalled Bible stories she'd heard in her youth. If ever she needed encouragement to believe in a mighty God, it was now. Samson had been a great warrior, she remembered. He had delivered God's people from evil people. She prayed that Corban and Titus had God's strength like Samson.

David and Goliath. Now was definitely a time to trust in a God who could raise up a meek shepherd to destroy the giant.

Militants outnumbered Corban and Titus, and yet, here they were. Corban was a believer, but what about Titus? She hoped God didn't hold it against their situation that Titus probably wasn't a Christian. If they survived this, Annette vowed to impress upon Titus the need to give his life to Christ. After all, she'd experienced His peace when in the most dire of circumstances.

Paul was another character she remembered. He'd been some sort of religious crook, but then he'd come to Christ. For years, he had braved other religious zealots who tried to kill him, but God kept him alive until it was time to take him home.

With this thought, Annette confessed in her heart she wasn't being faithful. She resigned to trust God with her life and situation, like Paul had with his whole life. And if God chose to take her home tonight, then what was the harm in that? She would be in the presence of God for eternity!

Meditating on that possibility, a peace swept through her heart, a peace that made her pains, hunger, and thirst pale in comparison. Eternity was before her, whether that night, or some night in the future. Yes, she would endure what God had placed before her. All she had to do was stand. Just keep standing. Until her Lord took her home to be with Him.

Nathan had lost track of what was under control, and what Corban may have failed to plan for. From his position near the door in the LED-lit room, Nathan could see a pool of blood under Corban's chair. His injury, or injuries, complicated their escape. If Corban insisted that Nathan save Annette Sheffield, Nathan wasn't sure he could—if it meant leaving Corban behind. The man had been like a father to him over the last few years. A spiritual father.

And that brought his eyes to Annette, the masked "militant" who stood like a pillar at Corban's right shoulder. She had barely shifted her feet during the hour, probably aware that Corban was her only safe ticket out of Gaza. Nathan couldn't wait to hear her story—surviving in Gaza for over two weeks. Had she been impersonating a gunman the whole time?

Then there was Titus Caspertein to Nathan's left, who had what sounded like a rabid monkey in the black case on the floor. Corban and Titus had spoken quietly in German upon Titus' arrival, but Nathan hadn't caught the conversation. Something was definitely afoot, but time was running out. Somehow, Corban had turned one of Crac Hassad's gunmen to take Rasht out, probably to safety. Now, Nathan hoped Corban had a plan for the rest of them. He scoffed at the thought. Wounded or not, when hadn't Corban Dowler had a plan?

Crac Hassad and a dozen Hamas militants walked into the room, anger evident on their faces. Nathan imagined why they'd be angry—since the promised canisters of nerve gas hadn't yet arrived. But that idea vanished when Nathan saw one of Hassad's men with the plastic chicken case. The chickens were awake and pecking curiously at their transparent confines.

"Hey," Nathan said quickly in German to Titus, "we're dead in thirty seconds. You must be here for something. Make your move now. I'll cover you."

"I'm here for Annette."

"Black mask next to Corban."

"Roger that."

Crac Hassad stopped in front of Corban. His gunmen surrounded him, and two men moved toward Nathan. Another two grabbed Annette by the arms and pulled her away from Corban.

Nathan couldn't wait to find out how Corban might talk his way out of this one. The chickens were alive. The nerve gas was a hoax, though it had gotten them in the door. In certain situations, the window to react is very narrow. Nathan judged that window in this situation to be now. He drew his NL-2 machine pistol from under his parka.

Next to him, Titus knelt down and unzipped his animal case, then kicked it toward the middle of the room. It slid across the dusty floor, a creature inside squealing like an unearthly monster that made the militants freeze in their tracks. They seemed afraid that a disease-ridden animal might emerge from the cage. Nathan hoped they remained still for a few more seconds as he opened fire, his pellets slapping across men's throats and chests as he stepped in front of the door. Crac Hassad couldn't be allowed to escape.

The animal case continued to slide across the floor until it came to rest against Crac Hassad's heels.

Instantly, two pink creatures shot out of the container. Their bodies glistened from the reflection of the lamp light, which cast eerie shadows against the walls. One of the creatures paused to change directions against the light, and all the devout Muslim men in the room could see its full, miniature features. Nathan's mouth gaped, and he wondered where in the Middle East Titus had found two little pigs!

Bringing piglets to a Muslim gunfight was a brilliant idea!

Hassad's men opened fire on the piglets. Bullets zipped past Nathan's head and smashed through a covered window. The glass shattered, and the night air poured into the room as Nathan dove to the floor to avoid sweeping gunfire, deafening in the room.

A lamp was knocked over and another was kicked across the room. To avoid the proximity of one pig, a militant fired his machine gun in a broad arc, shooting several of his comrades nearest him.

Nathan turned the valve of his canister and shoved it to roll into the fray. He knew that he and Corban were immune to the traditional liquid tranquilizer COIL chemists usually mixed, if this mixture was based on the same formula.

Crawling into the bleeding, squealing, screaming mass of bodies, Nathan searched for Corban. Adding to the confusion, two lamps were shot out and lighting was reduced. Annette might try to stay close to Corban, Nathan guessed. Suddenly, someone fell on top of him—whether shot dead or merely unconscious from the sleeping toxin, Nathan only saw it was a Hamas gunman.

The gunfire diminished. The rest of the lamps were knocked out. Men were yelling. A pig grunted and lightly trampled across one of Nathan's hands. Someone else fell over his legs and lay still.

"Corban!" Nathan called. "Corban!"

A firm hand grasped his collar, a breath in his face.

"Get Annette out!" Corban ordered. "I'm going after Hassad!"

A limp body was shoved into his arms. He couldn't protest

or argue in the dim chaos. And he certainly wasn't about to abandon Annette to the likes of the Palestinian militants again. Nathan felt Corban move along the floor amongst the others. Those who weren't tranquilized had apparently been spared by the open window which had surely sucked out much of the airborne toxin.

Someone turned on a flashlight. Nathan didn't wait for introductions. He lunged for the light and swung hard. His fist connected. The man grunted and fell. Recovering the flashlight, Nathan discovered the man he'd attacked was Titus Caspertein. Titus had a bullet wound in the shoulder—and now a swollen jaw.

The room was suddenly still, though several men could be heard running through other rooms, firing their weapons, presumably at one of the frightened piglets. Only one remarkably untouched piglet was on the other side of the room. It was nosing one of the unconscious militants, perhaps smelling something edible in his pocket.

Through the broken window, Nathan heard the faint thumping of a chopper. Its rotor sound was muffled by external cylinders as it approached in stealth mode. Having been in Special Forces operations his whole adult life, he recognized the sound and knew the danger it meant.

"Don't go anywhere," Nathan said to a sleeping Titus, then picked up Annette in his arms. Corban wasn't in the room. In one hand, Nathan gripped his NL-2, the flashlight in the other, and strode out of the room. Though still deep in Gaza, he'd feel much safer outside, in view of Chloe and Chen Li.

An explosion behind Nathan tossed him across a corridor and seconds later he realized he'd been knocked unconscious.

By the light of burning fires, he saw three walls had been vaporized, and the upper and ground floors had collapsed into the basement. The screams of what sounded like women and children pierced the suffocating air.

The flashlight and NL-2 weren't in sight. By the flickering fires, he relocated Annette's still body and crawled to her. Two more explosions farther in the building, presumably from IDF drone bombs, shook the floor. He prayed for Corban, and even for Titus, who he'd intended to return for. But now that whole section of the building was smoldering rubble.

Nathan was bleeding from the brow, and part of his parka and shirt were torn through to his skin, which felt burned.

One of Annette's legs lay at an odd angle, but Nathan couldn't worry about limbs when their lives were at stake. Corban had said to save Annette, so he would.

With her in his arms, he climbed to his feet and stumbled out of the hole in the wall where the front door of the school building once stood. Women and children ran past him and across the street. Militants fired assault rifles at IDF soldiers who crouched on the pavement.

Nathan looked up and across the intersection. How was he ever to survive crossing the street? Gunmen fired recklessly, the chopper fired at anyone armed, and the IDF ground troops shot desperately at anyone who wasn't wearing an IDF uniform.

A scared Palestinian kid with an AK-47 ran past Nathan and aimed at him. The boy suddenly fell, but without apparent injury. Nathan rolled him over with his foot, and still saw no bullet wound.

"Chloe," he said aloud, and knew she was indeed watching.

With Annette in his arms, Nathan walked straight ahead to the north. He wouldn't approach Chloe's location directly so he didn't lead anyone to her, but he would pass nearby, keeping himself visible to her line-of-sight.

On the left, a Hamas killer fell. On his right, two IDF soldiers dropped. Nathan walked faster, aware that Chloe was tranquilizing anyone who aimed even remotely in his direction. The existence of a mysterious sniper already on the scene would concern the Israelis as more of their numbers were taken out.

The IDF gave a signal, collected their wounded, and began to pull back. But the Hamas militants were too disoriented to notice anything except who they would shoot next. In their zeal, confusion, and fear, they massacred one another in full view of Nathan, until he reached the other side of the intersection.

Before he moved behind the corner of Chloe's multi-story position, he looked back. The school building was on fire and two choppers were still firing into the debris. Corban had entered Gaza knowing full well the IDF was actively hunting Hamas terrorists and their missile launch sites. He was in God's hands.

It had been Corban who'd found Annette and gotten her to him. Corban Dowler had died as he had lived—giving life to others. Tears blurred his vision, but still, Nathan stared at the scene. How could a body ever be recovered from such destruction? And in a war zone? This view on this terrible night would be Corban's memorial in his mind. Nathan would see to it that those who followed—other selfless COIL operatives, other sold-out Christians—they would all know how Corban Dowler had lived and ultimately died, protecting the helpless, bringing wicked men to justice, sparing his friends while he bore the pain.

Corban Dowler was surely dead.

†

CHAPTER TWENTY-NINE

GAZA / ISRAEL

When Corban Dowler awoke on his back, he couldn't feel his legs. Before he opened his eyes, he ran quick mental diagnostics over his body. Pain above one ear. One shoulder felt broken. Maybe a couple ribs, too. But that shrapnel in his spine . . .

He coughed and felt blood on his cheek. That meant something internal had been injured, maybe a lung by a broken rib. Opening his eyes, he took stock of his situation. Smoke filled the air, but the fire that caused it was several feet away and diminishing. Concrete slabs had collapsed above and beside his head, almost crushing him. Wires that hadn't had electricity since Israel last bombed the infrastructure hung in his face like ugly tentacles.

Looking to his left and right, he saw no way out, and didn't know which way to go even if he could crawl over the concrete slabs.

Then the stench hit him. *Death. Burning flesh.* He remembered arriving at a Nigerian village a couple years earlier. Boko Haram had been there an hour before, raping and killing Christians. Anyone who had a non-Muslim name had been tortured. The houses had been burned, some bodies left in them. It had smelled like this.

Corban closed his eyes again and moved his head left and

right. He prayed as he felt the extent of his injuries. Dying didn't bother him since his conscience was at peace, unburdened before the cross of Christ—because of the cross of Christ. At some point, he'd guessed he would have to retire from COIL . . . but not like this. Jenna, his blind daughter, wasn't yet in high school. Her brilliant way of seeing the world continued to astound her teachers and inspire her classmates. He prayed he wouldn't die before seeing her again.

And Janice—the only woman who'd loved him, even when he'd been around the world, focused on others, risking his life so others could live. Janice would understand why he'd died in a foreign land. She may not ever know which land, but she had prayed for his unsaved soul for years while they were married, and she knew him best now. Corban knew love only because he had been loved first—by Christ, and by Janice. He wished he could tell her that just once more.

It wasn't just love that made Corban, despite the pain, roll over onto his belly. He'd been ruining networks of crooks and devious diplomats for too long to see Crac Hassad escape this night. If nothing else, he wanted to know that the man had been captured or killed. Crac Hassad had to be stopped. Whatever the terrorist was up to in Gaza, the Gazan residents needed to see what could happen without Hassad over them. The Palestinian people needed life, and they'd never find life if Hamas was allowed to continue to use their streets, their homes, their clinics, their schools, their families.

Corban dragged himself over a steel beam. A new fire flared up, then died down again. He heard his feet clunk over the beam behind him, but now seemingly paralyzed, those feet meant very little to him, so he clawed forward.

Above, the rubble settled, sprinkling dust upon him. Other areas could settle as well, and crush him. He couldn't wait for rescuers. Perhaps days would pass before the Gazans arrived outside to search for survivors.

Someone called his name, but not his Muhammad name. The voice was distant, unearthly, as if from a dream. Shutting his mind out to the voice, Corban prayed for sanity, for clear thinking. The strange voice was an indication, he realized, of some sort of head injury.

Every time he moved, the nerves and bone in his shoulder pained him. And every time he breathed, his lung felt like it was about to collapse. But to stop was to die. He'd given the world his all for so long, he couldn't just lay still and perish now. God had given him a heart to preserve the helpless, so for Corban to do nothing would be to deny both himself and his God.

His fingers clawed through dirt and ash. The fires stretched behind him, and he dragged himself farther into darkness, into cold, into silence. It was some time after he'd begun to move forward that he realized he was completely alone—perhaps even dead, or dreaming. The earth below him was freezing, and no longer did the air smell of burnt flesh or charred debris. He paused and lay his cheek on the soil. Shivering, he wondered if he was going into shock.

A memory came to him. He'd once hunted with the Inuits of Northern Canada. A caribou had been shot, but only wounded in the spine. For two miles, they'd tracked the beast as it had crawled by its forelegs, desperately dragging its lower half. Corban was now that caribou, moving inches at a time, certain to die, seeking refuge, but finding no relief.

For hours it seemed he pulled himself forward, clawing a little more, and then drawing himself ahead. The pain in his collarbone and chest numbed him, and there were long moments of resting that turned into sleep, only to wake with a start, a purpose to complete some mission he couldn't quite identify. Behind him, that same voice called his name, drawing closer, like death stalking him through the blackness.

Suddenly, Corban stopped moving and tried to focus on what new thing he sensed. Voices. He'd been hearing them ahead for some time. They spoke Arabic. Yes, he was in Gaza. Terrorists were nearby. There'd been an explosion. He was hunting Crac Hassad.

As he left the haunting voice behind him and drew closer to the voices ahead, he saw the light of a room which illuminated Corban's position in a shadowy tunnel. The silhouette of a man moved in front of the tunnel mouth, but the man didn't enter the tunnel where Corban was. The man was working on something, facing away from Corban.

"The conventional warhead is enough," the voice said in Arabic. "We can launch it without Sohayb. He said it was already programmed."

"Yes, Crac. Please, stand back."

"Launch it now! We are out of time!"

Corban grit his teeth. Crac Hassad. They were together again, and some further evil was afoot.

Moving past several drums, Corban dragged himself into the recesses of what seemed like a wide garage. Above him hung a model airplane. He pulled himself under it, inches above his face. Nearby, feet walked around the plane.

"Clear the rail!" one voice said.

"Open the doors," another instructed. "Knock out the posts and check the street."

No! Corban realized it wasn't a model airplane. It was a drone—a drone with missiles attached under its wings!

He leaned painfully on one elbow and reached up to cling to one wing of the aircraft. If it launched now, he would fly out with it. Clutching the flap, he worked his fingertips into the crack, where the hinge made a gap. The sharp metal cut through his skin before the end of the flap cracked and hung loosely on a metal pin.

In seconds, he could die, once they discovered him, but Corban wasn't about to allow Hamas to launch an armed drone.

Reaching up the side of the fuselage, he unscrewed an aerodynamic fuel valve. With a hose, he could have quietly siphoned the fuel, but there was no hose around him. Panting from the pain, Corban grasped the port side wing and hung from it by both arms. The drone tipped on its runner, and fuel poured from the tank, pooling on the garage floor. Tipping the drone farther, he emptied the fuel completely.

"What is that?" someone yelled nearby.

"Stop him! Get him!"

Corban was kicked in the ribs under his left arm. He released the drone and fell to the floor of the garage. The drone rebounded, then rocked off the runner, falling to its starboard wing. Hearing it crack, Corban knew he'd at least temporarily caused their terrorist attack to fail.

By one arm, he was dragged away from the drone and dropped against the foot of the stairs that led to the house interior. The burns and wounds that covered Corban's body opened up from the abuse, and he fought to remain conscious.

"Keep him alive!" Crac Hassad ordered. "Throw water on him. Launch the drone now!"

"We can't. Look, the wings are damaged."

"Fix it! Get more fuel!"

Someone doused water in Corban's face, and the shock of the moisture startled him to alertness. In his condition, he wasn't sure how he would stop these men, but he had to try something.

"What is this?" Hassad tugged at Corban's fake beard. "Muhammad? I should have known! Who are you?"

In rage and fury, the crazed man attacked Corban, slapping and punching him. Corban felt the blows, but through the shock of his other injuries, he felt the numbness that many spoke of when close to death.

"You may kill me." Corban hardly recognized his own voice. His throat was choked with smoke and dust from the tunnel. Hassad took a step back, panting. "But know this: you are killing a child of God, a servant of Jesus Christ, the only—"

He was punched in the mouth. His head fell against the stairs and he drifted to unconsciousness.

...†...

Titus called and called to Corban, but Corban kept crawling away, through the flames, over concrete, beyond where Titus thought the school foundation ended. If it weren't for a slab of concrete that had crushed and pinned Titus' foot in the rubble, he would've crawled after Corban, but he was stuck sure.

For the first hour, there were others alive around Titus.

They cried and fainted, then woke again. They called for help, men of terror now beggars for mercy, and one by one they died and fell silent. Titus yelled for Corban by name, but said nothing else. He'd lost consciousness sometime during the brawl in the lit room above, but his wits were about him enough now to realize a number of missiles had decimated the school building. He and his fellow sufferers had fallen into the basement.

When Titus noticed his foot was trickling blood, he realized he couldn't wait for help. He would bleed to death if he didn't free his foot, and that meant the thousand-pound piece of concrete needed to be shifted aside.

As the fires around him began to diminish, so did his light to work to free himself. Quickly, he gathered pieces of rebar and conduit and chunks of concrete to act as leverage. He stripped off his shirt to prepare a tourniquet, then tore away his pant leg to better see the damage. The pain radiated so much that he thought his whole foot had been crushed, but now he saw it was just the lower half of his foot in the combat boot that was smashed.

The last fire went out, and no one else cried for help. Totally alone in the darkness, Titus remained still with unexpected thoughts flooding his mind. Memories. Stubbornness. Fear. Denial. Loneliness. And now this. It was undeniable that he'd been preserved while others hadn't been. And that fact led to the idea that Someone had preserved him. But why? Because he'd begun to believe in God finally?

"*Hell.*" The word came to his lips, giving him a chill.

Hell had been a fear of his for his whole adult life. Even before he'd become an international criminal, he knew he'd been born separated and distant from God. And since Titus had never given his life to God, only eternal separation had waited for him in death. But he no longer had that fear. Belief had changed everything. Christ had paid for whatever had separated himself from God. He had to find Corban to tell him. He had to find his brother and sister back in Arkansas. Everyone had to know the peace that was available through a spiritual surrender to God! Telling others had to be the only reason he was still alive.

Working by feel now, Titus used a piece of conduit to dig at the earth on one side of the slab that pinned him. As he removed the earth, one side of the slab settled lower, and the other side rose. He shoved pieces of concrete and rebar next to his foot to relieve the pressure as the slab move. It was slow work, measured by millimeters of progress. Twice, he thought he was free, and he pulled on his leg, only to realize he was still stuck. The wasted minutes required to recover from the agony of those attempts caused more blood loss.

Finally, the slab shifted into the earth and it fell free. He nearly blacked out at the fresh wave of pain from pinched nerves now coursing with life again.

Titus felt the wetness of blood dripping as he removed his cut boot and tossed it aside. He was disoriented and nauseous from the throbbing pain, but he worked quickly, wrapping his shirt around the crushed foot before he passed out.

With his foot bound in the shirt and with pressure applied to the areas of broken flesh, he relaxed, waiting for unconsciousness, but it didn't come. Instead, the pain lessened, and his next objective lay before him: Corban. Searching for Annette seemed a lost cause. She and Crac

Hassad's people had surely been killed in the devastation. If Corban was the only one still alive, then Titus would find him. He had to tell the old man his efforts of relentless preaching had broken through his rebellious heart.

✝

CHAPTER THIRTY

GAZA

Annette, carried by Corban's man, gasped against his chest as she sobbed. Though she'd never met him before, it was enough to know she was safe. But Corban and Titus had perished. For the IDF, the mere collapse of the building hadn't been enough. The COIL operative and the still-masked Annette watched as rocket after rocket flew into the rubble, and explosions shook the street blocks away.

Pulling away from the agent who introduced himself as Nathan, Annette looked to the west. Titus had been so bold, so confident. The moment he'd arrived, she'd known he was there for her. Sure, Corban and Nathan had come first, but Titus was the lone wolf, the thug who had seemed to care for no one but his own bank accounts. His presence in Gaza meant the most to her. Now, he was dead. It was little comfort knowing his last act was to save someone else.

"The tunnel!" She turned to Nathan, who continued to watch the scene three blocks in the distance. "Nathan, there's a tunnel under the school!"

"Makes sense," he said. "Keep your voice down. English shouldn't be spoken for anyone to hear in Gaza."

"Didn't you hear me?" Annette turned him toward her. "They could've gotten out. There was a tunnel into Israel under the school!"

"Point for me." Nathan was listening now. "Which way?"

"That way. It's a long, long tunnel. I know it's there. They were holding me in Israel, then I escaped through the tunnel into Gaza. You've got to believe me!"

"I believe you. Just stay back." He pulled her out of the street. "Israel must know there's a tunnel. That's why they're hitting it so hard. I'm sorry, Annette. There's no way anyone could live through that devastation."

"What if you're wrong?" Annette licked her lips and tried to visualize the perimeter wall of Gaza. It couldn't be more than a mile away. "Where are the people watching over us?"

"Back that way." He pointed toward the school. "Tunnel or not, I've got to get you back to Israel. We can't be found here."

"But, Titus . . ."

"We've waited long enough for them. They're gone, Annette. They're in God's hands."

For the first time, Annette noticed a strange gun in Nathan's hand, one of the non-lethal weapons that Corban's people used.

The assault on the school decreased, then ended. When Annette and Nathan reached the intersection, someone above them whistled. Annette looked straight up at a head poking over the edge of the roof."

"Eagle Eyes!"

"Chloe?"

"What happened? Where's Corban?"

"He . . . didn't make it."

"What do you mean he didn't make it? You were with him!"

Annette didn't know how Nathan could answer her. The events in the room that night had been so confusing prior to her passing out. Her memory seemed infected by some sort of nightmarish idea that Titus had released a couple of piglets in the room. She'd been next to Corban, and after two weeks in captivity, that's all that seemed important. For a little while, even with militants in the room, she'd felt safe, and even safer when Titus had shown up—for her. The fact that her last memory was standing next to Corban told her that the soft-spoken spy for Christ had helped save her life.

If there was even a chance that Titus was alive, Annette had to find him. No one else knew where the tunnel was. How would she live another day knowing she hadn't at least looked to see if the man who had come for her was still alive? An arm's length away from Nathan, Annette darted away, her eyes focused on a dark section of ground next to the burning debris of the school.

"Cover us!" she heard Nathan yell to the woman on the roof, then she heard his boots pounding the ground after her.

"Annette! This isn't safe!"

Next to the school, Annette ran through the bushes in the darkness when three soldiers with military helmets rose from their cover. They yelled at her in Arabic, but she could see they wore Israeli uniforms. She slid to a stop, her hands raised. When Nathan charged up behind her, two more soldiers broke cover and there was more yelling.

But suddenly, the first three soldiers flinched and fell over, tranquilized. The next two were incapacitated just as quickly, and then Annette was running again. Corban's people never ceased to amaze her.

That's when she knew for sure. She wasn't the same inside. Nothing she'd done had caused the change in her, but her contact with true people of God had planted a seed. What was in them was greater than anything she'd known in the world. And what was in them, was in her. She was like them. She was a Christian. For eternity, she would never be the same. And for some compelling reason, she wanted to tell Titus, if he was still alive.

...†...

ISRAEL

Crac Hassad was losing control. Israel and the Zionists were ruining everything. Even Sohayb had vanished. For years, the youth had obeyed his every word. Now, when Allah needed him most, Sohayb was missing.

"Weak, just like my brother." Hassad spat. He stretched out a piece of duct tape and passed it to his man under the drone.

It was righteous hatred, Hassad told himself—killing his brother's family, but keeping Sohayb alive to raise as his own son. It was a tale worthy of the legends of Allah's greatest warriors. Hadn't he become one of the greatest? Soon, Israel would be the scorn of the earth.

"We have to launch now," Hassad said to his men. Only three of his soldiers remained alive. If there were others, they had scattered into the night on the Gazan side of the tunnel. "It's daylight. The whole world can witness Israel's drone blowing up the Dome of the Rock."

"It won't fly. Not like this."

Hassad turned and looked down at the man he'd thought

to be Muhammad ibn Affal. The bleeding and now beardless man was duct taped to a pallet, but Hassad perceived the man was paralyzed; his legs were unnaturally positioned.

"Soon, you will die, and Allah will curse you to the fires of hell. Those burns on your face are a foretaste."

"That drone is a precision instrument. It won't fly with taped wings. You should repair it. Find the right parts."

"You just want me to stall even longer." Hassad slapped the man on the side of the head. "Your sabotage was ill-conceived."

Hassad's men opened the garage doors again, and another operated the controls from a laptop station. The drone's nose propeller came to life.

"Send her into the sky." Hassad folded his hands. He saw in the drone his life's work against Israel—the school, the tunnel, and now this final act. Nothing had gone perfectly, but the finish line was all that mattered. "Send her into the sky with Allah's blessings!"

The technician released the drone's brake. It shot forward on its rail and flew out of the garage door. Hassad ran to the open door and looked into the sky for the death-maker of Israel. But the drone wasn't soaring into the sky. Instead, it remained only a few feet off the street. With fury, Hassad realized even with its fuel replaced, the wings' damage was too great.

The drone arced to the left and slammed into the stucco wall around an Israeli courtyard across the street. The missiles didn't explode since they hadn't yet been armed. Its engine whined loudly for a moment, its nose damaged and stuck in the wall, then the engine died.

Hassad's rage rose within him. Never had he tortured anyone the way he would torture the man who had pretended to be Muhammad ibn Affal.

He stood over the beardless, crippled man and spat on him. They needed to leave the house. It was only a matter of time before the police arrived to investigate the drone crash. The IDF would soon follow. But at least he would have a prisoner, and he would be in Israel. The damage he could do with a few good soldiers, now already in Israel, was a tantalizing thought!

"Load him into the truck," he ordered his men, who stood around in uncertainty since they had failed him. He would punish them later for their incompetence, but for now, he needed them. "We're leaving!"

"I don't think so," a strange voice said from the back of the garage.

Hassad growled at the sight of the charred and ruffled blond man who stepped forward. It was Titus Caspertein, the Serval. Hamas intelligence reports had the smuggler's picture, and Hassad had known he was in the school when it had been bombed.

"Caspertein! You're just the man I could use now. You'll still be paid. Come." Hassad then noticed the strange gun in Titus' hand. "What is this? Caspertein! I didn't know they would attack the school. We have the same goals. Look at me! No one in Gaza is wealthier than me. Hamas will rise again. Last night was Allah's way of telling us to try harder. You'll be paid for even better weapons. What are you doing?"

"Back away from my guy." Titus waved his gun at the man as he hobbled closer. His foot was wrapped, but it left bloody marks on the floor after him. "You okay, Corban?"

"*Your man?*" Hassad glanced between the two men—the one called Corban and the Serval. "You are with this impersonator?"

"With him?" Titus scoffed. "I'd be lucky to be with him. He's always a step ahead of me. You okay, Corban?"

"A sliver or two. Glad you made it. Meet Crac Hassad. He about launched an Israeli drone against Israel."

Hassad looked around the garage for a weapon. For the last few years, he'd walked around unarmed, daring his enemies. Sohayb and Petra had always been nearby with their guns. Where was Sohayb?

"Crac Hassad, huh? On your knees, Crocker. Hands behind your head." Titus smiled. "Always wanted to arrest someone. Usually, I'm on the other end of that command."

"Allah will avenge me!" Hassad had never been so disrespected. No one ordered him around like this! "The blood of my ancestors—"

"Oh, be quiet."

Hassad knelt and interlocked his fingers behind his head. So, he would be arrested, but he would get word to Sohayb. The fight would go on. Israel could not win! He'd heard of Hamas commanders continuing the fight from prisons inside Israel, and sometimes the UN pressured Israel to release even the most radical Palestinians. Yes, he would not stop fighting!

The sound of running feet approached. Hassad's heart beat with new vigor. A masked man looked in through the garage door with a bearded man close behind.

"My men return to fight!" Hassad rose to his feet and pointed at Titus. "Kill this spawn of a Jew!"

Instead, the masked man removed his mask, and shook out his long hair. It was not a man at all, but a woman! Annette Sheffield! She glanced at Titus, then smiled at Hassad. Hassad's teeth clenched together so hard they felt numb.

"I'll kill you both with—"

Hassad was hit with a dozen pellets from the strange gun Caspertein held. Involuntarily, Hassad fell to his knees. His arms felt heavy.

"I was wondering where I dropped that gun," Corban said.

"It ain't easy keeping up with you, Corban," Titus said. "Didn't you hear me calling for you?"

Annette ran into Titus' arms.

With his mind swimming, Hassad's gaze fell on Corban. These people were not Israelis. It made no sense. How had they risked their lives against him—and won? He tumbled over, then everything went dark.

✝

Corban Dowler lay in his hospital bed, awake now, but he kept his eyes closed, taking in the softness of the bed under him, and the air that smelled like sunshine. The room he was in seemed far too small for so many people whose soft voices he heard around him.

"The doctor said most of the burns will heal within a month, but there'll be some scarring."

"Thank you for being here for him, Chloe."

Chloe and Janice. Corban's heart warmed at the thought of his wife being there to take care of him. She'd not tolerate him lying around.

"The boss'll never be the same without his legs."

"Hey, Scooter, at least you're not the shortest guy in COIL anymore!"

Corban, with eyes still closed, almost laughed as the others scolded Bruno, the bear-sized COIL teammate, for his words.

"I still can't believe you brought a piglet to a gunfight," Nathan said, and several chuckled. "A piglet? What were you thinking? Hassad's people went crazy, shooting at everything, even each other."

"I'm telling you," Titus said, "there were two pigs, and without them, we might all be dead right now. Tell them, Annette."

"One pig or two pigs, I'm staying out of this. I'm just glad to be out of Gaza, and there's a cease fire since Crac Hassad was arrested. But I'm pretty sure there was only one pig."

Everyone did their best to muffle their laughter. Corban was surprised the nurses were allowing them to be so loud yet remain in the room.

"Why does it matter how many pigs there were?" Chloe asked. "Any word on Rasht Hassad?"

"Only the boss knows," Nathan said. "A lot happened in the room that night that only he knows about."

"I still have a question." The room was still, waiting for Titus to continue. "I was gonna ask Corban when he woke up, but he's taking his sweet time. Now that I'm a Christian, shouldn't I join COIL or something?"

"That may be an option down the road," Chloe said. "You have some legal issues to sort out. Again, those are details to talk to Corban about."

"Stick with me," Annette said, "I know the way." There was a kissing sound, followed by a wolf whistle from someone. Probably Scooter, Corban guessed.

"Careful, you two," Chloe said, "or Nathan and Chen Li's wedding won't be the only one we celebrate while we're all here in Israel."

"As long as we all agree on one thing." Titus sounded serious. "There were definitely two pigs. I wouldn't have risked bringing only one. I always bring backup. It's a rule I have. There were two pigs."

"Well, Scooter and I have our own beef with the boss," Bruno said. "We want to know how long we have to put up with this bearded Nathan. I won't believe he's really still alive until I'm looking at the old Eagle Eyes—without all that scruff."

Corban let his mind drift through the laughter and company, and he thanked His Lord he was alive to be with them all again. His spy days were probably over if he was paralyzed now, but that didn't mean he would wash his hands of COIL. Too many Christians around the world were under COIL and his protection for him to just walk away. Or, rather, he couldn't just roll away. And maybe, when things were slow around the COIL office, he would fly to China and see if a wheelchair gave him an edge to smuggle a few Bibles into the closed country. The book of his life wasn't over yet; it was only a new chapter. With Janice at his side, and a faithful team of servants around him, COIL would continue to make a difference for Christ. The gospel would be spread, and God would be glorified.

And somewhere out there was an Italian who chewed more bubble gum than a man ought to chew—who was now a professing Christian. The future definitely held some exciting possibilities.

Corban opened his eyes.

"Hey, what's this about a wedding?"

Rasht Hassad opened the door for Colonel Yasof. The two shook hands.

"Thank you for meeting with me," the colonel said as Rasht led him into the living room. "How's the safe house working for you two?"

They spoke English, but Rasht was already learning Arabic.

"Sohayb is a little anxious, but we both know our stay here is temporary."

"I've reviewed your terms," the colonel said as he set a file on the table between them, "and I've spoken to Corban Dowler, who's recuperating in Jerusalem. COIL will send you and your son back into Gaza undercover."

"We're Christians now, even my son." Rasht gestured to the younger man who stood in the corner. He appeared to be uncomfortable in the strange surroundings. "Sohayb, say something."

"Please forgive me, Colonel," Sohayb said. "I'm still adjusting to all this."

"I understand. Corban's made it clear, as you have, what your humanitarian or religious status will be. All IDF asks is that you warn us of new Hamas uprisings. This is about keeping the peace and saving lives while you're in Gaza. We can help one another."

"You're fighting against an idea called Islam, Colonel." Then Rasht folded his hands. He knew he probably looked like a professor with his clothes pressed and beard trimmed. "Bullets and rockets won't do for us. My son and I are returning to the Palestinian people with love and the Truth. People must be changed by Jesus Christ from the inside out. It is the only way."

"Fine. This isn't the first time I've approved a reformed terrorist to help keep peace between our two peoples, but your son was—"

"He and I both know the deal. We'll take pictures and be in contact. Just don't ask us to compromise our priority for Jesus. We are Christians who work for COIL, and we'll assist the IDF regarding Hamas intel at our own convenience, if we hear about uprisings."

"Thank you." Colonel Yasof and Rasht shook hands. "When I first heard of COIL, I never thought it would have this much influence."

"It's not the organization that holds the power, Colonel."

"What do you mean?"

"Let me get us some tea. My son and I want to tell you about an empty tomb."

~

Dear Reader,

Thanks so much for reading *DARK ZEAL!* If you liked it, could you leave me a short comment or review on Amazon? That would help others notice the book. Thank you!

Though this is the last novel in *The COIL Series,* don't worry, I have <u>more COIL books to share with you!</u>

Please continue the COIL adventure with *DISTANT BOUNDARY,* Prequel of *The COIL Legacy Series* (as a FREE download!). You can find links to all my books on my website at <u>ditelbat.com/all-d-i-telbat-novels/</u>.

The COIL Legacy Prequel is followed by Book One, *DISTANT CONTACT,* and Book Two, *DISTANT FRONT. DISTANT HARM,* Book Three, will continue the series. I have many more clean, Christian novels to share with you. Watch for my latest book news at ditelbat.com/novel-lineup/.

You may want to <u>subscribe to Telbat's Tablet, my weekly blog,</u> so you never miss my novel news, Author Reflections, free short stories, or other related posts. Visit my website at <u>ditelbat.com</u> to enter your email address in the subscription form. (We will *never* share your email.) I also have exclusive <u>subscriber gifts and discounts</u> for you. Come join the adventure!

Again, thanks for reading. May the Lord be glorified.
David Telbat

ENDNOTES

As in my other *COIL Series* novels, I desire to focus on a Christian ministry that supports the Persecuted Church. This time, I bring you <u>Christian Aid Mission</u>, a ministry that <u>serves indigenous missionaries and ministries worldwide</u>. The following can be found on their website. Visit them at <u>www.christianaid.org</u>. All honor belongs to the Lord. –David Telbat

CHRISTIAN AID MISSION

<u>Mission Statement</u>: Christian Aid Mission seeks <u>to establish a witness for our Lord in every tribe and nation</u> (Matthew 24:14) by assisting highly effective native missionaries who serve with competent indigenous mission boards based in poorer countries overseas.

Christian Aid Mission is <u>a 60-year-old non-profit organization</u> serving as a non-denominational foreign mission board <u>assisting more than 500 ministries</u> overseas with <u>tens of thousands of indigenous or native missionaries in the field</u>. These ministries are <u>currently engaging more than 1,000 unreached people groups in more than 100 countries.</u>

Our <u>focus is on reaching the unreached</u>—areas in the world where there are few Christians, where Christians suffer because of poverty or persecution, or where foreign missionaries are not allowed.

Reaching the Unreached

<u>More than 40%</u> (2.58 billion and growing) of the <u>people living in the world today are unreached</u>, meaning they have <u>never heard the Gospel and there is no indigenous community of believers within their tribe or people group to evangelize them</u>. Many live in the least developed parts of the globe. Most live in countries that are closed to foreign missionaries.

Christian Aid was first established in Washington, DC as a missionary outreach among overseas students and other visitors from unevangelized "mission field" countries. Since millions of foreign nationals come to the US and Canada every year, our goal has been to reach these visitors while they are away from home, and <u>lead them to a saving knowledge of our Lord and Savior.</u> Hundreds of <u>highly educated men and women have gone back to provide leadership for indigenous missionary ministries among their own people</u> on every continent.

When they return home to spread the gospel, <u>we serve as their supply line.</u> <u>Indigenous missionary ministries do 95 percent of the pioneer missionary evangelism in the world today.</u> Indigenous missionaries know the language, culture, political structure and there is no traveling back and forth to their home country nor down time for adjusting to a new environment. Christian Aid has found them to be <u>the most effective and efficient missionary force for sharing the gospel.</u>

These ministries:

> --Train workers and send out missionaries
> --Plant churches
> --Translate and distribute Bibles and Christian literature
> --Help victims of natural disasters
> --Feed the hungry due to famine and poverty
> --Provide love and shelter for orphans
> --Offer medical missions
> --Dig wells for safe water supply
> --Support persecuted Christians

The majority of these mission boards are based in lands of abject poverty. A billion people, including many evangelical Christians in Asia, Africa, and Latin America, cannot find jobs that will provide cash income. They stay alive by growing tiny plots of rice, fishing or hunting insects. Those who do have paying jobs give generously and sacrificially; however, their wages are so low that the total sum of their tithes and offerings may only be a few dollars a week.

About Christian Aid

1. *Christian Aid* <u>seeks to establish a witness for our Lord in every tongue, tribe and nation</u> (Rev. 5:9) and to encourage and strengthen

evangelical Christian witness in countries where Christians are persecuted or few in number.

2. *Christian Aid* locates, evaluates, and sends financial help to indigenous evangelical ministries which are serving the Lord primarily in countries closed to foreign missionaries.

3. *Christian Aid* continually appraises indigenous mission groups, examines their doctrinal statements, and evaluates the fruits of their ministries. We make sure they are accountable and provide financial statements regularly. Each ministry is checked to insure that it is not linked—or is a branch of—any foreign organization, but is truly indigenous.

4. *Christian Aid* encourages American Christians to help these indigenous missions evangelize their own people. As we receive offerings from US Christians, we send them to indigenous missionary ministries in poorer countries. Then they send out native missionaries, who are getting the job done at a fraction of the cost of traditional missions. Christian Aid does not send out foreign missionaries.

More than 400,000 native missionaries are on the fields or ready to go. Approximately 100,000 of these have no regular support, but are evangelizing and planting churches in their own nations with the few resources they currently have.

As new churches are born out of evangelical revivals in Asia, Africa and Latin America, they very quickly begin to send out missionaries. Hundreds of these gospel workers have forfeited secular employment to serve the Lord full time in faith.

Thousands of indigenous ministries operate Bible institutes and missionary training schools that provide practical field experience with focused classroom teaching. *Christian Aid* has sent support to more than 150 Bible institutes in China that have trained and sent out tens of thousands of native Chinese missionaries. Many native missionaries have also opted to study abroad at evangelical colleges and seminaries in America, Canada, and Europe.

News/Stories of Missions Work & Persecution Around Globe

Christian Aid <u>serves as a bridge</u> between indigenous missions groups and Western believers. We <u>strive to inform you</u> about the desperate situations of millions of believers all around the globe as well as share with you evidence of the Love and Power of God among the nations. *Christian Aid s* <u>news articles offer you a glimpse into the lives of indigenous believers</u>, their struggles, and their triumphs. We hope by informing you of the needs of your brethren, <u>God will lead you to pray and support</u> indigenous missions groups.

Missions Insider Report

For 50+ years *Christian Aid* has championed the work of indigenous missionaries. Now, we gladly share with you <u>highlights of the com- pelling news received from Christian leaders</u> around the world. Periodically (currently about once a month), you can <u>receive the Missions Insider Report by email.</u> It will provide you a cross-section of the works and missions, the passion and commitment, the hard- ships and persecutions, the joys and victories of native missionaries working among their own people in some of the poorest, the most remote, the most difficult places in the world.

It is our <u>privilege to share with you the indigenous missionary's story</u>. We are excited to be able <u>to offer you "free of charge" the Mission Insider Report</u>. **Subscribe at www.christianaid.org.**

ABOUT THE AUTHOR

D.I. Telbat desires to honor the Lord with his life and writing. Many of his books focus on persecuted Christians worldwide—their sacrifice, their suffering, and their rescues.

David studied writing in school and worked for a time in the newspaper field, but he is now doing what he loves most: writing and Christian ministry. At this time, D.I. Telbat lives in California but keeps his home base in the Northwest US. Read his complete bio at ditelbat.com/about/.

On his Telbat's Tablet website, David Telbat offers FREE weekly Christian short stories, or related posts, including his novel news, author reflections, interesting research, book reviews, and occasional challenges for today's Christian. Subscribe to his weekly blog at ditelbat.com to receive his posts right in your inbox. He has exclusive gifts and discounts for subscribers as well.

Visit David Telbat's website to find links to all his Paperback books, eBooks, and Audiobooks at ditelbat.com/all-d-i-telbat-novels/. Follow him on Twitter at twitter.com/DITelbat. Contact him at ditelbat.com/contact/.

Visit David Telbat's Amazon Author Central Page at amazon.com/-/e/B004ULWX14.
You can also see his *COIL Series Page* on Smashwords at smashwords.com/books/byseries/5645.

Please leave your comments wherever you bought this book. Reviews tremendously help authors, and David Telbat would love to hear your thoughts on his works. He takes reader reviews into consideration as he makes his future publishing plans.

CPSIA information can be obtained
at www.ICGtesting.com
Printed in the USA
LVHW040750170520
655736LV00003B/161

9 780986 410352